I'd Walk
with
My Friends
If I Could
Find Them

I'd Walk with My Friends If I Could Find Them

JESSE GOOLSBY

Houghton Mifflin Harcourt
BOSTON · NEW YORK
2015

For information about permission to reproduce selections from this book, write to Permissions, Houghton Mifflin Harcourt Publishing Company, 215 Park Avenue South, New York, NY 10003.

www.hmhco.com

Library of Congress Cataloging-in-Publication Data
Goolsby, Jesse.
I'd walk with my friends if I could find them / Jesse Goolsby.
p. cm
ISBN 978-0-544-38098-1 (hardback) – ISBN 978-0-544-38102-5 (ebook)
1. Friendship – Fiction. 2. Soldiers – Fiction. 3. Homecoming – Fiction.
4. War stories. I. Title.
II. Title: I would walk with my friends if I could find them.
PS3607.O59254I96 2015
813'.6 – dc23   2014034425

Book design by Brian Moore

Printed in the United States of America
DOC 10 9 8 7 6 5 4 3 2 1

Portions of this work have been published, in slightly different form, in the following: "Be Polite but Have a Plan to Kill Everyone You Meet" in *New Madrid;* "Top of the World" and "Metatarsal" in *Epoch;* "Pollice Verso" and "Resurrecting a Body Half" in the *Literary Review;* "Neutral Drops" in *Northwind Magazine;* "Touch" in *Our Stories* and the *Breakwater Review;* "Safety" in *Greensboro Review;* "Thirteen Steps" in *Storyglossia;* "Two Things from a Burning House" in *storySouth;* and "No Doorbell" in *Nashville Review.*

For Joseph A. Goolsby Sr.

There was never any more inception than there is now,
Nor any more youth or age than there is now,
And will never be any more perfection than there is now,
Nor any more heaven or hell than there is now.

Urge and urge and urge,
Always the procreant urge of the world.

— WALT WHITMAN, *Song of Myself*

I'd Walk
with
My Friends
If I Could
Find Them

Be Polite but Have a Plan
to Kill Everyone You Meet

WINTRIC ELLIS, NEWLY ARRIVED, pushes his size 8 boot into the spongy ground and feels the subtle give of the earth run through the ball of his foot, up his leg, and settle in his camouflaged hip. *Green grass in Afghanistan,* he thinks, *water somewhere.* He smells damp soil and grass, unexpected but familiar — *Little League center field, Kristen in a California meadow* — and attempts to make this thick-bladed greenery stick alongside the everywhere, suck-you-dry desert he had imagined.

"Eyes open, everyone," Big Dax says.

Although Wintric knows today is a low-risk humanitarian mission, the words slide him back into his default, visceral nervousness: *Bombs, somewhere, everywhere.* Already he has been told that *roadside* means nothing in this country. Big Dax and Torres have shared stories with him — everything from far-afield livestock to massive diesel trucks igniting the barely buried hell, not to mention the bombs strapped to men, women, children, dogs. Bombs the size of tennis balls, soccer balls, tackling dummies. Under the rising sun Wintric replays the refrain repeated among his platoon for each of his eight days in country: *Don't go looking for a fair fight.*

Wintric watches the relaxed movements of the most experienced soldiers and he feels his body breathe. He pulls out his knife and crouches in the valley amid a mist of gnats. He plunges the blade into the soil and levers up a clump of grass. Silently he rises and collects his first sample of war in a plastic bag that he fists into a cargo pocket.

Nearby a group of mangy goats bleat in a grove of white-blossomed almond trees, their shepherd talking with the interpreter. For the first time since Wintric arrived the wind doesn't howl, and he wonders if any kind of omen awaits in the warming air, but he pushes the thought from his mind when he can't think of a single positive forecast. *The size of tennis balls, soccer balls.* He breathes and rubs his eyes. The shepherd laughs and nods and moves his hand to the interpreter's shoulder, then hugs him.

"Ten minutes till the party starts," Big Dax says. "Going to be hot. Hydrate now."

Wintric observes the men start toward the small mountain of bottled water. Torres passes by and slaps his shoulder.

"Drink up."

Wintric isn't thirsty, but he keeps his mouth shut — when they say drink, he drinks. He straightens up, pats his cargo pocket, and steps and stops. He looks back at the straightening grass and watches the indentation of his boot print disappear.

Ten-thirty and the children and limbless adults are starting to arrive, and Wintric scans the group heading his way, wondering if he'll be the one ordered to pat them down before the inoculation and prosthetic limb giveaway. He pushes his index fingers into his temples, then removes his camouflage blouse and tosses it on the hood of the dusty Humvee. Big Dax and Torres have been decent enough to keep him out of trouble for his first week, but they out-rank him, and each has only a few months left, so he knows he'll soon be the one palm-to-body with these incoming strangers.

Wintric studies his two superiors as they watch the ar-riving crowd. Big Dax towering and thick-shouldered, brick of a chin, dark, random freckles, scarred forearms, hands on his hips; Torres slim and handsome, black hair, side-burns, flat nose, outline of a mini-Bible in his pocket, hands interlocked on the top of his head.

"Ellis," Torres says, "check them. Old ones first."

Wintric nods and slowly walks over to the now settling group. The interpreter has his arms up, directing traffic, shouting at the dirty and quiet kids to stay in a single-file line along an outcropping of beige rocks. The adults are told to wait behind. On his short march over Wintric focuses on the adults, most missing a foot, a leg, or a portion of an arm. Light layers of clothing shield their bodies from the late-morning sun; various pant legs and shirtsleeves hang limp. He will have to touch all of these people.

Before Wintric begins the pat-downs, the interpreter says, "Don't touch ass, crotch. Easy with kids. No problems here. Medicine here."

"You know these people?" Wintric says.

"No."

"So you don't know shit."

Seventeen pat-downs later Wintric comes to a man who seems whole, tiny sweat streams around his eyes.

"Thank you," the man says before Wintric has touched him. Wintric glances back at the interpreter, who nods, then shakes his head.

"No problems here," he says.

"What's he doing here? He's not missing anything."

"No problems."

"Goddammit."

"Thank you," the man says.

"Yeah."

As with the others Wintric starts with the man's shoulders, pats down his arms to his wrists, up his sides, down from his clavicle, chest, to his belly, where Wintric feels something bulging, soft, ball-shaped. He pauses for a moment, and when the bomb vision arrives, he whirls around, head down, and sprints. In the slow-motion frenzy he hears the man yell something, sees his own arms reach out in front of him, and he knows he will die, right now, that the searing blast will take him from behind, open up his back and skull, liquefy his body. He is all heartbeat and screams "Bomb!" takes two more strides, and dives to the ground.

Behind him the man has lifted his shirt up to his neck, baring his torso, pointing at a fleshy protrusion.

"Na!" the man yells. "Na!"

"No!" the interpreter says. "No. Please. Nothing. No. Only." He pauses. "Skin. How do you say it?"

Wintric lies face-down in the grass, eyes closed, body flexed. He hears *skin* and pushes himself up onto his elbows. Big Dax and Torres run toward him.

"Crazy cells," says the interpreter.

Wintric still hears his heart in his ears, and he squeezes his hands, then opens them. He cut his left hand during the dive and wipes the fine line of blood off on his pants. He stands, still dizzy, and peers back at the man, who cups the ball of flesh below his ribs. Wintric shakes his head and glances down at his palm, where fine dirt is mixed with coagulating blood.

"Goddamn," says Big Dax. "Deep breath, Ellis. Breathe."

Big Dax touches Wintric's arm and Wintric shakes him off.

From the side, children's laughter.

"Cancer," Torres says. "Could be cancer."

"Ah, yes," says the interpreter, nodding. "Cancer."

Wintric stands in between Big Dax and Torres as they plunge syringes into children in the narrow valley. Three more soldiers from their squad occupy a similar station several feet away, and a med tech shuffles back and forth, observing.

The girls and boys come forward with lesions and growths, unhealed wounds.

"What day is it?" Wintric asks, still trying to shake off the embarrassment and confusion. It's been twenty minutes and nothing has worked.

"Doesn't matter," Torres says.

"School not in?" Wintric says.

No one answers.

"No school?"

The interpreter laughs.

"What?"

"Universities all on break," the interpreter says, grinning. "Maybe U.S. builds one right here?"

"Fuck you."

"I got candy bar in my pocket. Maybe bomb?"

"I got dick in my pants. Smack your face?"

"Easy," says Torres. "Dude is with us."

The interpreter smiles.

"Build one or not, I don't care. After this war I get my visa. I will move to Nevada."

"You're not moving to Nevada," Wintric says. "I've been to Nevada."

"Las Vegas."

"You'll lose all your money," Wintric says. "One, two days of slots. Good luck with that."

"No. You misunderstand. I will work at the casino."

"What?"

"Work there. Roulette. I've seen it. Wave your hand, put white ball in the spinner. Easy."

"There's more to it," Wintric says.

"No. That's it. Wave hand. Spin ball. Money."

"Never happen."

Wintric lifts a boy's sleeve up to the nub of the boy's shoulder joint and fumbles with, then drops, the cheap syringe. He selects another syringe and drops it.

"Hey. Relax. Focus on the kids," Big Dax says. "Hold their hands, sing, do whatever you need to do. Keep your mind working on the good shit."

"I don't need friends."

"Careful, Ellis," Torres says. "It's a long walk back."

Wintric pushes a new syringe against the boy's shoulder, presses the plunger, and the clear liquid slides in.

"It's not that long," he says.

"These kids," says Big Dax. "This one right here." A young girl missing her left nostril rests her neck in his hand. "She risks getting her arm cut off to come see us. It's why we only see the worst."

This seems like an exaggeration to Wintric, though he isn't sure of anything in this place. Another boy steps up for his shot.

"We're as safe as we'll ever be," says Torres. "You can almost relax for a few hours. No one ever shoots when the army inoculates and clothes and hands out money."

Wintric sees Torres glance over at the meandering goats.

"Still," Torres says, "stay close to the kids, especially the boys. They hate losing boys."

"That makes no sense," Wintric says. "We're safe, but stay close to the boys?" He glances at the naked mountain peaks above them.

"You from San Francisco, right?" Big Dax asks Wintric, hoping to help.

"Four hours north."

"Oregon?"

"No. California. The good part."

"Redwoods?" Torres chimes in.

"Two thousand people. A lake. Think Montana, but Bay Area assholes in the summer."

Wintric takes a drink of bottled water and motions to the next in line.

"They take our water," he says.

"A's or Giants?" Big Dax asks.

"Giants."

"You like Barry Bonds? 'Cause he's a prick. Probably got nuts the size of gnats."

"Hit three-forty-something, forty-five homers. He'll beat it this year. You'd take him in a heartbeat."

"Shit. Yankees don't need him. Don't make a hat big enough for his planet-sized 'roid head."

"Oh, damn," Wintric says. "Yankees fan."

"Maybe that's what we're giving these kids – some nice, fatten-you-up steroids," Torres says and rips another rubbing-alcohol pad from its wrapper. "Creating a superrace of Afghanis that can hit a baseball a mile."

"Torres, you dumbass, have some compassion," Big Dax says while tending to a girl with a goiter. She stares at him as he tries to wave her on.

"You're done," he says.

She doesn't move.

"Done. Go. Now."

She blinks twice.

"Go."

"She wants candy," the interpreter says.

"No candy," Big Dax says. He joins his right thumb and index finger, brings them to his open mouth, and shakes his head.

"No. Candy. No. Candy."

The girl stands still. The goiter bulges from the side of her neck, the flesh brushing her deltoid.

"No. Candy." He nods at the interpreter. "Translate, please."

"She understands you."

Big Dax grabs the girl beneath her arms, lifts her, turns her away from him, and sets her on the ground. He places his huge hands on her lower back and pushes her just enough so she takes her first step away.

"Come on now," Torres says, "where's the compassion for the greedy one?"

"They have nothing to do with us being here."

"You don't know that. These kids could have plenty to do with this," Torres says.

"Don't piss me off, Torres."

"Doesn't take much strength to dig a foot down, put something in the hole, cover it up. Bet some of these arms have done some digging."

Wintric sees Big Dax's left boot tap the ground.

"Fight your urge to be a little bitch," Big Dax says.

"We got staying-alive problems," says Torres. "So you're right, I'm a bitch. Guess I'm a scared bitch that wants to live." Someone off by the goats laughs. "I don't want the fucking dirt road exploding on our way back."

"Don't listen to him, Ellis. The road's fine. And Torres,

don't talk shit about these kids. You know the life expectancy of these dudes?" Big Dax asks, straightening his six-foot, eight-inch body. He pauses, and Torres scratches his neck. "Low thirties."

"I must've checked the Doctors Without Borders block instead of the U.S. Army," Torres says. "My mistake."

"If it was your kids in line here, you'd think different. If it was your kids that wouldn't see thirty-one . . ."

"These aren't my kids."

Stretching his arms above his head, Armando Torres examines the diminishing line of children. Not a single child appears nourished, and as he touches their arms and hair and holds their hands and the anger inside him, he thinks of his two daughters. His mind goes to Camila, his oldest and the prettier one, who refuses to eat anything unless she has a dollop of crunchy peanut butter on her plate. Four years old and tearless at his base sendoff. He was proud of her strength, but now he fears the indifferent expression she wore as he walked away.

Torres used to sing the ABCs to his girls every night while he tucked them in, and the tune comes to him now, in this gorge. It calms him. After a while he leaves out the letters and hums.

Wintric says, "You know any Metallica?"

Torres ignores him and continues to hum. He considers the minuscule amount his daughters are growing each day, how Camila will be old enough to play catch when he returns, how they might want to tuck themselves in.

"Incubus? Deftones?"

After delivering the shots, the men wait around with some of the now antibodied kids and a collection of Afghan amputees. The wind has picked up, and the injured glance up every now and again, waiting for their limbs to fall from the cloudy sky. The C-130 is late.

"Jim Abbott had one arm," Big Dax says as the men sit and pick at the ground.

"Who?" Wintric asks.

"He had an arm," Torres says. "Was missing a hand."

"Threw a no-hitter," Big Dax says. "For the Yankees."

"Did he use?"

"Why would you use if you have one arm?"

"One hand," says Torres.

"Jesus, Torres, who cares if it's an arm or a hand?"

"It's a big difference."

"He didn't use," says Big Dax. "Not like your boy Bonds."

"They'll never prove it," says Wintric.

"Look at a photo of him with the Pirates side by side with one of him on the Giants," says Big Dax. "I'm a Jersey-educated man and I can tell the difference. It's not broccoli."

"Your Yankees signed Giambi," says Torres.

"Yep. And he's sure as shit dirty. You see, that's how it's done. Just admit the worst and move on. What's jacked up is that everyone on the West Coast wants to believe. No one trusts their eyes."

Nearby an old man unfurls a red-and-brown rug as the children gather around and join the limbless adults in prayer, their voices echoing off the valley walls.

"They know not what they say," Torres says. Wintric guesses he means the children, repeating the chant they've heard since birth, but maybe he directs the jab at the entire group, kneeling and bowing and rising in unison.

"And they'll kill that one before too long," Big Dax says, nodding at a young man, maybe sixteen, standing and running his fingers through his dark hair as the others pray. "'Motherfucking infidel' is what the rest are thinking. They seem like they're praying, but they're begging for that dude to be hit by lightning."

"He's not praying," Wintric says.

"Holy shit, Ellis," Big Dax says. "You're a genius."

"But."

"Think about it, brother," says Torres.

"But the dude is . . . local."

"Do you know there's someone, right now, playing the trombone in Afghanistan?" says Torres.

"What the hell does that have to do with anything?"

"There's an Afghan right now, in this country, looking at porn," says Torres. "Someone planting a bomb, reading Hemingway. Someone building a bridge, listening to Celine Dion, getting off, not praying."

"Yep."

"Don't let it surprise you," Torres says.

"Fine," Wintric says.

"Not everyone wants to kill us," Torres says.

"Seems like they do."

"You haven't been here long enough to say that. You haven't done shit. You're a baby."

"I'm in this valley," Wintric says.

"You're a kid."

"I'm here like you are."

"You heard of the saying 'Be polite, but have a plan to kill everyone you meet'?"

"No."

"Too bad," Torres says. "It's some Marine shit, but it's perfect."

"Yep."

"There are a ton of people praying that we all die," Torres says. "Enough to keep us sharp."

But Wintric has stopped listening. He eyes the young man combing his hair with his fingers as the others rise and bow, rise and bow, not twenty feet from him. The move is something Wintric performed a thousand times before his enlistment, and he raises his right hand and rubs the stubble on his shaved head, still sensing the phantom weight of his once-long hair. Wintric wants to know what the young man is thinking, wants to ask him how he can just stand there, doing nothing. Is he afraid? Bored? Something else? The young man scratches his crotch and the atmosphere of wonder lessens. Still, Wintric wants to rise and walk over to him, but he fights the impulse and stares at the grass between his knees. He digs a clump up and inspects the individual blades.

Wintric isn't yet aware that Torres's comment will stay with him: occasionally, in the future, when he witnesses something out of the ordinary – in this country or his own – he will think, *Someone's playing a trombone.*

At last a C-130 lumbers overhead, drops a flagged transmitter, then circles back. High above, a parachute opens. Two crates full of prosthetic arms and legs float down to them. Torres recalls watching Air Force Academy cadets drift under blue parachutes, then he wonders out loud if the Afghans think Allah is a C-130 pilot, or the plane itself.

"Rain down the healing," Torres says.

Big Dax says it's all about personal will and raises his thick arms to the sky.

"Do they thank Allah for our bombs?" he asks.

Wintric stays quiet. He stares at the crease between his forearm and biceps, then fingers the skin there. At Fort Carson he saw soldiers with new carbon legs and arms, men and women, usually silent and alone, rubbing on their bodies, their stumps. He peers over and studies the armorless Humvee they will ride back to base. The hulking vehicle seems invincible, but he's seen videos of convoy ambushes: the dark cloud, pressure shock, and heavy Humvees slamming back to earth as mangled coffins.

Wintric already longs for his 1985 Ford Bronco. He installed a six-inch lift, a tow kit, and oversized, gnarly mud tires. The tire-tread hum on the highway drove Kristen mad, but he would take her mudding, or farther still into the forest to fool around. Sometimes he'd take his revolver and throw lead at squirrels, paper plates, or posters of basketball players he used to hang in his room.

But here, deployed half a world away, his back-slung rifle has the safety on, and he doesn't know when he'll need to summon his shooting skill. He considers the menacing but helpless Humvee and hopes that when they're done today, the dirt road will just be a dirt road.

Once the replacement body parts are sorted by limb, the three men help fit everyone. Most of the arms are too long or the wrong shade of skin, but the limbless smile, cry, hug the soldiers. After everyone has been fitted, a few artificial legs are left over, so the Americans send the confused villagers home with extras.

Before dark the soldiers climb into the Humvees, confirm emergency plans, coordinate with the other vehicles in their convoy, and start the engines. As they drive away, Big Dax rolls his window down and gives a thumbs-up to the newly limbed as they limp away, grappling with plastic legs piled high.

"Vote for us," he yells.

A month and a half later, late on a hot July morning, red and yellow kites fly above Kabul. They veer and shake. One darts off, away, descending toward the roofs.

On a street corner, Big Dax, Torres, and Wintric scan the foot and auto traffic and swap stories. Smells of chai and lamb mix with exhaust from gridlocked vehicles. Wiping the sweat from his face an hour into their four-hour patrol, Torres oversells a harrowing skiing experience at Breckenridge. Someone whistles to their right before a car bomb explodes, the pressure fire blowing the men back.

Torres vomits on his boots and Wintric is knocked unconscious, then comes to with Big Dax cursing and dumping water onto his face before running off.

Bodies and flames, shit and screams litter the street. Dazed people run and stumble away.

Torres picks a scrap of metal out of his biceps, then reaches down to drag a silent girl away, and with his rescue yank the girl's shoulder detaches, the surrounding skin separates, and her thin arm slides from her body.

A man runs in to help and Big Dax almost shoots. A bearded man in white linen snaps photos, steps over slithering bodies. He covers a charred corpse's genitals with a blue cloth before clicking away at the carcass. He kicks the corpse before hurrying away.

Wintric tries to yell to him, but nothing comes out, and Wintric goes to walk, but nothing happens, and he feels wet inside and sees in waves. He screams but hears nothing, now aware that he is somehow trapped within his body.

Smoke and sky, someone firing a rifle into the air, then Big Dax, running nearby, waving at Wintric, saying something, nodding, thumbs up, then reaching far down, lifting him up.

Ambulances arrive in the dissipating smoke, then leave. People with various flags on their uniforms fill out paperwork, take photos, then depart. Afghan men and women shriek in the streets, then go, and workers tend to the debris that covers a once-busy intersection.

That evening, as Wintric dozes off in the corner, cleaned up save a smattering of dried blood spotting his throat, Torres listens to the calls to prayer. Torres's limbs and mind ache, and he sifts through the day's events. He touches the bandage on his arm and ponders the size and shape of the future scar. He monitors his fingers and wills them to stop trembling, but they refuse. Emotion pools within him and he finds himself on his knees, hoping to tap into some communal source of faith and belief. He tries to focus, but soon his mind drifts to the millions of people praying against him and his country. He pictures a vast field, an enormous crowd of white-robed men and women bowing in unison, the haunting force and beauty of mass synchronization.

Torres thinks of how he has taught his daughters to pray and what to pray for: safety, food, recovery. His younger daughter, Mia, is old enough now to speak a simple offering. Torres's wife sent an e-mail with the words Mia recited every night, said she always finished with "Thank you." Torres envisions his wife, Anna, and Mia at the side of her bed, kneeling, with their elbows on the *Finding Nemo* comforter. Anna said they were working on "Amen," but she thought that "Thank you" was just as good. For the first time Torres considers the purpose of "Amen," and after whispering the word three times realizes he has no idea what it means. He considers waking Wintric, but he won't know, so he says the word one more time as the melody from the minarets filters through the window. In Afghanistan everything he knows about the world has a different name and, worse, he doesn't know the meanings of the English words he uses for salvation.

Big Dax smokes outside, his dirty, dry skin irritating him. He takes a drag and thinks of his high school friend Alston, how surprised he would be by Dax's cigarettes, even more so by the confident, uniformed man smoking them. He remembers when Alston left town in the middle of the night with his girlfriend, headed for Key West. Alston's last postcard had a picture of a clear lake, a small boat, and a golf course putting green floating right in the middle of the water. On the bottom: "Coeur d'Alene, Idaho."

Dax has heard that the army is building a new public pool nearby. What he would give for a few laps without his Kevlar vest and helmet and heavy boots – to purge the dust from his ears, mouth, and chest. Dax pictures all the pools he has swum in. Not that strong in the water, he still desires the chlorinated depths. To immerse himself in a swimming pool would be to return home. He misses the cool water and the chemicals, the tanned female lifeguards, community pools, post pools, a banana-shaped pool at a Vegas resort he once visited. His neighbor's pool in Rutherford, New Jersey, where he grew up. That one had a four-foot-tall diving board, way too high for the six-foot-deep pool, but Dax and the neighbor kids would cannonball and jack-knife off the board and float in the summer air and bet each other to belly-flop, although no one did. But while he starts to dwell in his comforting memory, he imagines a shadowed man there, in his neighbor's back yard, strapped with explosives, in a slow-motion diving board jump. The board fully flexes before launching the man high into the air, and eleven-year-old Dax and a couple of local kids watch the terrorist click the handheld detonator again and again, but nothing happens, only a violent fall into a too-shallow pool.

Big Dax wasn't in Rutherford the day the towers fell. Up visiting his grandparents in Watertown, New York, already signed up for the army but waiting for basic training, he watched the news for two days straight in disbelief. Dax pictured himself in camouflage, taking aim at people, missing, and he felt the nerves in his body ping. He would have to kill now, something he'd hoped to avoid when he signed up for the G.I. Bill and travel. In his transforming world, this is why he despised the terrorists: people dying, diving from the towers, it was dismal business to be sure, but now, after joining the army in a time of relative peace, he would be asked to shoot, and probably be shot at.

After returning home to three funerals in a week, Dax stayed up late replaying television clips of people jumping from the buildings. The news had stopped running them, and he couldn't understand why. Without these clips the whole disaster was like any other demolition of steel and concrete, but these scenes showed living men and women falling through the air. This is where the pain lived, in impossible choices on a clear late-summer morning. Dax had never considered choosing between flame and gravity, but watching the people fall to their deaths, weighing which way to die, he guessed he would pick gravity.

One night his father spied him watching the clips.

"We think we're more important than we are," he said. "Each one of us. It's our biggest mistake. Remember this— you can love God, but God doesn't give a shit. You want to celebrate births and winning the lottery and graduations? You give credit to the heavens? Fine, but you better celebrate this shit as well."

Dax hadn't thought much about God, about intervention or justice, so he sat there in his living room and stared at his sober father pointing at the television.

"It's okay to feel good when you make them pay."

Tonight, in Afghanistan, Big Dax smokes his third cigarette down and snuffs the nub out on his forearm before flicking it away. Typically he performs this forearm trick in front of others, but lately he continues the move when alone, the singe becoming more and more bearable.

As he enters the room he sees Torres on his knees. Big Dax considers saying, "No one's listening," but he swallows it down easily and walks to his bunk, lies back, and lets the nicotine work.

•　•　•

One day while on patrol in a mud village in the midday heat, Big Dax, Torres, and Wintric drink tea with a man rather than detaining him because there's no sign he's killed four Americans and a Dane over the past five months. As they leave, the man smiles and waves at them.

Later in the afternoon, an elderly man offers what the men guess is his daughter to Wintric. It's the opposite of what they've been briefed, that Afghan men would purposely disfigure – often with acid – the faces and bodies of adulterous women. Brown-eyed, short, and thin, the daughter smiles and widens her eyes when her father taps her leg with his cane. She offers her hand to Wintric in the narrow alley, and he steps close and takes back the girl's hijab to reveal her dark hair. The men are hot in their gear, but the shade of the alley helps.

"Hey," Big Dax says, "don't do anything. There, I said it."

"Second that," says Torres, and strokes his rifle. "But seriously, don't do anything. You have five minutes to check that house for weapons. She can help. Be careful. We're not screwing around here."

The father moves down the street, and Torres follows him for a few steps.

Big Dax leans on the thick mud wall of the building, waiting, thinking about the shade and the smell of roasting meat. He catches some kids staring him down from a house nearby, and he wonders if he had been born in that very alley what Afghan Dax would think of this man, with this rifle, leaning against this wall. He senses empathy there, but in scattered, fleeting fragments, not enough to care, not now, not with a few months to go.

After Wintric enters the shabby dwelling with the girl, he takes off his helmet and she turns to him and smiles. She motions him to a back room, but Wintric stays a couple steps inside the door. The girl walks back to him and touches his chest, but he can't feel the pressure under-neath his Kevlar vest. He hasn't touched or been touched by a woman in months. She keeps her hand on his chest and raises her eyes to his. He watches the girl, not sure what's expected of him or why he's here, but he takes his time. On her right cheek, a tiny circular scar. Her lips are dry. She re-minds him of no one and he feels a focused but nervous de-sire to touch her face.

Wintric reaches out and the girl's arms fall to her sides and she closes her eyes. He stops his hand inches from her face. He lifts his left arm and senses a weight and remem-bers he's holding his helmet. He sees it in his hand. He's here, in this home. He's in Afghanistan. When she opens her eyes, he turns and leaves.

The men walk in the dusty afternoon, and they soon pass a quail fight inside a tiny hall. Dozens of men circle a brown mat and cheer the frantic, bobbing birds.

"My state bird," Wintric says. "Little bastards are easy picking where I'm from, and good eats."

"Jersey doesn't have a state bird," says Big Dax.

"I thought every state had one."

"Isn't Jersey's the Shit Bird?" says Torres.

"We do have a horse and two ugly bitches on our flag," Big Dax says. "That much I know."

"We got a grizzly bear on ours, but no grizzlies," says Wintric. "We got black bears. One ate the dog I grew up with."

"Torres," Big Dax says, "we found a true California hick."

Wintric seizes the opportunity and talks about his ru-ral hometown of Chester, about playing football on a los-ing team that carried fourteen guys total, about his respect for those who leave the logging town for other parts of the country.

Big Dax and Torres let him carry on. They don't ask any questions about the girl in the alley, but later, after drinking enough smuggled booze to feel something, Wintric tells them that he began to undress her but stopped himself. He says she grabbed his hands and placed them on her bare shoulders, and he left his hands there for a moment before walking out. He says he wouldn't be able to live with himself – a girl waits back home.

"No one's ever waiting, my friend," says Big Dax. "They're living and moving on. And don't get mad. It sucks, but it's true."

"That's bullshit," says Torres.

"You know it's not," says Big Dax, raising his voice. "You know about Billings and Winston and Henlish. What are their wives doing right now?"

"If you had someone at home, you'd know," says Torres. "I feel sorry that this is all you have. It's pathetic."

Big Dax turns to Wintric. "Billings and Winston and Henlish are trying to stay alive over here and their wives are banging the shit out of dudes at home."

"Okay," Wintric says.

"Okay?"

"Okay. I don't know them. That has nothing to do with me."

"Fine," says Big Dax.

"You have right now," says Torres. "Then, when that's gone, you have the next moment, then that's it. What do you look forward to, man? If all it is is surviving, that's shit."

"I see," says Big Dax. "I'm crazy for seeing things the way they actually are. Reality tells me it's dangerous to believe that someone's waiting for you back home. Their lives are shit. We stay busy, keep our minds working. They get to worry and pretend they're fine with us dodging bombs over here. And you know they have to act as if they're fine with it because if they don't, if they actually speak their minds, they're unpatriotic and bitches and everything else. You hate me for saying it. Fine."

"Her name is Kristen," says Wintric. "The girl at home. It's my fault. I haven't e-mailed. I told her not to. I don't know why."

"One day the people we're trying to kill will be in charge again," says Torres. "One day soon we'll negotiate with these fucks, even though they've killed us and tortured us and today we're trying to kill them. No one will remember 2004 or us breathing in the fucking burn-pit smoke or the bomb that almost took off my arm. None of this will have happened. So yes, I think about who's waiting for me, because if I think about all this, I'm done. I got kids, man, so be careful."

"I'm not commenting on Anna, your kids, or whatever," says Big Dax, "just reality. Dude, you may be a lucky one. People change. That's all I'm saying. They're living every day that we live."

"That's enough," says Torres. "Don't say this shit again."

"You guys believe what you want to."

So Torres believes. He lives his return home in advance. He feels the departure out of Afghanistan, out of Kyrgyzstan, out of Germany, the packed jet, restless legs, nervous energy, the Atlantic, the boredom, the squiggly coastline of Maryland and Delaware, landing at Baltimore, buying a magnet of Colorado in a gift shop, flying across farmland, the Rockies bringing him to tears, into Colorado Springs. He sees his family running to him in the airport, his daughters jumping into his arms, them arguing about who gets to ride on his shoulders, walking into the home Anna bought while he was away, and after his girls are tucked in, Anna's skin and weight pressed against him, her hands and mouth on him, on top of him, under him, the pressure build and release, home.

Wintric sees Kristen naked on the shore of Lake Almanor late at night, standing on a stump in the low beams of his Bronco, waving her arms, singing, urging him out of the water, to come to her and this place, his home, again.

Top of the World

THE TOP OF the World is a clearing cut into a hill outside Chester, California, and from that height Wintric
watches a column of white smoke pushing out hard from
the mill. Inside, men strip and cut trees into boards. Some
of the workers tell their children they're making clouds –
Wintric's father had told him this years ago – but from the
Top of the World Wintric can see the plume dissolve into
the air well below the slow-shifting cumulus.

The bet is up to thirty dollars, and the .38 special feels
just right in Wintric's callused hands as he squeezes the
gun's handle. He's gathered his long brown hair behind
him in a band, and his left big toe claws at a fresh hole in
his shoe from a nail he caught working construction out by
the sewers. He kicks some of the construction paycheck to
his mom and dad to keep the electricity on, but the betting
windfalls he keeps for himself.

Young men he passes every day in high school shout
obscenities as Wintric takes aim at a target the instigators
squint to see. Today there's a run on *motherfucker* and *bitch*.
The rules: they can shout and move about, anything except touch him. Tall trucks with gnarly tires line up at their

backs. Ponderosa pines surround them, many with white chalk lines around their trunks where they'll be cut.

Kristen sits in Wintric's Bronco, swings her long legs out the side, and sings to Metallica. Her green eyes look out through mirrored sunglasses on a scene she's witnessed plenty of times, and she wonders if this is one of those outings when he'll purposely miss so the second round of bets nets over fifty bucks. She stays in the truck in case they have to leave in a hurry, but she feels relaxed as she hears her voice mesh with James Hetfield's. She watches Wintric take the verbal abuse in his green Levi's T-shirt, his young face, the squint he never seems to lose. To her, he seems most alive on these betting runs and other afternoons when he drives her deep into the woods on back roads and chances getting the Bronco stuck. She knows Wintric's routine and senses that he's about to perform the wipe-the-forehead move. It's hotter than usual for late May, and she guesses that if everything goes well she may score an ice cream soda out of this if he leaves in a good mood.

A new smile rounds at the corners of Wintric's mouth. He knows this game's conclusion, but he lets the boys in their flannel shirts go at him a little longer. He has to play the whole thing up, even lose sometimes, or people will stop wagering. He drops the gun to his side and shakes his head. He wipes his sweatless brow. His toe digs at his shoe. After a theatrical exhalation he lifts the handgun and pictures the new boots he will buy: black steel-toe boots on sale down in Chico. The advertisement he saw on television says you can drop a thousand pounds on them without so much as a dent. He keeps both eyes open and visualizes the bullet's trajectory all the way to the target, a skill he's been able to conjure for as long as he can remember. One of the boys calls Wintric's mother a cunt, which he would normally fight over, but the money's too easy to take the insult as an insult. *Just a game,* he thinks. Still, the word hits Wintric enough for him to say, "Through the capital *P*."

The boy replies, "Make it fifty, motherfucker, and when I win, I'll give half to your mom for services rendered."

Wintric has cocked the gun, so the trigger pull is light. A Pepsi can falls in the distance and he's wearing new boots.

Marcus ruins another black-and-white sundae. A little chocolate sauce on the bottom of the glass, a fat scoop of vanilla, marshmallow cream, a scoop of vanilla, chocolate sauce, whipped cream, nuts, and a cherry. The dessert construction isn't hard, but Marcus flusters easily, and the grayhaired woman in front of him shakes her head, trying to talk above the crowd and the spinning milkshake machines.

"No. Marshmallow in the middle, son. Not the bottom. The middle."

Already Marcus's fourth mistake and he hasn't hit the lunch rush, but this summer has brought temperatures in the high nineties, and the line for the Lassen Drug Old-Fashioned Soda Fountain snakes out the door. These rushes exist only in the summer, when the lake brings the crowds up from the valley to their second homes and the mainstreet town awakens.

Marcus stands short and muscular behind the counter in a white shirt with a banana-split patch sewn onto the front. His work shirt is the only one he owns that isn't black, and it showcases the drying splatter of an exploded strawberry shake. His hair is parted down the middle, and he doesn't yet realize that a sliver of banana is lodged in his eyebrow. Two female coworkers shoot around him, filling orders for milkshakes, ice cream sodas, and cones. He dumps the ruined sundae into the sink and grabs another glass from beneath a NO OUTSIDE FOOD sign.

He turns back around to face the crowd and sees Kristen. She stands inside the glass front doors, touching one of the painted ceramic bowls for sale. Wintric is there.

Marcus is seventeen years old, and at the moment completely aware of his attire. Kristen has seen him working many times before, and even though their families have been close for years, her presence still unnerves him, and now, as she plants a cheek kiss on her boyfriend, the volume in the store lowers and he can hear his insides working. His vision blurs for a moment, and when he comes to he sees that the marshmallow ladle is at the bottom of the new sundae glass. He wants to throw the whole thing, wants to take off his shirt and burn it. The gray-haired woman turns to her companion and says, "Moron." More people squeeze into the store. Some of them wear shirts printed with his town's name on it. Marcus has the ladle in his hand and marshmallow at the bottom of the glass.

He reaches back for another glass, stealing a glimpse at Kristen in the large mirror, her gaze intently fixed on something, as are the other reflected faces, and several customers now point. Over his left shoulder a woman has her hands locked around her throat and her female friend bangs at her lower back with a closed fist. Like the others, Marcus freezes. The choking woman shades to maroon in seconds. Her forehead veins bulge, and one of his coworkers joins the woman's friend beating at her back. Marcus knows what to do, as do many of the people in the shop, but something stays them. The back beating isn't working, and he holds a sundae glass in his hand. A few people huddle closer, and Kristen takes a step in as well. Marcus stares at her and her frightened face, but suddenly she bounds forward, pushes the swinging women away, and reaches around the choking woman. Kristen vises down and Marcus notices the long muscles in her tanned forearms before they disappear into the woman's midsection. A violent moan, and a thick pretzel segment explodes out.

The tense atmosphere flushes out after a minute and the crowd invites Kristen to the front of the line. Playing into Marcus's simultaneous fear and desire, she and Wintric take seats at his section of the counter.

"Hey," Wintric says, and Marcus nods.

"Maaarrrcus," Kristen says. She buries herself in the menu, and despite her confident tone, Marcus can tell she's still coming down off the adrenaline. Kristen only ever orders one of two things – a cherry or lime ice cream soda – and he's never seen her peruse a menu before.

"That's why they have the policy about outside food," Marcus says, pointing to the sign above the glasses. "We only sell ice cream. Can't choke, you know, on ice cream." Kristen peeks up at him with a polite smirk before returning to the listings. Marcus would tear his tongue out if he could. Wintric orders a chocolate malt and she gets a banana split. The malt is easy, but at the store they have a policy on the order of the strawberry, vanilla, and chocolate ice cream in the split – each has a specific position and topping – and although Marcus can recite the last twelve U.S. presidents in order, he can't remember the flavors' bananasplit positions at this nervous moment, so before he scoops the ice cream he tilts his shirt up and examines the patch.

Marcus places their orders in front of them, but before he turns away Kristen reaches over and touches him on the arm and draws him closer. Confused, Marcus glances at Wintric, but he's already into the malt. Marcus hesitates, but leans in after she says, "Come here, Marcus," his name from her lips like magic. Her vanilla perfume intoxicates him as he advances ear first, but she repositions his head straight on. She stares just above his eyes and swipes at his lower forehead twice.

"There," she says, leaning back. "A little banana."

Wintric and Kristen swim naked in Lake Almanor while the Bronco's stereo plays Incubus out the open windows. The water appears mercury silver and dense just after midnight. They tread out past where they can touch, and slithery plants rub at their feet and calves. The low water level reveals random stumps poking up from the beach. The moon blooms full. To the west, a cloud of lit smoke from the mill.

They laugh about a teacher who always has coffee breath, about the future occupation survey they were forced to take in class, and Wintric tells Kristen he signed papers to enlist in the army. He leaves two weeks after graduation. He'll pocket a bonus for signing up. She's guessed at a departure of some kind for a while—he said he'd never work the lumber—but Wintric's casual announcement while she treads water surprises her. She lets herself sink to the lakebed, only a few feet below. Her feet settle in cool mud and she stays there for a moment, inside herself, wondering what she'll do next.

She crests the surface splashing but silent, and retreats to the shore. The moment deserves a scene. She wants to cry, wants the tears. She needs him to witness them running down her cheeks, but they aren't coming. For a reason she can't capture, the news itself troubles her only lightly. She knows the town sends lots of people into the military, and her father has told her that the service has saved many of the local kids, but Wintric? Her mind spins, but comfortably, and she searches for a response that makes sense. He should have told her weeks, months ago—only a month's warning after two years together?

Some of her classmates already celebrate their near-future plans to leave Chester for faraway towns and universities, a course she hasn't pursued, and she knows couples who have promised to stay together when one half leaves, but long distance rarely ends well – it just ends. In the forty seconds she's had to process the news, she's decided that if Wintric asks, she'll stay together, will, if he asks, maybe even go with him, but everything is too new, there's no expectation, only a calmness, this unanticipated reaction to his announcement.

She walks to the shore and the lake recedes down her body and the mud at her feet hardens to pebbles. Her skin throbs with a recovering sunburn and the soft air evaporates the moisture away. She poses in front of Wintric's lifted Ford, low beams at her back, disappointed that she can't recall all the words to the song playing. After a minute the rocks dig at her bare feet so she steps onto a nearby stump.

She calls out over the stereo, "How much is the bonus?"

Wintric has stayed in the water, letting her go about her business. He's witnessed her productions before, and is a little surprised there aren't any tears. He swims in to where he can touch and revels in the sight of Kristen's moonlit body, her constant, unabashed confidence.

"Thirty thousand."

"You're going to the war."

"Is there anything else?"

Something swims between his legs and he grabs his genitals. He isn't sure of all the details of his enlistment, about what he'll be asked to sacrifice, but he knows the posts are nowhere near this place, that the travel will take him away from these pine-filled valleys that cut him off from what he calls "civilization." There are other lakes in the world like the one he stands in. He would struggle to name any, but he's sure there are cities with lakes right in the middle of them, and when you're done swimming you walk a block to your apartment or to other city things that await your call, and the sun shines warmer. He wants more than a taste, he wants to stay, and not in Chico or Redding or Red Bluff. Farther. He longs for strangers surrounding him, people who don't know about his family's crumbling house or his father's bad back or his repeating sixth grade. He needs the separation, even if it means aiming a weapon for real.

Wintric watches Kristen balance on the stump. He's sure she will never leave this place. Once when he asked her about her fantasy vacation, she said she'd always wanted to drive through the massive redwood over near the coast. She wasn't sure of the tree's exact location, only that she'd seen photos of cars halfway through the trunk. It was so close by, her dream getaway, he had to laugh. She argued that people come from all over the world to drive through that tree. "If you're from Japan or France, driving through the tree is a big deal. Why can't it be a big deal for me?" He knew she was right, and he thought about how the only thing interesting about travel was that it's away from where you are.

Kristen turns around, faces the low beams, and Wintric studies her silhouette, her lean shoulders, the lines of her slightly spread thighs up to their intersection. Her hips have filled out, and Wintric pictures his hands there.

Wintric hobbles out of the lake and strides to her. Her skin smells like fish, and he smells his own arm and it's the same. His face comes to her stomach and he kisses her belly button. She sways her hips and he places his hands on them and listens to her singing.

They decided early never to say "I love you" to each other. Even so, Kristen is all he has known of romance and trust. He kisses her right hip, then runs his tongue along where it meets her thigh.

"Wintric," she says.

Though he can't fathom what death or war means, he'd want her to get the folded flag if everything came to that, and he wonders if that's what love is, and he thinks that it is. He reaches up from her hips and runs his palms down her sides, up to her breasts, down her ribs, her stomach.

"Not here," she says.

"Please," he says.

Wintric squats down and kisses the inside of her left knee, and she runs her hands through his wet hair.

"You'll have to cut your hair," she says. "You'll look bad with short hair."

He kisses the inside of her right knee, her inner thigh.

"I could look great. You never know."

"A bowling ball," she says. "A tennis ball. Round."

His hands on her hips.

"The lights are on," she says. "At least get the lights."

"Low beams."

Her hands through his hair, her fingers on his scalp underneath. Can he feel better than this?

"They charge for haircuts in the army?" she says. "Stupid if they do."

"Are you kidding?" he says. "It's thirty grand a cut."

Marcus prays his erection will go down before the bell rings. He has about ten minutes left in class, but Kristen sits two rows ahead to the right, wearing a white cotton shirt, and every time she leans over to talk to her friend he catches a flash of the top of her breasts. He untucks his black shirt. A female voice trickles down through the air, something about lawyers.

The results of the career questionnaire rest on Marcus's desk. He darts his eyes back to the top of it: (1) Doctor, (2) Teacher, (3) Accountant, (4) Lawyer, (5) Services. A week ago he filled in the far-right bubble on each line and let a computer tell him what career options there are for high schoolers who answer "Very Interested" to every question.

Even after glancing at the results multiple times, seeing his name above "Doctor" sends a warm surge through him, but when he closes his eyes he can't picture himself in the white coat, can't feel anything but the word and the sound of it from Kristen's mouth, the same mouth that he dreams of at night. He imagines her naked in his bedroom doorway, walking toward him, taking back the covers, saying his name, and going down on him.

The lecture ends and the counselor weaves up and down the rows, helping anyone with his or her hand raised. Marcus's hands are in his lap, but Miss Sheroll stops beside him. She appears tired.

"They don't have an ice cream question so you blow it off? Keep the paper, Marcus. Keep it and think of what you won't be. When you wake up, we can talk."

The bell rings, and she leans in with bad coffee breath. "Not everyone has to go to the mill." Then, with a smirk: "I wouldn't assume they'll be hiring."

Marcus stays put, waiting, and Kristen walks up his row, books at her chest. He flexes his right arm, leans in enough to get a whiff of her vanilla perfume.

Wintric and Kristen eat lunch in Reno before his flight to basic training. The slot machines near the casino buffet bang out their solicitations. The carpet underneath them is a dated turquoise-pink-and-black stew. He wears a gray shirt with *Army* across the front, and his hair reaches the middle of his back. He has put away four platefuls of shrimp.

Wintric has never been on a plane before, and his buddy told him to watch for the turbulence, but he isn't afraid.

When he imagines the inside of the plane, the images are from the movies and the seats are large and flight attendants in tight uniforms carry trays of drinks.

"Are you going back for more?" Kristen asks.

"No, I'm good."

"Is it time?"

"You want me out of here?" Wintric says, and stares at her to make sure she feels the joke, but he knows she's his equal.

"As soon as possible," she says. "Don't worry, you won't miss anything. Afghanistan has world-class shrimp."

"Got to get through Fort Benning first."

Kristen wears his favorite outfit, but she hasn't caught him glancing at the plunging neckline.

From the casino floor, *Wheeeel ooooff Fortune!*

"Will you send me your hair?"

"What?"

"Your hair. It's something. Stick it in the mail."

"You want me to overnight it?"

"Stick it in the mail."

"Fine."

"They're gonna wonder where the heck you came from with your hair."

"The army has to have people like me. That's the point. Rich big-city people don't enlist. Why would they?"

"It saves the kids of our town."

"What does?"

"The army saves. That's what my dad says."

"We'll see. Not sure what I need to be saved from."

"No. I didn't mean . . ."

"It's okay."

She spoons soft-serve vanilla ice cream into her mouth.

"They take girls, K. I'm only half joking."

"Yeah. Well. I haven't thought about it."

"I don't know if I want you to think about it."

"Be fair. If it's good enough for you . . ."

"Okay. Let's not talk about it right now."

"So you're going to send me your hair?"

"If you want. I'm serious. I will."

At the airport Wintric checks his bag, and they walk together through the central lounge. A band from the local middle school plays a poor version of the *William Tell Overture* in the lobby and they stop to listen near a hand-painted sign and a donation bucket. The clarinets are especially awful – a squeak emanates every third bar – and the trumpets fail to keep the momentum even at half tempo. Neither Wintric nor Kristen imagined a soundtrack to their goodbye, but they hear the music and stop. The aging carpet stretches another fifty feet to the metal detectors, but this is the spot. Behind them on the wall is an advertisement poster for Harrah's Lake Tahoe. Wintric has asked Kristen not to write until he gets settled, and even then he isn't sure how many reminders of home he wants right away. They hug, and as he pulls away he looks down her shirt.

"I have a window seat," he says.

He walks away, the bottom of his ponytail bouncing in step. He doesn't wave, and when he passes through the metal detector he lifts his hands up.

Marcus has twenty minutes before he enters, stage left. He realizes that everyone is worried about him, even though the cast is mostly people from the retirement home and other high school kids who don't mind a horrible-paying summer gig. The director told Marcus that it would be okay to sit out until he is more comfortable. Julian, an ostentatious seventy-year-old with a bad hip, has memorized Marcus's lines and could cover for him, but Marcus refuses.

Marcus knows the words, but his demeanor in and out of character is the opposite of what the director needs: his character is supposed to be fiery and impassioned – a man fighting the railroad for his land – and Marcus is neither, though he may look the part with his impressive wrestler's body. He has done poorly in rehearsals, but this is community theater in a small town, so they let him keep the part because he knows the lines and helped paint the backdrops.

His mother sits somewhere in the darkness of the half-filled elementary school auditorium. He wonders if she smells of Beam, her familiar breath-scent since his father lost a hand delimbing trees for the mill. The smell no longer bothers Marcus. His mother never drives drunk, and at least she's there in the uncomfortable folding chair when other parents are not.

The actors sweat under the lights. Three pages before he goes on. Marcus wears thin overalls. His hat is too large for him, but he's ready. He wonders if Kristen has come and decides that she has: he imagines she has sneaked in alone for his performance and she's leaning forward, mouth slightly open, waiting for his entrance. She smiled when he told her about the play, and although there's no reason to think that she's there, Marcus doesn't care. A hand pats him on the back and he steps out onto the stage.

The space is larger than he remembers, and as he takes the long walk to the aged railroad man, his mother shouts his name. The crowd laughs. Marcus is supposed to address the railroad man, but he stares out to the darkened back row as he speaks his lines. The conversation lasts six minutes, and Marcus maintains his focus. The railroad man ad-libs "Look at me" twice and then gives in and gazes at the back of the room as well. The other actors follow.

Marcus doesn't realize that Kristen is actually sitting in the fourth row, where the cusp of stage light fades out.

One of her girlfriends is playing a corn farmer, and Marcus had jokingly told Kristen that she should come and watch him forget his lines. Kristen hears Marcus speaking to the railroad man, a possible deal and a rejection, but they don't look at each other, and quickly the play has changed in a way no one quite understands.

The audience listens closely, the awkwardness forcing them to shift in their seats. They want to know what they're missing. They want to understand why no one looks at anyone else. Several glance over their shoulders to the back of the room to check if something is there. The railroad man angers, demands the five thousand acres: "Forty thousand dollars is more than fair!" But the farmer is trancelike, as if he can't hear the offer or the threat that follows.

Marcus is in the middle of his monologue: "My land! My soul! Inseparable! The rebirth of our lives in the soil! This seasonal passion! Roots of my land! My Nebraska!"

He stands with his arms at his sides, slightly hunched over, gaze still locked onto the back row. He speaks to Kristen in the seat he can't see. He's placed her there and put her in a white cotton shirt. He enchants her, seduces her now. He hurls his lines forth, body slouched but his voice powerful and confident.

Kristen spots the farmer's hat sliding down, his strong arms at his sides, everything odd but captivating. His voice has taken on a desperate but fierce rhythm, and his pleas fill the room like nothing else in Act I. She compares this actor onstage to the Marcus she's known: playing in the back yard at family barbecues, looking at her longingly in ninth grade, exchanging daily pleasantries in the high school hallways, working at the soda fountain, wrestling, his singlet and triceps at the one match she attended. She's heard he might get on with the mill.

The door opens at the back of the auditorium – a late arrival – and the hallway sheds enough light to illuminate the empty back rows. Marcus hesitates long enough for the director to whisper his next line. His hat has slouched down again, and he grabs the brim and flings it into the crowd. He glances around at the railroad man and the other actors as they all stare at the back of the room.

Kristen watches the farmer's hat fly up and float down into the ambient light. The room is silent, and the entire cast focuses on a far-off point as the farmer takes in their faces for the first time. The farmer appears confused and stammers: vocal heartbreak. His hair is crazy.

"Her bosom! Her long reach around us! The spring like a . . . like a slow kiss!"

His pace is fast and his voice cracks. His eyes dart back and forth across the auditorium, and the audience squirms, some now staring at their feet, the awkwardness too much, but a few reach out to meet him, entranced. Kristen squeezes her knees. Her feet tingle. She sees his eyes pass over her. Is any of this for her? Is it all for her?

The farmer appears lost onstage, and he delivers his final words exiting, apparently too soon, because he's still speaking even after he's past the ruffled curtain: "And my heart in the wheat!" There is no scene break in the play, but the actors are speechless, the audience silent. Everyone hears Marcus, offstage, stamp his feet on the floor and call out, "Shit!"

He hits himself on the side of his head before leaving the building. He has more dialogue in Act III, but he doesn't return. When someone has to deliver the farmer's triumphant monologue about the unrailroaded land, a confident Julian limps out to center stage in the retrieved hat, but before he reaches his mark, the crowd buzzes and Marcus's mother screams out "Bullshit!"

• • •

Above an old pair of Nike basketball shoes and Kristen's prom dress, on the top shelf of her closet, sits a box containing two feet of Wintric's hair. She hasn't moved the box in four months. Wintric's absence no longer occupies her daily thoughts, but when she does think of him — when she spies the box or when he sends a postcard of the Garden of the Gods, letting her know he's been stationed at Fort Carson in Colorado Springs — his presence arrives, intense and warm. He has contacted her only twice, and each time he has written he has asked that she not contact him, said that he is still sorting out the military life and that her words would make him lose focus. When friends ask her if she and Wintric are still together, she pauses and answers "No," but she despises the way that answer arrives more quickly to her lips with each passing day.

On the far right of the closet hang four white shirts and three pairs of brown pants, her work clothes. The supermarket — the only one in town — loans the employees a logoed apron for each shift. The block lettering reads, *Holiday*.

An athlete in high school, Kristen was all-district in basketball and volleyball, and she's considered asking her old basketball coach if she might serve as an assistant, maybe one day take over the volunteer job. She thought about college until the nerves and lack of money became real, so she took the checkout job after graduation and promised herself that she'd earn an associate's degree from Lassen College over in Susanville, but already she can't imagine a future in which she'll start classes. She doesn't love or hate her job; it's just her life now, and most days she doesn't allow herself to dream up alternatives, save maybe the coaching gig in a couple years. If she keeps out of trouble, she can get a fifty-cent raise every six months.

After work one evening Kristen grabs her sleeping bag and drives out to a campsite at Domingo Springs. When she pulls up, her two girlfriends are setting up a tent near a stand of dead trees, and one of them holds up and shakes a bottle of rum. Experienced outdoors, Kristen knows her friends have picked the worst possible October location. There's not much protection from the breeze, the bathrooms are upwind, and the comforting springs are a good fifty yards away, but Kristen cares little – this is how she relaxes. Local places like Domingo Springs, Willow Lake, Drakesbad – the trees, clean water, Mount Lassen nearby – form the limits of the world she knows and support her personal edict: *Why go somewhere else when you're happy where you are?* The campsite is only twenty minutes from town, but far enough. She drops her sleeping bag and backpack by the nearly assembled tent and heads off to find dry wood for the fire.

Newly hired, Marcus drives his Forest Service truck up to the payment box at the campground. He opens each numbered slot and marks his camp sheet. His uniform almost matches the light green truck. He drives ten miles an hour through the one-way maze of campsites, each with a crusty barbecue grill and picnic table. Some of the campers haven't paid, but it's mainly locals this time of year, and he ignores their five-dollar sins and motors along with the window open, returning waves and stares. He enjoys it out here – he recognizes a few of the people, and they treat him with respect.

As he rounds a curve he sees Kristen's car and the three girls huddled around a fire too large for the pit. The truck stops, and before he can convince himself otherwise he is halfway to them, kicking at pine needles along the way. One of the girls tosses the bottle at the tent, only to have it slide down the zipped-up screen entrance. He attended school with all of them and expects them to call his name in relief, but it's too dark and all they make out is his uniform. One of Kristen's friends has hit on Marcus a couple times, and he's disappointed she's among the group.

Kristen, not quite drunk, stands. She has to focus hard to recognize Marcus, but when she does she says his name, and his shoulders relax. The girls invite him to join them and Kristen fetches the bottle, which Marcus accepts.

He says nothing about their payment, nothing about the tall fire so close to the dry trees, but he does talk, sparingly at first. Yes, he works for the Forest Service now. He patrols campgrounds throughout the area. He's self-deprecating and fit, and soon chugging the bottle. One of the girls stares at him and smiles.

Marcus avoids Kristen's eyes, and for the first time she wants him to look at her. They all laugh and talk about high school, and Kristen tells a story about a girl fight she thinks is new to him, but halfway through she remembers that Marcus was there. She asks him why he didn't interrupt her, why he's so quiet, but he just nods and stares at the fire. She talks to the other two girls now, recalling the summer play, breathless and stunned, this Marcus a genius. "The fucking wheat!" she says. She describes the farmer, the silence, the frantic tension, the craziness in Act III.

Marcus glances over. He can't feel his hands.

It's eleven-thirty when one of the drunk girls asks Marcus if he has to report back. He's an hour late, and they'll think he fell asleep, or worse. Marcus tries to stand up straight, and his legs take a moment to support his weight. When he starts the truck, the fuel gauge shows empty and the orange light is illuminated. He's excited and over-whelmed, but he keeps the truck on the road while scanning for deer. After he coasts into the Forest Service station lot on fumes, he picks up his phone. No missed calls.

Late morning in early February, and the Forest Service supervisor tells Marcus they're letting him go. He doesn't argue, but the supervisor lists the reasons besides overmanning: sleeping on the job, failing to prevent the tree fire last fall at Domingo Springs, having an ambivalent attitude. She tells him that she thinks the mill has started hiring again.

Marcus senses his own smile. It's been two months since he started seeing Kristen, and although there have been no promises, they meet up regularly and have agreed to get together later that night.

The station is a mile out of town, two to his apartment, and Marcus walks back in the dirty snow. He has yet to save up for a car, but an old yellow motorcycle stands for sale in his neighbor's yard for a hundred and fifty bucks. He stays off the shoulder of the road – the last level inches before the mounded snow berm – and passes the airport. To his right are a couple single-prop jobs tied to the tarmac and a refurbished WWII fire bomber that's about to take off to hit an incredibly early blaze far south in the canyons. Marcus has heard about the winter fire, but there's no smoke to prove it's real.

He passes a worn-down storage shed and a decent Mexican restaurant – the sixth restaurant in the doomed location – and he raises his arm to slap the green city-limits sign and reads the familiar POP 2200 and ELEV 4525. A couple years ago rumors floated that they were taking a new census, but no one ever came to his family's door. Then, without notice, the sign changed: the town lost twenty-four people. No one knew who the departed were. The county didn't repaint the elevation, and the last 5 has almost faded away completely.

Marcus strolls past the entrance to the mill, by the red barber shop/laundromat combo, by the Pine Shack Frosty, and he smokes a cigarette as he gets to the Beacon gas station. The smoking is a recent habit. He can't get enough of the smell on his clothes and in his apartment. He doesn't cough at all, and he jogs to equal everything out. Kristen won't touch cigarettes, but she keeps quiet about the smell when she heads over to his place.

Marcus takes a drag, and from the gas station door someone appears dressed in camouflage, and for a moment Marcus's world explodes and he projects in flashes – *Wintric, home, hero, breakup, Kristen, empty, a gun* – but the man turns and he sees that he's not Wintric, just a no-name hunter returning from a morning out. Marcus's blood runs back to his legs and his heart settles. It's at this moment that he imagines, then wishes for, an accident wherever Wintric is – *Afghanistan? Fort Carson?* At first thought it's not Wintric's death, just disfigurement, a lost hand, leg. *But no,* he thinks, *it has to be his face, turned unrecognizable.* He pictures a mash of swirled flesh, but he wonders if there's too much sympathy and attention in that, no matter how repulsive. Having heard about ill-equipped Humvees from his uncle, Marcus considers an IED ripping Wintric in half from the bottom up – an instantaneous death. *There's sympathy there,* he thinks, *but it won't last.*

Marcus walks past the Holiday supermarket and a silent surge hits him from being this close to Kristen, only a parking lot, a brick wall, four small eat-in tables, a rack of magazines, and two cash registers away. He could go in and surprise her – she might like that – but he talks himself out of it.

He walks by the Kopper Kettle and the U.S. Bank and pauses in front of the ice cream shop where he used to work. A woman dusts the empty barstools. He passes the old theater converted into a church and the park with bent basketball rims and stops on a bridge over the North Fork of the Feather River. He works his mind toward hopeful images of the evening: Kristen sliding her pants off, her bra, standing in his doorway. He pauses to survey the cold water of the river, and he wonders how the lake can sit low in the summer with all the water running underneath him.

When he arrives, his apartment is cold, icicles hanging from the eves in front of the living room window. He turns the thermostat up to eighty, hoping it'll hit sixty-five. Uncooked pasta sits in a pot for the dinner he had planned to throw together after work. The living room recliner calls to him, and he lights another cigarette. Marcus stares out the window, over at the post office, an old building with two flights of stairs. They're finishing construction on a path for the handicapped. Marcus has never been in a wheelchair and wonders if anyone in the town will use the ramp. The route to the doors will be longer but easier on the legs.

At dinner Kristen gives him a plain red shirt before pouring herself a glass of cheap red wine.

"Something new," she says.

He hates the shirt but promises her he'll think about wearing it.

After the pasta they relax on the couch and flip through the television channels. Channel six, eight, eleven, twelve, and Kristen tells him to stop.

"Keep it here," she says. The evening news.

Marcus holds the remote, index finger on the black channel button, ready to press. Colin Powell inside the UN, photos of Iraqi buildings taken from space, arrows, ultimatums. Marcus stays silent and listens for Kristen's breathing, but all he hears is his apartment's undersized heater humming and Powell's voice: "We know that Saddam Hussein is determined to keep his weapons of mass destruction; he's determined to make more." In his peripheral vision Marcus sees Kristen put the tip of her finger in her mouth. As the segment winds down, he prays for anything except a piece about car bombings or friendly fire or any mention of Afghanistan, and his fears soon dissipate when a mug shot of Phil Spector appears in a small box near the left side of the news anchor's head. "Producer of *Let It Be* arrested for murder."

Marcus turns off the television and puts his arm around Kristen.

"We should get out of here. Go somewhere."

"Yeah," she says. "I'll go."

"Mexico is warm."

"Dreams. Only dreams."

"We can drive."

"You're not serious. We work, remember?"

"Closer?"

"Marcus."

"I'm serious. Any place in the world you could go, where'd it be?"

She pictures the gaping hole in the gigantic redwood, envisions her car driving through, a thousand growth rings surrounding her, but she feels Wintric in the vision, feels him in the car with her.

"San Francisco," she says. "Go see Bonds."

"Doable. In a couple months, it'll be perfect."

Eleven at night, and she asks Marcus if he wants her to do anything special, and he summons the courage to say yes. He's nervous, but after hundreds of classroom daydreams, he can give her detailed instructions. He undresses, positions himself in bed under all the blankets, closes his eyes, and waits. The streetlight shines in enough that when he opens his eyes, he sees her in the doorway and knows it's no longer a fantasy.

"Kristen," he says.

She stands in the doorway. She hears her name and waits in the near darkness. She knows he'll call for her again.

3

Pollice Verso

THREE MONTHS AFTER his prison stint for starting a forest fire that killed a man, Armando's father drives his family past the Supermax outside Florence, Colorado. He's in good spirits.

"You know the guy that invented the Richter scale? Dude was a nudist," he says.

The Torres family laughs together inside their minivan as they head back to Colorado Springs after an overnight campout in the Wet Mountains. Fifteen-year-old Armando rests in the back seat with his younger sister. She holds her stomach and smiles. Armando half listens, half mentally undresses a girl in his grade named Marie who sports a pinkish birthmark on her cheek that resembles Wisconsin.

"I can't help but imagine a naked guy, poolside, when an eight-point-oh strikes a couple miles down the road. Bet he wishes he had pants on."

Armando's mother smiles and play-punches his father in the shoulder.

"So you got gladiators," he says. "And they battle it out and finally one stands over the other one, sword high, and he checks out the emperor to see if the near-vanquished will live or die, and the crowd gives the thumbs-up. You say, 'Good news,' right? No, my dear family. Pollice verso. With a turned thumb. The movies have it wrong. Thumbs down, sword down. Thumbs up, dead."

"So we should give a thumbs-down when someone does something right?" Armando's mother asks. "Weird."

"There's a flower that opens up at night," his father says. "Bats do the work, not bees. Your turn."

Armando extends both thumbs up and smirks at his sister. His mind works, and a school bus passes the other way. "There's blind fish in caves."

"One huge, linked cave. In Kentucky. What else you got? Give me something good."

"My English teacher says Shakespeare ripped off his stories."

"Shakespeare didn't rip off anything 'cause he didn't write the plays," his father says. "Edward de Vere, Earl of Oxford. That's a fact. Listen up kids, read widely, but only pay attention to de Vere's stuff and three others – William Blake, Bill Watterson, Jane Austen. That's it."

"You're full of it," says Armando's mother, "but you're right about Austen." Then, smiling back and winking at Armando: "Listen, a half, maybe a quarter of what he says is true." She reaches and squeezes his shin.

"Ask me anything about sports. Anything."

"We got the Olympics," she says. By "we" she means Mormons. The Torres family has visited Salt Lake City twice: Temple Square, the tabernacle, two Jazz games. "We're going."

"Luge and ice hockey," says Armando's father.

"Maybe we can get him into luge," his mother says, thumbing back at her son. Then, tone rising: "How many people can be into luge? A hundred?"

"A thousand, worldwide. Still good odds."

"What do you say?" his mother says.

"That's headfirst, right?" Armando says.

"It is? Forget it, then," she says.

"But you'd be okay with feet first?"

"Drop it," she says.

"Figure skating," says his sister. "I can see you in skates."

"I could wear pink," he says.

Armando's father whistles, sees the approaching dotted yellow center line, flicks the left turn signal on, and accelerates out into the left lane to pass a brown truck doing forty-five, but as their van draws even the truck speeds up, so he pushes the accelerator, but the truck matches him, and four seconds in he peers over and spots two shirtless boys, the young driver smirking, glancing at his speed, and nodding to his buddy, and Armando's father presses the brake, but the truck slows as well, and Armando's mother reaches up and touches her window and says, "Hey. Hey," and the dotted line goes double yellow and Armando's father smashes the accelerator down and they fly along a bend, the van tilting hard, and a car coming for them in the far distance flashes its lights as the van's engine wails a high-pitched squeal, and Armando freezes in the back seat, and his father's head leans forward as the van gains a bumper ahead, then a full car length, and his father turns the wheel and cuts the truck off and the oncoming car whips past, horn ablaze.

"Shit!" his father says, lifting his right arm up with a fist.

His mother moans.

"My God," she says. "Slow down. Slow down. Now. Please."

Armando's father lifts his foot from the accelerator, but the pedal sticks. He presses the brake and the van shakes.

"Stuck. Pedal's stuck. Shit," he says. "Help me."

Armando glances outside and watches the red rock and pine trees flash by. Amid his still-forming fear he wonders if they're doing a hundred.

Later Armando will understand that his father's mistake was not shifting the car to neutral and not making any attempt to turn off the engine, but no one in the minivan knows that now, so while his father hammers down his left foot on the parking brake and his right on the main brake pedal, his mother unbuckles her seat belt and leans over the center console and yanks on the accelerator. The burning brake stench overpowers them. From the back seat Armando watches his mother's lower back jerk and jerk. He has never seen her body move so wildly, and the sight scares him more than anything that has happened up to this point, until his body launches sideways, then presses taut, and he hears his father yell out "Na!" as the van begins its roll.

His vision straightens and Armando makes out his sister's wet face and the ground at the window behind her. Something presses on his neck and he reaches there and grabs at flesh, bone underneath, and he moves it away from him. A dangling, shoeless foot on a leg – his mother's leg extending out at an impossible angle toward her body. He hears voices nearby and reaches out in the space in front of him, toward his sister, and sees his hands there before darkness overtakes him.

One afternoon, eight weeks into Armando's mother's coma, Armando's father picks him up from school in their loaner van and drives them past the luxurious Broadmoor resort and out on Gold Camp Road toward Pike's Peak. Aspens flank the packed dirt path. They talk about the Broncos beating the Redskins, about John Elway, how he may have a couple more seasons left in him.

His father says, "The guy once knelt on home plate at the Stanford baseball stadium and hurled a baseball over the center fence from his knees."

Armando pictures young Elway kneeling on home plate before the throw. Elway's in uniform, warming up, windmilling his massive right arm loose as a crowd gathers near the backstop. A baseball appears in his hand, and in one superhuman motion he flings the ball high and deep. The ball still climbs into the sky as it passes dead center, headed for the clouds. Young Elway grins as Armando shakes the vision away.

After a crest in the road his father turns south, guiding the van into a valley. A mile down the bumpier road he pulls the van off by a stream and parks.

They follow the stream for a while and piss at the base of a rusted-out sign before peeling off and hiking up a hill, then resting on a granite outcropping.

"Never eat an armadillo," Armando's father says. "Leprosy."

"I'll never eat an armadillo."

"You never know when you'll be tempted to try. Wyoming. New Mexico. Weird freaks out there."

"What's the weirdest thing you've eaten?"

His father smacks his lips. "Weird, of course, is relative. But to answer your question, human."

"Human?"

"You believe me?"

"I guess."

"Be careful."

"Okay."

"I ate a rabbit eyeball for twenty-five bucks."

"Dad."

"Hard Jell-O marble."

Armando looks out on the modest vista – gray rock and

trees scattered together. He picks up a flat rock and tosses it down the hill. Tiny dust eddies circle into the afternoon. He sees dirt on his jeans and swipes. He imagines Marie calling his house and leaving a message he'll find later that night. He recalls the yellow shirt she wore at school, the freckles on her neck. Near the end of the day she mentioned to him that she wanted to see *Se7en* — he's heard something about a severed head in a box.

"Your mom will wake up," his father says.

"Yep."

"I mean it, son. She'll be back with us soon."

"You gave her a blessing?"

"Doesn't have to do with that."

"Okay."

"There's free will, but there's God's plan. There's volcanoes and shit too. God's always watching, which is a pain in the ass. And, of course, Freud is always watching, which is less a pain in the ass, but still. So there you go."

The wind blows through the trees and they hear the branches move.

On the way down they stay silent, but as they near the van, his father tells him to wait by the stream, ambles to the vehicle, and returns with a glass jug and matches.

"It's getting darker," his father says. "Okay." He uncorks the jug and holds it out to his son. "Smell," he says, smiling, but Armando can smell the gasoline from where he stands.

"Little smoke 'cause there's no green on it," his father says, stepping close. "Always pick dead ones."

Only then does Armando notice the tree next to him. It's largely limbless save a few dead branches near the top.

"I'll do this one," his father says. "Now listen. You just burn one. I got too cocky. Out of control."

He steps to the snag and pours gasoline over the bottom two feet of the tree.

"Wow," he says. "Yeah. That's the smell." He pinches a match and holds it in his left hand between his thumb and index finger.

Armando stares in wonderment. "They'll see the smoke," he says.

"Getting dark, son." His father shakes his head. "And there's no *they*."

"Okay."

"Most of the law is good, but some of it's shit." He shakes out his arms. "You already know that. You may think different, and I don't care. Just never say I didn't know what I was doing. You understand? Don't ever say that." He points the match at his son's chest. "That's the worst thing you can say about someone, that they don't know what they're doing. Doesn't matter how old. We should hang kids that kill people. They know enough." He pauses and examines the unlit match. "If you have a drink, that's fine. Your mother will wake up and disagree."

"I try things."

"Good."

"Some things."

"Always believe in God. You'll be tempted. People believe in gravity. No one knows what the hell it is. There's no difference."

"What?"

"Be suspicious of Jesus. No one understands what's going on there."

His father strikes the match on the side of the box and cups the miniflame. Armando's head buzzes, and he steps forward.

"Can I?" he asks, but his father ignores him, and Armando sees his father's mouth move, but no sound emerges. His father flicks the match at the base of the tree and the flame catches and climbs. The tree lights up quick – a twenty-foot torch.

Armando can't find words to say, but in his mind many cartwheel by: *beautiful, free, power, hot, trouble, crime, glorious, God, coma, dead, Marie, prison, run.*

Then his father's voice.

"She said I was a slob or something. Things go back and forth, then you dig up the good stuff, and I end up calling her an über-bitch. So she says she's going to stay at her sister's in Cortez. Fine. 'Good,' I say. And she gathers her stuff, her priceless diploma. Gets in the car. All ready to go. But she sits out there forever. She's not crying. Not doing anything. Just sitting. Not even touching the wheel. Finally she comes in. 'It's Sunday,' she says. 'Can't spend money on gas on Sunday.' That's it. She stays."

"Mom?"

"Can't spend money on Sunday? Can't live like that, man. Don't talk about it." He takes a step toward the fire.

"And they say I killed a man. Bull. He killed himself. Intent matters. We pay people to kill. We give them awards. We call people heroes because they get shot down trying to bomb people. How does that make you a hero? You survive the Hanoi Hilton and you're a hero? You firebomb Dresden or Tokyo and you're a hero? Ask about LeMay."

"What?"

"You need to know I've never killed anyone. Doesn't make sense. Why would I do that?"

"You wouldn't."

"Go," he says. "I want you to go."

Armando doesn't move, still mesmerized. His father walks over to him and gently squeezes his neck.

"Get in the car," his father says. "I'll see you at home. I mean it." He turns his son to face him and smiles.

"Dad, I don't have a license."

"It's okay. Drive slow."

"Dad."

"Now, son."

Armando opens the driver's door and gets in. He lowers himself onto the seat and takes in the burning tree, his father's back to him, and he squeezes the wheel hard and he reaches his feet out to touch the brake and gas pedals. He has practiced driving twice in their old van, but this is a newer Aerostar, electric doors and windows and side mirrors, and already he has decided not to adjust anything, but the seat is too far away and it takes him several nervous seconds to find the button that brings him closer to everything. Armando turns the key in the ignition – keys left in the van – then lights on, dashboard to life, a little brake, and he grabs the shifter and slides it to reverse, off the brake, and movement. The lights of the van spotlight his father as he pulls back, and once Armando reaches the road leading out, he shifts to drive but keeps his foot on the brake. He wipes his hands on his pants and peers over. A thought comes to him, and he watches the lit tree, his father's hands on the top of his head, a piercing certainty: his mother will never wake.

On the drive back Armando keeps it at thirty miles per hour. He focuses on the road, how close the van's right-side tires parallel the shoulder, anticipating oncoming headlights, late-night loggers, but after thirty minutes of slow driving he enters a space of half awareness and replays the tree lighting, the glass jug, his father's shiny face ranting, the invisible smoke flowing into the night. He considers his father, a man who seemingly knows everything but knows how to do little, who showcases benevolence and service, a diehard Broncos fan, a hugger, quick to smile and encourage. He's also someone who attends every fire station open house to climb on the trucks, a man who lights a match and blows it out after every bathroom trip, a person who, no matter the intention, has burned someone to death.

While his father was in prison, his mother would tell him and his sister that the fault was the dead man's for not heeding the warnings as the fire crept toward his log home. Never a passionate vocal defense, but it was practiced, and soon she stopped talking about blame altogether. Sometimes his mother wouldn't come home at night, and he'd call the dentists' office where she worked, and they'd inform him that she'd left hours before. Once she called him from Raton to tell him that there were extra frozen waffles in the freezer in the basement, that this would take care of him and his sister until she returned, but she was always home on Sundays, when she would dress up and haul them to church, a family procession he didn't dread unless it was NFL season and the Broncos played the early game.

Driving down off the Front Range he passes a large truck heading in the opposite direction, and although he can't make out the driver, Armando imagines a Forest Service uniform and a sidearm. He slows the van and pictures his father standing near the fire. When the truck pulls up to the still-burning tree, will his father run? Laugh? Align his wrists for cuffs? Then the startling thought that he might have to be the one to pull the plug on his mother if his father is in jail. He doesn't know the rules, but as he speeds back up for home, he thinks of standing over the hospital bed when the doctor hands him the form to sign, points, says, "Sign here." His messy signature materializes.

When Armando arrives home, his sister is watching *Xena: Warrior Princess* and eating a bowl of Corn Pops.

"You stink," she says.

The next day there's nothing in the *Colorado Springs Gazette* about a fire, no rumors at his school, and when his father shows up at their house two days later he wears new clothes.

"We're going out to eat," he says.

Armando's mother wakes up twenty minutes after O. J. Simpson is acquitted. Thinned out and shaky, she carries some internal organ damage, but the doctors tell the Torres family that their mother will be relatively fine, save a limp and the need to regulate her insulin for the rest of her life.

The first thing his mother asks for is a chocolate pudding pie in a graham cracker crust.

"Just this once," says the doctor. The dessert is Armando's favorite, and after she tears into the pie and nears the last couple of bites she asks him if he wants some.

"No," he says, amazed.

In the weeks after his mother's return home she discovers that she no longer likes to read, she has perfect pitch, and the color yellow brings on headaches. Armando never hears her complain about the needles.

What he does hear is her singing voice. Never one to carry a tune outside of church – and even then quietly – his mother devours CD after CD and sings along at top volume. Her favorites are Chicago's *The Chicago Transit Authority* and Tower of Power's *Tower of Power*. One day Armando comes home from school and his mother hands him a trombone.

"Learn, for me," she says, eyes wide and expectant. "You don't have to play at school."

Soon Armando finds himself with his trombone in hand, sitting down for private lessons in a padded room inside a rancher on the east side of town. The instructor is a blind man pushing seventy.

"'Hot Cross Buns,'" the man says, face toward the ceiling, already nodding. "First, second, third position. Ready. Play."

The first thing the Torreses buy with the $400,000 settlement from the car company is a two-story stucco home on a hillside near the Broadmoor.

This is the home where the family watches *The Empire Strikes Back* on an April Saturday night.

When the film ends, Armando's mother says, "The Force is the gospel. That movie was inspired. I believe that."

"Mark Hamill plus car crash equals ugly Skywalker," his father says. "Kind of resembles Joseph Smith."

"You're not serious," says his mother.

Later that night, while his family sleeps, Armando watches *Risky Business* in his bedroom. They have a free six-month HBO trial, so he's been staying up late. As Tom Cruise starts fondling Rebecca De Mornay onscreen, he feels himself go hard. He doesn't know if there's actual no-masturbation doctrine anywhere in the Bible or the Book of Mormon, but there are enough context clues in Sunday school to guess that God would be pretty pissed at a young man jobbing himself hours before taking the sacrament. But still, he's sixteen now and this feeling is back again. De Mornay is ungodly hot, and he thinks he might come even if he doesn't touch himself. He begs for a concession between release and salvation somewhere in the night, and within ten seconds he thinks he's found a compromise as he grabs his penis but doesn't move his hand. *If something happens,* he thinks, *then it happens.*

Armando's eyes and groin sync in heartbeat rhythm. He lets the pressure build as De Mornay straddles Cruise, and for a few seconds he thinks he may suffocate. He squeezes himself slightly and briefly considers dry-humping the new couch, and he hates himself and absolves himself: he didn't seek out this I-want-to-do-this-beautiful-woman-for-days urge, but here it is, undeniable and strong, and yet this sensation collides with the vision of a white-robed, muscular, Caucasian God peering down, shaking his head, shaking a tiny bottle of Wite-Out, taking out the thin Wite-Out brush and painting over "Armando Torres" on the "Welcome to Heaven" list. Then, too quickly for Armando and his racing insides, the sex scene ends, and fully clothed actors talk onscreen in daylight, and his blood slowly settles. He feels a dull ache, and already he thinks about how he'll be okay if he's asked to say a prayer in front of people in ten hours. He is still clean.

On the eleventh hole of the Broadmoor's West Course, Armando clips his tee shot off to the left and the white ball splashes into a pond. Early afternoon and the clouds have begun to gather over the peaks. He reaches into his bag for another ball, but he's out. He's a poor golfer, which he accepts, but he still waits a second before asking his mother for one of her balls. She used to be a scratch player but now carries a four handicap. "My car-crash four," she calls it. She still maintains an effortless swing, but there's a hitch now when the weight transfers to her damaged left leg, as if she tries to stop everything a split second before it happens.

Armando's mother wears a blue visor and a form-fitting white polo. She is thirty-six years old and attractive, her slim waist and long hair often a target of silent male acknowledgment. Armando notices the minor nervousness of the two strangers who play with them. One wears a bright yellow shirt. The other, he overhears, is a retired Air Force Academy economics professor. Mr. Yellow Shirt shifts his gaze to the sky and smirks each time Armando's mother flattens her back and sticks out her butt during her preshot routine.

Armando's parents married when his father was twenty-two and his mother nineteen. He was a return missionary from England, smart enough to showcase a sliver of his bad-boy status by drinking Coke and growing long sideburns. His mother was a sophomore at Cornell. Within a year of their marriage she was pregnant with Armando. His father never finished his studies at Brigham Young, opting for a decent-paying job in the diamond business, but his mother keeps her framed diploma in their study on the wall above their new Apple computer.

While always weary of the attention his mother's beauty receives, Armando is proud of her golf talent when they are alone on the course, but he's not thrilled to be humbled in front of strangers – including a stranger who responds to "Colonel" – by asking his mother for a ball, which he knows will be a pink Slazenger.

"Need one, Mom," he says.

His mother opens the side of her golf bag and reaches in, and he sees a gun among the golf balls – his father's black 9-millimeter. The Colonel and Yellow Shirt don't notice, and Armando's body clenches.

"In the ancient days these used to be made by stuffing goose feathers in a leather pouch," his mother says, impersonating her husband's voice. She fingers the ball before tossing it over. "Swing hard." She grins.

The rest of the round Armando catches himself staring at the Ping logo on his mother's bag, thinking about the weapon behind the light-blue fabric. He loses two more of his mother's golf balls and each time watches as she unzips the bag and chooses a replacement.

On the way home he works up the courage to ask about

the handgun, but his mother strikes first. "Tell me about Marie. How much should I be worried?"

That night he and his mother sit at the kitchen counter eating chocolate pudding.

"You had a gun today," he says. "In your bag."

She swallows a bite, then takes her spoon and swirls the remaining pudding in her bowl. Her elbows rest on the polished granite slab.

"You never know," she says. The tone in her voice signals the end, but Armando presses.

"For bear?"

"You never know."

"Where else?"

"Let's see," she says. "I carry a smaller one pretty much everywhere. I don't care if you know, but don't tell your sister. Got it?"

"To Broncos games? Supermarket?"

"Yes."

"Why?"

She spoons up some pudding and eats it.

"I grew up with guns, and you drive around long enough and you see bad situations. It always comes across as this random thing, but it's not. Do you understand?"

"I guess," he says, mouth full.

His mother stares above him. "I never want a fair fight. I don't understand why anyone would."

"Yeah. That makes sense."

"Now eat your dessert or I will."

Armando spoons the pudding to his mouth and peeks over at his now quiet mother. Her face has thinned, and Armando wonders what she's thinking about: *Guns? Fights? Pudding?* Although his dad is the talker, almost all decisions for the family end with his mother's approval: trips, major purchases, allowances, movies. This power enchants Armando and his sister – their father talks and talks and talks, then, in the end, waits for their mother's nod, smile, or grimace. When she was in the coma the family would encounter unsettling swaths of silence after a debate, no matter how minor, before realizing that her approval was absent. As Armando thinks about it now, he wonders if he'll always seek her consent, especially in challenging times, and it comforts him to think that he will. He doesn't yet know what he'll ask her, or what adult choices he'll face, but he hears his mother's confident voice in the space before future difficult decisions. Next to him, she stares beyond her bowl at the gray and white and black swirls of granite. Armando sits and listens to the sound inside his mouth as he swallows his pudding.

Under a cloudy and warm autumn afternoon, Armando and his father rest on the corner of South River Boulevard and West Walnut Street in Independence, Missouri. The manicured grass surrounding them is a gorgeous, shiny green. Armando's mother and sister are in one of the Temple Lot's visitor centers.

"We'll never know if all this is true unless we find out it isn't," his father says. "But if we're right, God is supposed to come down from the heavens and land right here. We'll get the message, drop our stuff, and congregate at this exact spot. It'll be busy." He breathes in. "I tend to believe it. You'd think God would choose Tahiti or the Yucatán. But that's too easy." He scratches his forehead. "Missouri. Damn, it'll take God coming down here to get me to relocate. Lots of fat people running around."

"What about Jerusalem?"

"Jerusalem sounds more important, but it's not. You

know, someone in Jerusalem right now is high on dope or banging a prostitute or reading the Bible or sharpening a knife."

Armando, confused, notices the perfect mower lines in the grass.

"Come on, Kansas City or Jerusalem or Berlin – it won't matter. I wouldn't mind touring Germany."

A city bus stops near them, then drives away. A man walks by with an ice cream sandwich. The scent of fertilizer floats around them.

"Do we have to walk here?" Armando asks.

"That's the rumor."

"Is that written down?"

"Good point. I doubt you were trying to make a point, but still."

"But we have to walk?"

"Walk to salvation with all our friends."

"People in Europe are screwed."

"Good point."

"But what would happen if you didn't? Say we drove here. Is God or Jesus going to tell us to go back home?"

"Put down your lendings. Put down your lendings." He laughs. "'The Fourth Alarm.'"

"What?"

"Cheever. You'll get to him one day."

"Who?"

"If the difference between driving and walking to Missouri is the litmus test for eternal life, then most are in trouble. Yes."

"So the prophet will let us know when?" Armando says.

"I figure when we see the red chariot flying in the sky, we'll start our trek."

"With bolts of lightning."

"No, you're confusing mythology with Revelation." His

father balls his fists. "You're too young sometimes. Soon you won't be. It's my fault. I've wished you older."

"I know the difference."

"Good."

Armando watches his father pick at the grass between his legs, then toss it at his shoes. His father does this repeatedly, picking away a small circle of lawn.

"Let's not talk," his father says.

Armando leans back and stretches out on the ground. The day is too hot to get comfortable in his slacks, and he is starting to sweat through his gray shirt. He closes his eyes and listens to the traffic and his father picking blades of grass. He imagines walking here, to this place. His legs hurting, sleeping on the side of I-70 as cars and diesel trucks zoom by. *How many will be with them? Then what? Do they live here forever? In Independence? What would they do? Look up at the sky and wait? Would they get bored? Is there a choice?* He recalls a vampire book where the eternal bloodsuckers get bored out of their minds and need antidepressants to get through their days. Then a Sunday school talk comes to him. The well-dressed speaker had said that when contemplating the notion of "forever," the kids should think of how long it would take a hummingbird to peck away at a piece of granite as big as the earth. "Well," said the speaker, "eternity is a lot longer than that."

Colorado driver's license finally in hand, Armando chooses Gold Camp Road as his make-out parking location with Marie.

Marie is patient and understanding of his quirks: no gum, fascination with her birthmark, U2 and Bon Jovi ballads. And he of hers: breaks for air when she says so, and once in a while a lazy George Strait song.

After school one day, while he and Marie hang out in

the living room watching reruns of *The Wonder Years,* Armando's mother walks into the room holding a banana and an unopened condom. She'd watched a television special the night before in which Tom Brokaw lectured a town hall meeting on safe sex. She asks if Armando can put the condom on the fruit. Though unsure, he says he can.

"I'm not condoning premarital sex," his mother says.

Marie buries her face in her hands.

"If you're using this, you're past the point of trouble. But if you're past the point of trouble, use this."

Armando's mother puts the banana back in the fruit bowl and leaves the condom on the counter.

Armando's father corners him one night after he breaks curfew getting back from Gold Camp Road. His father holds up the *Sports Illustrated* swimsuit issue and points at the cover, two beauties instead of the regular one, leopard-print bikinis, gleaming smiles, gleaming bodies.

"The lineaments of gratified desire. Say it with me. The lineaments of gratified desire."

Armando squints and shakes his head.

"An orgasm is pretty awesome, son. You know this. But it's not mystical. Semen shoots from your penis. It feels good. These pictures have nothing to do with that. People were having orgasms long before photography and papyrus. The women in these photos aren't real. That isn't their real skin. That isn't the real sun, real light. They're smiling, but they don't know why."

"Okay."

Armando waits for more from his father, maybe something about masturbation, pregnancy, late-night HBO, Armando has no idea, but his father only nods, somehow satisfied, and tosses the magazine at him and walks away.

• • •

Part of Armando's chores now involves stacking his mother's dialysis fluid boxes every week after a large truck unloads them in the driveway. The machine in his parents' bedroom stands on his mother's side of the bed and makes puffing noises as her blood circulates through the contraption. Often this is where his mother will dispense her advice – hooked up, ready for bed – including her opinion that nothing good happens to teenagers after eleven at night. Sometimes she says after nine at night.

On weekend nights Armando and Marie drive out on Gold Camp Road and pull off in the trees, kill the lights, and try their best in the cramped back seat. He's the novice, and while he's unsure of the extent of her experience, he knows she has endured a couple boyfriends, good and bad. At sixteen, he doesn't comprehend the vast possibilities that separate good from bad.

One night they drive out to the spot where his father torched the tree by the stream. They maneuver past their normal shirts-off, bra-off endpoint, and her hands start to show an interest in his jeans. In that moment he wouldn't say "Stop" with a gun to his head. He feels Marie at the top of his jeans, running her fingers in the thin space between denim and skin, then fumbling with the button, then unzipping him. The roof closes in and spins. In this dark space in the Rockies he only wants to live forever, and for a moment he believes he will, weightless, on fire, and then he hears her, barely at first, crying.

"Marie?"

"I'm sorry," she says. "I'm okay. Lie back down. I'm fine."

He lets her cry for a while with night all around before reaching out for her and holding her, feeling her breasts and warm skin on his skin.

"It's not you," she says.

"Okay," he says.

There's no talk about her crying that first night in the shadow of Pike's Peak or any other night. Not even after several late-night parkings and other attempts at unzipping him and the tears that follow. He never asks her to try again, but she does. Even after he tells her "No, you don't have to," she ignores him and pushes him down and straddles him, her hands on his chest and stomach and hips, moving down.

Often, after their drive out into the Front Range and the mix of limbs and jaws, around midnight Armando lies staring up at branches and white stars through the rear window, listening in pleasure and fear for a sign, waiting for her mouth on him but always hearing her short breaths, then gradual sobs coming from the dark before he takes her in his arms, then dressing and driving home.

On the windy drive home there's plenty of time to ask anything he wants, but they stay quiet, sometimes holding hands, having an occasional chat about Marie's dream of living in Arizona, but normally they just listen to Jon Bon Jovi belting out "Bed of Roses" or "I'll Be There for You" as they wait for the city lights to greet them below.

Pairs of men in tailored suits begin to show up in the Torres family kitchen. When Armando gets home from school they are crouching around the worn dining table, jabbing at papers while his parents nod along. They never glance in his direction, but their disinterest doesn't bother him. Soon he finds out they are life insurance men.

One night after the latest set of buttoned-up men have fled, Armando hears his father say "Uninsurable" over and over before flinging a stack of papers and stomping off to the back yard. His mother sobs while warming water on the stove. Armando thinks about going to her but stays on the couch. She adds macaroni to the boiling water, then steadies herself on the kitchen counter, head down. His father reappears and takes her face in his hands and kisses her on her lips. Armando knows they love each other, but anything longer than a public peck is unusual. He glances over, then down at the carpet, then back. His father runs his fingers down his mother's blue blouse and then pulls her close, keeping his right hip angled away from her injection site.

Armando isn't interested enough to ask why his parents are in the market for life insurance – or what life insurance even is – and his parents don't volunteer the information, but he is interested in this lengthy kiss, and he stares at the strangeness of his parents pressed together for so long. Not sure why he wants to cry or how he knows to stay silent, he watches as his mother tries to look away and his father pulls her back and kisses her again, but she's crying too much now and the kiss has moved from pressed lips to pressed faces, chin to forehead. When his father says, "Go somewhere else, son," Armando walks to his room, where, after thinking about his parents and his forays with Marie, he questions why no one has ever taught him the right way to touch someone you love.

Eventually one pair of insurance men circles back with frequency. The older one, with gray hair, always messes with his paisley tie, and his crumpled suit struggles to cover his bulging midsection. He and his younger partner come back time and again, and after one particular visit Armando guesses they will never return, because his mother hugs them and kisses them on their cheeks and his father shakes their hands and hugs them and calls them "my brothers."

That night Armando's parents take the family to the

Cliff House in Manitou Springs, where the family drinks Martinelli's sparkling cider from champagne glasses. His mother sings "Saturday in the Park" on the way home.

One January morning Armando's mother undergoes a kidney-pancreas transplant in a Denver hospital. Two nights later – just he and Marie are home – Armando paws through his neighbor's trash and swipes a five-foot-long, thick cardboard tube used to ship fly-fishing rods. He gathers up a few racquetballs and tennis balls, a screwdriver, and a red gasoline can from the garage. From his father's gun safe he grabs a can of black powder, a fuse, and two M-80s. On their way to the snow-dusted back yard, he asks Marie to get a set of tongs and oven mitts from the kitchen.

He positions the tube at a 45-degree angle over the back fence, aiming toward the lights of downtown Colorado Springs. With the screwdriver he punctures the tube near the base and threads the fuse through. He places the M-80s in the can of black powder and the can of powder in the tube, insuring that one of the fuse's tips rests deep in the small, dark kernels. The pungent smell surrounds him. Once the contraption is stable, oven-mitted Marie dips two racquetballs and four tennis balls into the gasoline with the tongs, then drops them down the tube.

Armando pulls a lighter from his pocket and walks over to Marie, still mitted, and she backs away.

"Holy shit," she says. "This is a great idea."

"God, forgive us," he says. "Get the car ready. If it's big, we'll take off." He smells his hands.

"I want to see it."

"Okay."

"Wash your hands first," Marie says. "We should wash our hands."

"Good."

His still-damp hands hold the lighter and the fuse. A helicopter flies overhead, so he waits. Then another.

"Fort Carson," he says. "Invasion."

"Red Dawn?"

"Go, Army. Start up the tanks."

Armando flicks the lighter and a miniature flame jumps to life. He lights the fuse and backs away.

"Cover your ears," Marie says, hands on her ears.

"No."

"Cover them."

He can still hear the helicopters in the distance, the spinning rotor blades compressing the air tight. He watches his cardboard cannon, all potential, all rush, blood racing in his ears, floating, and a fire illuminates the tube from within, a split-second reverie of light and heat before the orange-tinged explosion rocks the night.

Armando's mother returns home three weeks later with someone else's organs tied inside her body. Her face bloats from anti-rejection drugs, and she sprouts light blond whiskers on her chin and a few strands hug her cheeks. If the new hair humiliates her, she never says so, and once in a while she still manages a toothy smile. Still, he wonders why she refuses to shave, but he lacks the nerve to ask.

His community service for the back-yard cannon explosion doesn't start for another month. His father told him two things when the judgment was handed down: never confess and never do the same thing twice. They pay someone to fix the fence.

Armando doesn't recognize the life draining from his mother until she grows scared of leaving the house, then of walking, then of standing. Her singing stops, and now, lying on their green living room couch, drinking 7Up and chewing saltine crackers, she will not speak unless spoken to, and even then she offers only one-word answers.

Armando, his father, and his sister try to play games with his mother or read to her every now and then, but mostly she lies there with a glassy stare. Still, at the end of the nightly story, or when he wins at Sorry or Uno, she says "Yes" or "Good" and strains a smile. But the Torres home grows sullen with the February snow, and he finds reasons not to return home until late at night. He kisses his mother on his way to bed and she stares up at him, still somehow knowing him, and although he hates himself for thinking it, he crawls under the sheets wondering if the person confined to the couch is still his mother or if she is something else now. On the worst days, when she barely moves or eats, he battles himself, wondering if he should pray for a swift, pain-free death, but then the anger overtakes him and he forces images of resurrection—his mother standing, walking, singing again.

One night his family plays the game Taboo. The score isn't important to them. Armando's mother mainly stays silent anyway. This time Armando draws the word *tower*. The taboo words eliminate most of the clues he would use, so he starts out with "It's tall, straight, and long," and before he says another word his mother shouts "Penis!" Armando, his father, and his sister freeze for an instant, dumbfounded, and then his mother laughs, and laughs again, and her giggles swell into full-throttle, full-belly roars. The implausible sound fills the room, and she sits up and doubles over, grabbing at her belly.

"Penis," she says, and her eyes water and she laughs and hoots and snorts uncontrollably, and Armando's sister and he laugh, and his father wipes at his eyes, and his mother keeps saying "Penis" and busting up and grabbing at her stomach, and she can't stop herself and they don't want her to stop, and she roars then says, "It hurts. It hurts," and she grabs her body, and all of them know she's in pain, but she keeps laughing.

"It hurts," she says, and her cheeks are wet with tears, and she presses her hands to her midsection.

"Stop," she says. "Stop it." But she can't stop, and she laugh-speaks "Help," but it takes them a while to understand, so his mother says, "Help me," and his father rises and goes to her. He places his hands on her stomach and asks, "Here?"

"Yes," she says, her laughter swiftly shifting to groans. "Press." Armando's father presses his hands and they sink into her scarred belly. His mother brings her hands to her face and wipes at her cheeks.

"Harder," she says, so his father presses further in, and she moans and clenches her hands. When his mother calms down, his father helps her recline on the couch, easing her head down onto her favorite red pillow. With their bedtime near, Armando and his sister pick up the word cards and put the game away. His mother's laughter still wafts in the room. They kiss their mother's forehead and say good night. They walk down the short hallway together.

"Mom's okay," his sister says. "She's getting better."

"Yes," he says.

"What was the secret word?" she asks.

"Tower," he says.

"Tower," she repeats, then pauses. "But you said 'long.' That doesn't make sense. A tower isn't long. You should have said, '*blank* of power.' She would've gotten it." She shakes her head and turns and walks away.

• • •

One morning, after another week of his mother's slow sink into the couch, soundless, his father comes into his room while Armando readies for school.

"She wants you to play," he says. "It's no big deal. Relax. But please. She's asking for you."

"Dad."

"Just do it. It's okay. I know what you're going to say. Please."

Armando brings his fingers to his lips and his insides evaporate. He visualizes his blind instructor, his words: "No. Again. No. Again. Are you trying? Have you practiced?" His trombone has been untouched for weeks, and he hasn't progressed past basic scales and simple kids' songs.

He grabs his trombone and walks downstairs to the couch with his head hanging. His father and sister have pulled up chairs. His mother is covered with blankets, and they've propped up her head. She stares off into the distance above, somewhere in the air below the vaulted ceiling.

"Mom," he says.

"Chicago," his mother whispers.

He shakes his head at his father.

"Play anything," his father says. "It's okay."

"Anyone. Know. What. Time. It. Really," she says.

"Mom, I can't."

His sister nods at him. His father holds his palms out.

"Play. Anything."

He brings the instrument to his trembling lips, smells the slide oil, breathes in, and exhales hard into the mouthpiece. A metallic belch echoes in the room. He lowers the instrument.

"Dad," he says.

"Chicago," his mother whispers.

"Play. Just play, son." His father walks over to him and lifts the trombone up. "You can do it."

"Chicago."

Armando feels the humiliation, the impossibility, and the mouthpiece on his lips. He doesn't know the song. He inhales through his nose. His father mouths "Anything." Armando closes his eyes and thinks he may be able to get out "Twinkle, Twinkle, Little Star," and he opens his eyes. His father mouths, "Anything, son, anything." Armando closes his eyes and blows.

Two in the afternoon, and Armando and Marie leave school early, drive up to the Air Force Academy, and watch cadets fall from the sky. Adjacent to the overlook, a pedestaled T-38 jet points skyward. Facing east, traffic zips by on I-25, and high above is a slow-circling airplane. Wave after wave of tiny dots escape the plane in five-second increments before blooming blue parachutes. On the other side of the lookout, a group of tourists take photos, their bus hulking behind them.

Marie has her notebook out and is drawing landscapes, mainly high-desert-cacti scenes. She leaves a four-inch-by-four-inch square at the bottom right of each page for poetry. Armando has his hands in his pockets. He watches the level airfield and watches each cadet's impact – a couple graceful, upright landings, but for most a weirdly managed feet-to-hip crash. Somehow they gather their chutes and walk away uninjured.

Although he lives just twenty minutes from this place, it's only his third time on the base, the other two to watch the Thunderbirds perform at the academy graduation, but when Marie saw him with his head buried in the crook of his arm during fifth period, she tapped his back and said,

"Let's go." She didn't plan to bring him here, but driving north they noticed the parachute-spotted sky and pulled off the interstate.

Marie finishes a drawing and leans over to show it to Armando.

"What's the first word that comes to your mind?" she asks.

"Water."

"Too many cacti?"

"I like cactus."

"Have you ever seen the big ones?"

"Sure."

"The big ones are almost extinct. Phoenix and Tucson and places like that cut them down. There's some at White Tanks by my grandma's house."

Armando stares at Marie and nods.

"You always stare at my birthmark," she says.

"Not always."

"Always."

"I like it."

"You don't like it. You say that so I won't feel bad."

"Am I allowed to like it?"

"I don't know. There's no way to get rid of it. Anything I do will make it worse."

Armando looks back at the crash-landing cadets. A pressure grows near the back of his head and he squeezes the base of his neck.

The plane has circled back high above. New dots fall and bloom.

"My mom's growing a beard," he says. "You don't want to come over."

"No."

"I don't blame you."

"I'll come over. I will."

"Listen to me. You don't have to."

"If you want me to."

"No. You shouldn't."

"I'll come. Please. Just tell me."

Armando kicks at the sidewalk and his shoe squeaks.

"She doesn't care that she's growing a beard." He wipes at his cheek. "I want her to care about that. Shouldn't that bother her?"

"I don't know."

"How is she supposed to get better? We have to feed her."

"I'm sorry."

"All we do is sit her up. She opens her mouth. That's it. We don't even move her to the bed."

"Maybe she wants to be there. It's comfortable for her. She can see you."

"But she should stand up. How is she going to get better when she never stands? She has legs. We can help her get stronger."

Marie clutches the notebook to her chest. Armando kicks the ground.

"You're helping," she says.

"All we do is feed her."

"I don't know."

"No one knows. That's the problem. Why can't she stand with our help?"

"Maybe she doesn't want to."

"What does that mean?"

"I don't know."

"You think that?"

"Armando."

"She wants to stand, Marie. We'll help her. My dad on one side, me on the other. Lift up. It's that easy."

In the near distance a blue plane lands and idles on the

runway while a new group of jumpers loads up. Through the air, the low hum of the plane's propellers. Behind the airfield buildings, northbound interstate traffic has slowed to a crawl.

Marie strokes the cover of her notebook. She looks down at the ground, over to Armando's shoes jabbing at the pavement. His black Nikes. The white swoosh a misshapen smile, a slanted *J*, an ice skate.

A week left of school, restlessness everywhere. Armando's government class watches the television as a Colorado jury sentences Timothy McVeigh to death for the Oklahoma City bombing. McVeigh is largely emotionless, but many of the jurors appear tired and squeamish.

His teacher mutes the television. "The sad part is, they'll make it as comfortable as possible."

Marie's voice brings him back. "Who's that?" she asks.

On the television screen, two elderly people weep uncontrollably behind McVeigh's lawyers.

"Everyone has parents," says the teacher.

The class moves on to a halfhearted discussion of the judicial system. Armando daydreams about a clear Oklahoma morning on which he spots the moving truck, McVeigh at the helm, at a stoplight two blocks from the unbombed building. He imagines pulling a gun from a shoulder holster and putting a bullet in each McVeigh kneecap and one in each shoulder. When the cops show, he holds up a photo with the alternative, no Armando Torres intervention—a gutted building, 168 dead—and they proclaim him a hero and decide on the spot to keep the bullets in McVeigh, to take him to some dank garage and foster life and pain as long as possible.

That afternoon his father arrives at the school's baseball field in the middle of PE. The sun shines and Armando stands in the dugout shade, joking with friends.

"Your dad," someone says.

He watches his father slide through the gate in the outfield fence and step on the warning track. Armando stands and waves, but his father only nods, and Armando attempts to walk, but his legs lock up and he sits. His shoulders sag and he remembers to breathe as everything slows down. His father walks toward him, and it all seems to take too long, the length of the field, how many steps his father takes without getting any closer.

"Armando, your dad," someone says.

As he hits second base, Armando's father scratches his chest. The PE teacher meets him at the pitcher's mound and the teacher nods his head and points at the dugout and stares.

Armando stands and hikes the dugout steps into the sunshine. The sky seems close.

His father crosses the base path and takes his son in his arms.

On the way home, Armando's mind pounds out images of his mother on the couch—*7Up sips, Uno indifference, trombone disappointment*—and he can't get his mind to work back far enough to when she was whole.

When his father misses the turn for home, Armando doesn't ask where they're headed. His father drives past the Broadmoor and its blooming flowers, past stucco mansions with rock walls, and turns right, heading up into the mountains. They gain altitude and Armando peers out over the valley, all the way across the city to the eastern plains curving toward Kansas and Missouri. Once the pavement turns to dirt his father says, "When Tesla was up here," but he stops the sentence. His father rolls his window down, inhales, mumbles, "She wanted to see London and Naples, the Thames," then flips a U-turn. On the way back down, the city rises up to them.

When they walk through the front door, his sister rests on the couch where their mother spent the last months of her life.

Armando retreats to his bedroom and sits on the edge of his bed and stares at a white wall holding up his room. His father comes in and sits down. Armando wants to tell his father that he thinks he's okay, that he worries about his sister, that he wants Marie near, but he keeps quiet and sits next to his father, who begins to rub his son's back, first slowly, then faster. Armando listens to his father breathe and feels his father's hand circling fast, warming his back as they stare at the wall because neither of them knows what to say with the words they have left.

4

Neutral Drops

ALSTON MIXES VODKA and cherry Kool-Aid in his water bottle before his high school doubles tennis match.

"Gatorade," he says to his doubles partner, Dax, then gulps down the red concoction and smirks. No one cares enough to notice Alston's drinking because Dax and Alston are terrible, even stone-cold sober. They play for the short-skirted girls who never pay them attention and the spring weekday afternoons out of school. Dax, who sticks with actual Gatorade, has a single goal on the court – he takes aim at the other team's net player and tries to smack the ball as hard as he can into his opponent's head or nuts. If he gets four or more direct hits before he and Alston are blanked 6–0, 6–0, he considers the damage a victory.

Alston is fast, sinewy, and handsome with his square jaw and narrow blue eyes. He likes to rile Dax up and tell the other team what's coming – "Dax, the dude at the net says your sister likes it blindfolded with a midget watching," and "Hey, Freckles, your nuts are about to get fucked up!"

The other team typically responds with mock anger or withdrawn cowardice, never neutrality, but Dax doesn't mind whatever animosity comes his way. Already six foot six, two hundred pounds in eleventh grade, armed with a cannon forehand, he has a stature that alone deters the most ardent opponents.

Dax's friendship with Alston is cemented by past loyalty and subtle envy. Alston showcases none of the shyness that Dax battles, so Dax attaches himself to Alston's moments of outward exhibition and feels the alluring intensity, but not the consequences, of a life without restraint; even now, though Dax has no sister, he plays along with the blindfold taunt and lets the net player decide which body part to defend. The choice may seem easy, but Dax's coach often sees talented players hunched over, peering through the heads of their meshed nylon racquets, praying that Dax will aim high.

Alston handles his liquor well, but one day he throws up in the middle of his serve.

"Damn," he says, wiping his mouth. Then: "Love thirty. Second serve."

"Wait," the nervous but skilled opponent at the net says. "We're not playing with that shit on the court. Somebody's got to clean it up."

Alston studies the foul puddle of alcohol and Kool-Aid.

"Dax, you want to keep playing?"

"Whatever," Dax says.

"We're done," Alston says.

"Then you guys forfeit."

"Bitches," Alston says, already swigging from his water bottle.

Dax and Alston walk over to the top of a grassy hill overlooking the courts and check out the girls' matches, their attention focused on the hiking hemlines and swaying asses of girls awaiting serves. Their earnest coach leans forward in a lawn chair next to the fence, shouting encouragement. Dax stretches his body out on the grass and stares up at the crisscrossing contrails. Alston sits and wraps his arms around his knees.

"Hey," Alston says. "Tall one."

A new girl at their school speaks with the coach, her hands rubbing her hips, then turns and walks toward them. She crests the hill and stands close to the boys.

"They're talking about you two," she says. The hill is empty save the two boys and her. Dax shakes his head and rises onto his elbows.

"Bad flu," Alston says.

"I can smell you," she says.

The girl lowers herself to the ground. Dax watches her long limbs fold. She clasps her hands and slides them between her thighs. Dax notices a dolphin tattoo above her right ankle, a scar running along the outside of her thigh, disappearing under her shorts.

"You on the team now?" Dax says.

"No racket," she says.

"Oh." Then silence, except for the grunts, shoe squeaks, and score recitations of six high school tennis matches.

The match they all ignore features the two best girls from each school. The girl from Rutherford High is the better player, quicker to the ball and with smoother ground strokes, and she produces a high-pitched squeal every time she strikes the ball.

"There need to be more tennis sluts," Alston says. "All this grunting for nothing."

"Alston," Dax says, and nods at the girl.

"Relax, Dax. Your name's Jean, right?" Alston says.

"Janelle."

"How come you don't play?"

"I'm new."

"So? Aren't you living with the Conleys?"

"Yeah."

From down below the coach yells something about backspin and gives a thumbs-up. The boys Dax and Alston forfeited to stand across the way, talking to their coach and pointing to where the three of them lounge. Dax stares at his feet.

"Don't the Conleys have a bunch of foster kids?" Alston says.

"Jesus, A," Dax says.

"Yeah," Janelle says.

"You been in other foster homes?" Alston says.

"It's not my first."

"Where you from?"

"Delaware."

"The whole state?"

"Dover."

"Why are you in Rutherford if you're from Delaware?"

"You talk too much," she says.

"Bitch, please," Alston says, "people should talk more." He reaches into his shorts, pulls out a pack of Camels, selects one in the middle, and lights it.

"Here," he says, holding out the pack to Janelle. "I can tell you smoke."

She accepts one and Alston reaches across Dax and lights it for her, cupping the flame with his opposite hand although there's no hint of wind. Dax glances at her face, her thin nose and dark eyes, then her long legs. His body tightens, but when she glances back at him he knows right away she's not interested. She looks at him as many have, as a slight physical freak – a grown-man body at seventeen – that's worth a second glance, and that's all. Dax shakes his size 15 basketball shoes and wonders when he'll stop growing.

"I'm trying to get this one to start," Alston says, exhaling a cloud of smoke.

"Not a chance," Dax says. "I like my lungs without the crap they put on the roads."

"It's different tar," Janelle says. "This is good tar. Helps you breathe." She smiles for the first time and shows her perfectly white, crooked teeth.

The three of them stay quiet for a while under a partly cloudy April afternoon. The low grunts of the Rutherford girls' number one rise to high-pitched shrieks as she volleys, retreats, then hammers a cross-court winner to take the first set.

"Druggie parents?" Alston says.

"No," Janelle says.

"So?"

"So what?" she says.

"So what's the story? You're what, seventeen? Eighteen? You're in Rutherford, New Jersey, sitting with two fucks at a stupid-ass tennis match, and you don't play tennis. You probably already know you're going to take off if you've spent over a week at the Conleys'. But we're not there yet. What's up with your parents?"

"You're pretty stupid, aren't you?"

"Yes, but you're still sitting here with me and Dax."

"Dax isn't a name."

"He's sitting right here," Alston says.

"Are you stupid like this one?" she asks Dax.

"He's not the most talkative," Alston says.

"I'm talkative," Dax says. "What do you want to know?"

"Tell me about anything."

"Okay. If you keep throwing up at our tennis matches, coach'll kick us off the team and we'll have to sit through history class more often."

"Did you throw up?" Janelle says.

"Do I seem like someone who throws up in the afternoon?"

"You look like someone who flinches."

"What?"

Dax yanks up a balled fist and Alston jerks away.

"I'll kill you, Dax."

"You're a shit talker, but I didn't say that was bad," Janelle says.

"Shit. I've never flinched. I've hurt people."

"Where?" she says, smiling.

"Where?"

"Yes, where did you hurt people? Tell me where you were when you hurt all these poor souls."

Alston takes a drag.

"Everywhere. That's what you need to know. In the Bronx. In Canada. In your back yard."

"That doesn't make sense," Dax says.

"I'm not done. Here, in Rutherford. In fucking Finland and Egypt and Iraq."

"Wow," Janelle says. "World traveler."

"Where you going to go?" Alston says.

"When?"

"When Conley accidentally walks in on you taking a shower."

"You don't know shit."

"Yep. But where?"

"To your house."

"Take Union to Springfield, couple houses on your left."

Alston and Janelle light two more Camels and somehow end up sitting next to each other. The sun warms Dax's face, and after he gets a flirty wave from an overweight girl from the opponent's school, he forces a nod. An ice cream truck pulls into the nearby parking lot, thin music box tunes tinkling out, and for a moment Dax thinks back to when his parents were still together.

Later, with only one match continuing in the far court, Janelle fingers her right earlobe.

"A refrigerator fell on my dad in Iraq," she says. "In Desert Storm, unloading crap. Damn thing crushed his neck and most of his chest. After we got the army money, my mom split." She takes a drag and exhales white smoke. "She's in Wyoming, I think, but I'm not sure. Every now and then she sends me thirty dollars cash."

"What's the return address on the envelope?" Alston says. "If you want to know where she's at, check out the return address."

"You think I don't know that?"

"Yes. I think you don't know that."

"Damn, A," Dax says.

"And a fridge? No bullet to the heart or anything?"

"Nope."

"What kind?" Alston says.

"What?"

"A Maytag?"

"Alston, come on."

"I don't know," she says. "I know it was big. Someone said it was brown. That's what I know."

"A falling refrigerator," Dax says.

Alston runs his fingers through his hair and looks at Janelle.

"Fuck Saddam."

Drew Barrymore sits behind Dax, Alston, and Janelle in a New York City theater just before *Die Hard: With a Vengeance* starts. Early summer and hot, and Dax and Alston have traveled the short distance to the city from Rutherford for basketball camp and sneaked out on the third night to the show. Dax didn't anticipate that Janelle would show up, but nothing surprises him about Alston and Janelle, now that she's a permanent fixture.

Dax is too nervous to talk to Drew, but Alston turns around and says, "*Poison Ivy* was your best work," and for those words he receives a condescending pat on the head before the lights dim and they all watch and cheer Bruce Willis and Samuel L. Jackson as they kill, maim, and solve logic puzzles to save New York City from pissed-off foreigners.

On the sidewalk after the show a disheveled and serious old woman begs Dax never to cut his hair because she's certain the Japanese will soon invade the country searching for American locks. Dax takes a step back and the woman holds up a paintbrush as evidence.

"Promise me," she says.

"Yes," Dax says.

"They have unfinished business here."

"Okay," Dax says.

"Oklahoma City was two months ago. It was just the start."

"Yep."

"I was alive for Pearl Harbor."

"Okay."

"Promise me."

"Fine."

"Your hair."

"Yes."

A block later, Dax, Alston, and Janelle stroll along the night boulevard, and a boy around twelve years old walking in the other direction pulls up his shirt to reveal a white-handled revolver stashed in his pants. He contorts his fingers into a practiced gang sign. Once Dax notices his weapon, he allows his shirt to fall back down, nods his head, and continues down the street. Dax's body shakes and Alston says, "Calm down. It wasn't loaded."

"You can't tell that shit from the handle," Dax says, trying to settle himself.

"I can tell."

Dax is in awe of Alston because of his ignorant surety — an unabashed confidence that Dax desires for himself — and because Alston teaches Dax things he's not supposed to realize until much later in life, stuff like honesty is rarely the best policy, a car runs even if you don't have a driver's license, and people do whatever you want them to do if they're scared enough.

Alston's father left when he was eight, and his undisciplined mother saw Alston as a miniature version of his wayward father — same verbal energy, blue eyes, and attraction to alcohol — so Alston largely takes care of himself. Most nights dinner is frozen chicken nuggets and a Coke from the corner store. His father still shows up once a year and takes Alston up to Bear Creek Camp near Wilkes Barre to shoot a .357, camp out, and sip a mix of whiskey, vodka, and root beer, a drink Alston's father calls root root.

Dax's father, a tired, below-average dentist, gave fatherhood a shot when Dax had to make a decision during the divorce but has since focused on golf, his new girlfriend, and his timeshare in Hilton Head. If he had to do it all over again, Dax wouldn't pick differently — he has all he needs, and his father kicks him extra money whenever he asks. Plus the freedom gives him more time with Alston, the one person he considers a close friend.

One of the things Alston teaches Dax is neutral drops, the art of shifting an automatic vehicle into neutral, revving the engine, and simultaneously "dropping" the shifter to drive. One Friday night Dax and Alston neutral-drop Dax's

1984 Toyota Camry in the Lincoln Elementary School parking lot, listening to the front-wheel-drive vehicle skid on
the old pavement. Alston nurses a fifth of Black Velvet, and
even though he has never had a driver's license, he dem-
onstrates particular talent at the neutral-drop maneuver,
seemingly oblivious to the grinding sound the shift produces after each drop.

"You need a six-cylinder," Alston says. "But hell, you
have a car." He pauses and takes a sip. "Drink this," he says,
offering the bottle. "I know you won't. And that's okay. If
you did it, I'd hate you. You've fucked yourself into expecta-
tions, my friend. Always the good guy, huh?"

"Never," Dax says.

"Guy with your size should be fucking shit up. You know
that?"

"I am."

"No. You're not. Listen, it's easy. You need to be louder.
Even when you're wrong, be loud. It works."

"Where do you get this stuff?"

"I have eyes and ears."

"Fine."

"I mean it. A guy your size, they'll tuck their dicks and
run. Girls coming out of their minds."

"You should teach, A."

"Volume up. Free lesson, my friend. And you should
play football. Everyone likes football. You watch it enough."

Dax loves college football and follows the games closely,
especially the New Mexico Lobos, from where his father
went to school, but actually playing football would mean violent contact, speed, and inevitable pain.

Alston revs the engine and drops the shifter and the
tires squeal.

"Not bad," he says. "Hey, what about Janelle?"

"What about?"

"You know she's messed up, right? That family she lives with – they got all those dumb-shit foster kids."

"Okay."

"Weird shit. Foster dad jacked up."

"The dad messes with them? Did she say that? I don't want to know."

"We're going to take off. This is the last time you're going to see me."

"Don't tell me."

"Why not?"

"I don't want to know. You tell me too much."

"'Cause you don't know anything."

"Where you gonna go?"

"She wants Key West. Figures rich people need help around their mansions. Plus if we got to live, why not live there?" He takes a swig of the Velvet.

"I don't think Key West is real. But even if it is, it can't be all that great or everyone would live there," Dax says.

"I always wondered why people don't move to the vacation spots. If you have so much fun there, just move, get a job, boom, done."

"Sounds too simple. Like when you're ten and say you're going to run away when your parents piss you off and you don't make it out of the driveway."

"I'm not ten, and besides, how hard is it? Get on the bus, get off at Key West."

"You think Greyhound goes to Key West?"

"Close enough."

Weeks pass and Alston and Janelle haven't gone anywhere. Autumn sweeps in and basketball season arrives. Dax finds himself starting at power forward. He's big but not very strong, and outside of the summer camp with Alston he has largely ignored the sport, but the team needs height, so Dax clogs the lane and keeps his arms up.

Alston comes to the home games with Janelle and sits in the front row trying to pick fights with opposing players, which, while funny, still surprises Dax. He has seen Alston in three fights, all of which he lost badly.

After one home game – a rough night when Dax's best efforts and Alston's "weak dick" chants fail to keep Dax's man from pouring in thirty-three points in a blowout win – Dax, Alston, and Janelle neutral-drop in the post office parking lot. Alston drives first, drinking root root from a Natural Springs water bottle he then passes to Janelle. Dax lounges in the back seat, feeling the jerk and lurch of the car from neutral to drive, neutral to drive, and the dirty smell of brakes and tires. Tired, he thinks of the player that lit him up in his home gymnasium, how the guy was smaller than him, not that much faster, but had seemed so much better at everything. He wonders why it's so damn hard to get his body to do exactly what he wants, as fast as he wants it.

When it's Dax's turn to drive, Janelle and Alston climb into the back seat and disappear into the darkness.

"Put on some Biggie and drive around," Alston says, so Dax does. He drives down Montross to Pierrepont to Riverside with the music loud. A cop car appears up ahead and Dax rolls his window up. He turns on Passaic and something pushes at the back of his seat. Alston told Dax that the first time he and Janelle screwed he used Saran Wrap and a rubber band, so this is what Dax can't shake out of his infected mind: Alston, back at home, unfurling a rectangle of clear plastic and snapping it off with the carton's sharp teeth.

After a song titled "Who Shot Ya?" beats out of the factory speakers, Alston hops into the front seat. For a while no one says anything, and for the first time Dax notices that he has to hold the steering wheel an inch to the right to keep the Camry straight, but he's unsure what this means.

"I fucking hate people that play instruments," Alston says. "Seriously, who has time to learn to play an instrument? There's nothing better to do? Let's learn notes over and over. Dumbasses."

From the back-seat darkness, Janelle says, "I played the piano for a little bit."

"You're a foster kid," Alston says.

"So? You're a shit. I can play a Beethoven song, a song from *The Nutcracker,* and an overture."

"What's an overture?" Dax says.

"Did I say I was a fucking music teacher?" Janelle says.

A right turn.

"Where did you get a piano?"

"Electronic keyboards at Walmart. They got them set out and plugged in and no one's ever there, so you go in and practice and keep the volume low. Sometimes I went to Target, but mostly Walmart."

"Radio Shack?" Dax says.

"Did I say Radio Shack?"

"Foster-kid trick," Alston says.

"When we're married we're having ten foster kids," Janelle says.

"You're too tall for me," Alston says.

"You're too small for me. And by that I mean your cock."

With that, Alston jumps into the back seat.

Dax slides a Boyz II Men CD in and thumbs the track to "I'll Make Love to You," knowing it'll piss off Alston, but there's no reaction. After the first chorus Dax only wants to escape from his car, so he drives to his high school, parks the car facing the grass field, leaves the stereo on, and gets out.

The grass is still wet from the previous night's rain, so Dax walks the length of the field and leans on a damp picnic table. He looks up at the city lights' dirty hue, then over at his Camry, a tiny light from the stock stereo illuminating the interior.

Dax smells the night grass, considers how there's a good chance that no one, anywhere, is thinking of him. He thinks of his mother, her hands on his face the day she left, her eyes on his eyes, her voice whispering. "I love you, but you chose *him*." Dax imagines his mother in Dallas, where she now lives, strolling down the street in an oversized cowboy hat with her Texas husband. They hold hands and laugh and push their set of twin girls in a wide stroller. The last he heard from her was three years ago, when she sent him a Troy Aikman jersey for his birthday. A New York Jets fan, he burned it in his back yard with Alston.

Dax fights the tension in his chest and glances over to his car — still the stereo's glow, but he's not sure how long the battery will last. His dad has shown him how to jump the car, but he's not sure he remembers, something about grounding. Janelle will probably know.

A helicopter overhead, with a searchlight scanning. A pain in Dax's back right molar, then gone. Dax thinks about his dad, the new girlfriend who resembles his aunt Karen, how his dad has been harping on Dax to consider the army, how it'll pay for school, how he'll have no one to fight, just train and train, maybe stub a toe or two, then go to college. Even Alston thinks it's a good idea: "Sweet outfits? Rugged, hot army bitches? Bazookas? Fuck, yeah. Do it." Dax pictures himself in camouflage, running in formation, hiding in the woods, and wonders what kind of disadvantage he may be at in blending in with the surroundings. He's a big man, easier to see. That can't be good. But who's shooting?

He hasn't been swayed toward this army idea, but when

he imagines college or a job, nothing comes to him and he hears his father's low voice in his head: "A paycheck, free post living, free food, free school." Dax thinks, *How can everything in the military be free? When was the last time we really got into a fight? Vietnam? Iraq? Does Iraq count? A few days of bombs. Night-vision tracers on CNN. A falling refrigerator.*

Dax has fired a gun once outside Watertown with his WWII army vet grandpa, who has also been pushing the military route. Empty beer bottles near a creek in autumn. He remembers the silver revolver, the bunny-eared rear sights, the fierce percussion, and the still-standing bottles. His grandpa's voice – "Fun, isn't it?" – and Dax thinking it was something, but fun?

Dax snaps out of his dream when a lifted truck pulls into the spot next to his car and someone jumps out. The person races in front of the truck's headlights, then jerks the Camry's back door open and reaches inside. Dax stands and starts walking back, and by the time he's close enough to see clearly, a man towers over Alston, punching and punching, and Janelle, pantless, is at the man's back, tearing at his neck and face. Dax's body comes alive, and he races across the field and lunges at the man, but Dax is thrown off and he feels a punishing pounding on his face and chest. He tries to rise but can't. The man lifts a grunting Alston from the pavement and rams Alston's head into the Camry's door. Janelle lies in the first cut of grass holding her stomach, her naked lower half kicking at the sky. The man walks over to Janelle, pulls her up by her hair, walks her to the truck, throws her in, and leaves.

Dax's chest burns; rocks dig at his back. Alston moans.

"Al-ston," Dax says, trying to find his lungs. "Alston."

"Shut the motherfuck up."

Dax touches his body, but everything is too new to know

anything. He goes to his knees, then stands and staggers over to Alston, who drags himself up into the passenger seat.

"Drive to my house," Alston says.

"What the fuck, Alston?"

"Conley, that sorry-ass, messed-up dick. I'm killing that motherfucker." Alston says this calmly, and Dax worries that he might be telling the truth. Dax flicks on the interior lights and sees Alston's inflating face.

"Call the cops, A," Dax says.

"Drive to my house. I'm not asking."

"I'm calling the cops."

Dax reaches for the keys in the ignition.

"Fine. Listen, you won't see me after tonight."

"What?"

"Don't call anyone."

"What?"

"Stop and listen to me."

Dax has his hand on the key but doesn't turn it. He stares at Alston, who seems transformed, happy.

"Give me a sec." Quiet everywhere, then the soft sounds of traffic a couple blocks over. Alston touches his own arms and neck, then smirks.

"You're not gonna see me after now. I knew it was coming."

"What?"

"Shut up and listen. That dude should've killed me."

"Alston, don't be crazy."

Alston shakes his head. He pulses his hands into fists, in and out, in and out, each time slower than the next.

"Damn, he's a tough fuck," Alston says. "Didn't see that coming." He laughs. "Okay, all right. Okay. Thinking. I'm thinking. Just sit here for a bit."

"Alston."

Alston slaps his face and blinks three times. His eyes narrow and Dax wonders if he'll cry.

"Okay, brother. Here it is. If you go into the army, shoot first. Prison is better than dead."

"What? Calm down. Calm down."

"You aren't listening, Dax. Listen for a sec."

"Fine."

"Be a medic or something, but if you get a gun, shoot that motherfucker. If ever in doubt, shoot first. Prison is a ton better than dead or paralyzed or no arms or eyes or whatever."

"What the hell are you talking about?"

"And one more thing."

"We're not fighting anyone."

"And one more thing. Listen. You're not going to see me again."

"Sure."

"And one more thing."

"What?"

"I forgot."

"Fuck you, A."

"Don't worry about me. I know you will," Alston says. He opens the door, stumbles into the night, and disappears around the corner of the gym.

When he arrives home, Dax steps into his living room. His father and his father's girlfriend, Angela, sit on a blue leather couch.

"I'm okay," Dax says before they can ask.

"You don't look so bad," says Angela, a fortyish brunette whom Dax believes is too good for his father. She likes her martinis, but she's well-spoken and even dragged Dax's father to a couple of Dax's basketball games. "Did you take an elbow during the game?"

Dax sees himself for the first time in the living room mirror and realizes that Angela is right: he appears fine, with only a scratch on his left temple and a black mark on his red T-shirt.

"Dax, sit down," his father says. "I was just finishing this story. You won't believe it."

"I'm tired, Pop," Dax says. "Alston's out of his mind. Got the shit kicked out of me. I'm headed to bed."

"Here's the story, honey. Someone called him the *n*-word on the golf course," Angela says.

"Angela, please."

"But you're white," Dax says. He touches his stomach, surprised there's no pain.

"No shit. That's the point. How does that make sense? There weren't any black guys around. And even then."

"It doesn't make sense," Angela says.

"Who was it?" Dax says.

"Another golfer," she says. "What do you say to that?"

"I should've laughed, I guess. I don't know. Bizarre."

"So what's the point?" Dax says.

"There's no point, honey," Angela says. "People don't know how to speak."

"I'm white," Dax's father says.

"It doesn't matter," she says.

"I don't know."

"Okay."

Angela reaches out and holds Dax's father's hand.

"I'm sorry," she says.

"Why are you sorry?"

"It's just I'd be sorry for anyone being called that."

"It shouldn't mean anything."

"Well."

"To me, I mean," Dax's father says. "I don't know."

"It doesn't mean anything. It can matter to you but not mean anything."

"I was playing golf. Wild."

Dax waves good night, walks down the hallway to the bathroom, pisses, brushes his teeth, inspects himself in the mirror, washes his face, walks to his room, undresses, and climbs into bed. He glances at the Cindy Crawford poster on his wall before turning off his bedside light. He touches his forehead and runs his fingers through his hair, finding, then flicking away a piece of gravel. His chest lifts and depresses. In a weird way, he wishes he was more badly hurt; maybe then he'd have the courage to call the cops. He runs his fingers along his rib cage twice, then down his sides to his hips. Alston's stupid, but Dax doesn't believe he's kill-someone stupid, so he has no one to save, as long as Alston saves Janelle.

Dax shifts to his left side and wonders how Alston will break Janelle out. He imagines a near future with Alston and Janelle at the local bus ticket counter, wild and nervous, and then the dim, southbound Greyhound filled with grim-faced nocturnals with little to lose. He knows Key West is near Miami, but he's not clear on exactly where Miami is, only that there's water everywhere. He pictures a map of Florida, then alligators, then an island with high-walled mansions. He imagines Alston strolling around in a pink shirt serving drinks at a party and sneaking one for himself every time he refreshes his tray.

What Dax can't imagine as he drifts off to sleep is what will actually happen—that he'll receive a postcard from Alston nine years from now, and on the front a photo of a mountain lake with an island golfing green right in the middle of the water. On the bottom: *Coeur d'Alene, Idaho.* And the handwritten words on the back: *Yeah, Idaho. Shoot first. A.* Closing his eyes on his dark room, Dax can't fathom that he'll receive the postcard in Afghanistan on his second tour there, or that later, on a dirt plain, he'll peer through his rifle's scope as a girl sprints toward him. So tonight he visualizes Alston in Florida; Janelle on a beach in a two-piece bathing suit; hurt Janelle in the night grass holding her stomach, her long naked legs, somehow inviting and cursed; Notorious B.I.G.; Janelle in a well-lit, cavernous store, an ELECTRONICS sign overhead.

She stands at the keyboards, alone. She's picked a new model with a large CASIO on the side, and she turns the volume up and presses middle C over and over. Using just her right hand, she keeps to the white keys first, "Mary Had a Little Lamb," then "Twinkle, Twinkle, Little Star," easy and boring but still magic, the connected sounds from her fingers; then she moves to the black keys, the tone shifting, somehow ominous and tender at once. She doesn't recall a song for the black keys, so she presses each one in order, working her way left to right, then back down again. She starts into the one *Nutcracker* song she knows, "The Dance of the Sugar Plum Fairy," playing slowly, biding her time. Every now and then she peeks over her shoulder for a ticked-off employee or a one-in-a-million keyboard seeker, but as always no one notices her, so she decides to stay and play until someone does.

5

Unbomb

Two months after the car bomb in Kabul, Big Dax sees nothing but dirt and a road extending from him bisecting more dirt. Two miles away, an Afghan town of a thousand he can't make out through the windswept dust.

The checkpoint he mans is set up for car inspections, but there have been only six in the past two days. Two weeks on this duty and Big Dax, Torres, and Wintric are bored – they oversee this lightly traveled road, more donkeys than cars, and the loaded donkeys and their handlers often circumvent the checkpoint, far enough off the roadway to ease the nerves but close enough for the men to scope with their M4s.

Torres and Big Dax are a month away from heading home. The invisible clock ticks in their minds, but they refuse to talk about time. Torres has asked his family to stop sending care packages, since they won't arrive until after his return, and something about that absence of the tangible – no cookies, no kids' handwritten letters on the way to him – fills him with equal parts longing and dread. His wife, Anna, listening to the advice of the spouses back at Fort Carson, has been sending e-mails with reminders of their courtship and has attached photos of the Royal Gorge Bridge, Michelle's ice cream shop downtown, Bishop's Castle with its dragon head, Breckenridge, the master bedroom in the new house, a self-portrait in leopard-print lingerie.

Big Dax hasn't told anyone, but he has submitted his separation paperwork. In moments of admitted weakness he already allows himself to daydream about leaving Afghanistan and Fort Carson behind and returning to Rutherford, getting his own place, the Meadowlands, the Jets, the Lincoln Tunnel, cargo shorts and T-shirts every day, how everything can once again become routine.

Big Dax spits and performs a short in-place jog to keep his legs alive. Behind a wall of sandbags Torres listens to early Pearl Jam and writes in his journal while Wintric spits tobacco into an empty Dr Pepper bottle and plays hearts with a lieutenant they all like. Wintric has won four games in a row since the lieutenant told him the 49ers suck.

"Call this payback for Montana and Young," Wintric says as he shuffles the cards.

"Luck," says the LT, wiping at his eyes. "And I mean they suck now. At least you have nice childhood memories."

"They'll be back."

Torres uncovers an ear.

"Big Dax, what up?"

"Ass nothing," he says.

"Beautiful," says the LT.

"Not beautiful," says Wintric, placing down a ten of spades. "Not beautiful. Need a little something every now and then. Nothing crazy, just something. I'm tired of beating you at this game. Need something to find. To do. We're looking for nothing at all."

"It's true," says the LT. "We're looking for nothing. Absolutely nothing. That's the game. And after a year of finding nothing, we leave. That's the best way."

"That nothing happens?" Wintric spits into the bottle.

"Yes."

"That shit isn't in the recruiting video."

"You could be in Iraq."

"Fuck Iraq."

"How much you wanna bet that our boys are sitting there saying, 'You could be in fucking Afghanistan where no one cares that a war is going on'?"

"No one is saying that," says Torres.

"Sure, LT," says Wintric. "But our job is to put holes in bad people. I'm realistic. I'd take an easy kill. Get one of these ragheads into the open. I don't need no gray-area shit."

"You're wrong." He pauses. "Our job has always been to unkill." The LT inhales, feels the rattling phlegm, suctions it up to his throat, and spits.

"What? No word games, LT."

"It's easy. We unbomb and unshoot billions of people every day. There's nothing we can't destroy. Call up the bombers, the ICBMs. Punch in the code. What do you think the air force is for? We can end this world if we want, right now."

"That's fucked-up beautiful," Big Dax says. "You've practiced."

"That's why we're saviors. I'm not shitting you. This is serious. We save the entire world every single day. And we're kind as hell, because a lot more people deserve to die than we kill. Remember that shit and you'll sleep."

"I'm sleeping fine," says Wintric. "And if Bin Laden walked up right now, I'd happily blow his fucking head off. There's no gray area there."

"In a mountain somewhere, or Pakistan," Torres says. "He deserves to die a hundred times over, but that's one committed man. Whole world searching for you, millions on the table, and no word."

"He's dead," Big Dax says. "Smartest thing they ever did was not to talk about his death. We'll spend billions more searching for a dead man."

"He's not dead," Torres says. "We'd know."

"Torres, really, man. The smartest thing they could do is burn his body, spread the ashes, and walk away. It's the story, the myth that has the power. They aren't idiots. You expect a press release?"

"Everyone thinks they're dumb shits," says the LT. "Big part of our problem is that they're as smart as us, but we can't admit that."

"They won't burn him," says Torres. "Muslims don't cremate."

"Only when we help them with a bomb from above," says Wintric.

"Whatever," says Big Dax. "They buried him, then. The point is, I doubt we'll ever know. No Hussein hiding-in-a-hole shit."

"We'll know," says Torres.

The LT coughs, spits. He draws more phlegm, spits again.

"Fuck me," he says, and pinches his nose.

"Jesus, LT. Get some meds."

"Burn pits, man. Call me in five, ten years. It won't be good. The odds say we won't be shot. You know that, right?"

"I know."

"We breathe in the smoke instead," the LT says. "No meds for this crap."

"What we burning in those things beside our own shit?"

"Everything and nothing. Listen, guys are already complaining, but we're in a war. Put it this way, no one's bitching back home if it's a bomb or our burning shit that takes someone out. Don't take that the wrong way. But just wait, when we're all sixty the government will admit that we poisoned ourselves, give the living ones a couple grand, maybe some VA bennies. That's it. Thanks for volunteering."

"So you're saying we're burning more than our shit?" Wintric says.

"Will do more damage than these Taliban jerk-offs."

"No offense, LT," Wintric says. "I hear you, but it could be a flu."

"Damn, Ellis. You're making sense to me. You're an optimist. They need you at West Point. Stay with it, man. Stay with it."

The next two days, nothing. Dust and distant helicopters and heat. Scan horizon, clean weapons, sweat, scan horizon, drink water, scan horizon, sweat, repeat; a two-hour argument on Stallone versus Schwarzenegger, an hour on Liddell versus Ortiz, an hour dispute on the hottest porn star followed by a half-hour debate on who among them would let a woman stick her fingers up his ass. Two yes, one no, one "has experience."

"This one's for everyone," the LT says. "Five division-one football teams don't have *university* in the name of the schools they represent. Go."

Silence.

"Three you should get, being in the military."

"Shit, LT, don't help. Service academies."

"There's three. Other two?" The LT coughs into his fist.

Big Dax scratches his neck. "Football's for pussies. Except Peyton Manning and Jonathan Vilma. Jets are two and oh, baby."

Torres stands and raises his rifle. "I think better when I'm aiming."

"You'd make a hell of a tight end, Big Dax. Tell me when you all want a hint."

"I like that Tennessee orange," says Big Dax. "We need Peyton on the Jets, LT."

"Jets need Elway," Torres says. "The greatest ever. First answer, LT, Georgia Tech."

"One more to go. Not bad."

"In Georgia you get free school if you've served, right?" Wintric says.

"I don't know," the LT says. "A few states . . ."

"Yeah, Texas, Illinois, Georgia. G.I. Bill or not. Doesn't matter. It's in the constitution or something. That's what I've heard."

"You going to school?"

"Sure. I'll move to Texas," Wintric says.

"What you majoring in?"

"Does it matter?"

"Not really," the LT says.

"The Citadel?" Torres says.

"No."

"Virginia Tech?" says Big Dax.

"No. It's actually a mouthful: Virginia Polytechnic Institute and State University. Think gold helmets."

"Seven months left here," says Wintric. "A few more months at Carson, then my commitment's up. Drive to Texas with my papers."

"Austin?"

"Is there water near there?"

"Yep," the LT says. "Lake Travis. It's right there. They'll

make you a longhorn. The other obnoxious orange, Big
Dax."

"They call it burnt," Big Dax says. "And I don't like to
talk about Texas. Too many crazies."

"Sounds good, LT," Wintric says. "Lake Travis, huh?"

"Supposed to be nice."

Several moments of silence as the wind picks up. Wintric has rarely considered Texas, and as he does now he pictures long-horned bulls, the Dallas Cowboys' blue star, Em-
mitt Smith, oil dikes bobbing. *Lake Travis,* he thinks, *right
there,* and he tries to imagine the lake, but all that appears is
a replica of Lake Almanor without the pine trees.

Big Dax runs through his mental catalogue of gold helmets. *Notre Dame, Florida State, Colorado, UCLA, Purdue?
Wyoming?*

Torres lowers his rifle.

"I'm ready for a hint," he says.

"Big Dax?"

"Fine," Big Dax says.

"Doug Flutie," the LT says.

"Doug Flutie?" Torres says.

"Boston College," Big Dax says.

The next day, during a cloudless afternoon, and Big Dax notices a child in the far distance, but he doesn't yet realize it's
a girl. He's been on watch for two hours and nothing, and
now this kid, a wide-open dirt plain, wind, and a heart he
now hears inside him. Two hours since his last cigarette and
he feels it in his blood. A mongoose darts across the road,
surprising him, and he thinks about the little nondescript
mammal tearing up cobra after cobra. *Do they ever lose?*
Then his back tattoo. He had asked for a boa constrictor, but
for thirty-three dollars outside Fort Benning you get what

you get, so he sports a green creature along his vertebrae that appears more eel than snake. He's nicknamed it Snake.

Again the child, now walking toward them.

"We got any candy left?" Big Dax says to no one in particular, and no one answers.

Big Dax thinks he sees the kid wave, but no, just a child in a white shawl and pink pants, ten, maybe twelve years old. She walks alone, holding something round.

"Guys, where's our candy?" he asks.

Big Dax lifts his rifle and peers through the scope at this walking girl – no shoes, a soccer ball in hand. *But all alone?* A gust lifts her white shawl, and something silver, metallic, flashes. Another gust and he gets a peek at a silver vest. His insides pulse, then expand, and he calls out to Torres, "Scope her. Scope the girl."

"Call it in, Ellis," Torres yells.

The girl tosses the spotted ball to herself. Big Dax flips the safety off and his heartbeat throbs and he hears the LT on loudspeaker: "Estaad sho yaa saret fayr meykunam." *Stop, or I'll shoot.* She strides toward them, all alone with the flat earth.

"Two hundred out," Torres says.

"What did you see? Talk to me," the LT shouts.

"Vest. Vest."

"Vest?"

"Metal. It's not right. No one is here. It's metal."

"What the fuck?"

"Vest?"

"Look!"

"No one is here."

"Shit!"

"Where is everyone?"

"A girl?"

"There's a vest. Something's there, LT."

The girl stops. Big Dax sees the silver glint under her shawl and her moving lips through his crosshairs. The girl has an odd lump of skin hanging from her jaw.

"Something there, LT," Big Dax says.

"Got it."

"Not right. Not good."

"Easy," says the LT. "Wait."

"I see metal," Torres says. "Silver something. It's not right. The girl isn't right."

"Yes."

"She's talking to herself."

"Make the call."

"Wait," the LT says.

She walks toward them, alone. A soccer ball in her hands.

"Make the call, LT."

"Warning shots one-fifty. Shoot at one hundred," the LT says.

The girl shakes her head at something off to her right, then walks again. She keeps her gaze off to her right but walks straight. Torres raises his rifle and the girl stops again and touches her chest—*A skin-and-bones chest? A wired chest? Silver-strung explosives?*

"Estaad sho yaa saret fayr meykunam."

Wintric mimes opening his blouse over and over.

"Look here!" he yells.

Torres's voice: "Dax, your shot. One-fifty. Your shot. Your shot."

"Warning shot," LT says.

Big Dax peers through his scope, from the girl to the clear sky. Aiming high, he pulls the trigger and feels the rifle's kick as a bullet hurtles away. Back to the girl, who stares off at the openness, seemingly unaffected, her moving lips, the skin sac hanging off her face. He smells gunpowder.

Please, Big Dax says to himself, then repeats out loud, "Please."

Wintric has his rifle up; he peers through the scope, sees his bullet's trajectory from his barrel to the girl's chest. *A girl?* His mind works question and answer. *A girl. A girl? A girl.* He pictures his bullet tearing through her heart.

For a moment everything stops save the girl, standing still, turning the soccer ball in her hands, her small hands on the ball. They scope her and she turns the ball. Quiet.

Then, in one fluid motion, she drops the ball and sprints at the men, arms up in a *V.*

"Estaad sho yaa saret fayr meykunam!"

"One-twenty-five," Torres says. "One-ten. Fuck." A pause. "One hundred. Your fucking shot, Dax. Now. Now."

Big Dax sees the girl growing bigger and bigger; his weapon's crosshairs meet on her expanding chest. Torres's gun bursts and the girl still runs in long strides, uninjured.

Big Dax takes a quick breath and holds this afternoon, this moment, this white shawl, pink pants, glinting chest, bare feet. He fires.

Wintric exhales and squeezes the trigger.

The girl falls down, curled, and they hear the rifles' simultaneous report and smell the gunpowder and heat. Then quiet. No wind now. No talk. Everything has been swallowed. The girl's body jolts on the road, legs kicking, the soles of her bare feet exposed in the afternoon. Her legs jolt again, then still. Her bare feet. One heel digging at the road, then still. All quiet. Not calm. Quiet.

6

Tattoo

DAX FLIES TO Salt Lake City, rents a car, and drives past the salt flats, Bonneville, the state border, past Wendover and Wells, to Elko, Nevada. Alston, as lean as he was in high school but now sporting a shaved head and a *Janelle* tattoo on his left forearm, greets Dax in front of his mobile home on half an acre on the south side of town.

"First off," he says, "you're still a big son of a bitch. Second, Janelle stayed up in Idaho, and there's nothing more to say about that. Third, I'm gonna let you talk about the war. Get it all out. No one's listening out here. Let's go inside and get to the tough shit first."

Framed prints of large bucks and antelope hang on the walls inside. A dusty but clean smell hangs in the room, as if it's been recently vacuumed.

"Elko's got water and gold," Alston says over beers. "You don't need anything else. Listen, a lot of people are going to freak the fuck out about losing their homes, losing their jobs, all that bullshit. Just wait. I don't feel sorry for them one bit. What do you expect, living in San Francisco or L.A.? You gonna spend a million bucks on a two-bedroom fixer? Big cities, they're not taking anything out of the ground that people want. Of course you gonna eventually be screwed. We got water and gold. Other places have one or the other. We got both. I'm never leaving. I paid one-fifty for this house. It's worth three hundred, easy. Okay, that was the icebreaker. Talk to me, man. Are you fucked up in the head? Are the movies true? You got all of your limbs, right?"

Alston pauses long enough for a sip.

"Talk to me, man. Look at your fucking forearms. What'd you do? I'm not joking, Dax. I want you to talk. All these guys and gals come back and they all say that they got no one to talk to, no one's gonna listen. I believe them. No one wants to hear the stories. Who has happy stories? You don't even have to go to war. No one has happy stories. Good jobs here, but where's the gold going? You'd think we'd keep a couple chunks for ourselves, but trucks leave every night at 2 A.M. headed for somewhere that's not here, digging the gold, killing the mountains, dumping it in the trucks and hauling it away. Listen, I don't ask too many questions, but why is gold so damn important? Who's wearing gold these days? It's all platinum. Janelle wore gold. She loved that shit, but only with the turquoise in it. So fucking weird. No one makes the gold with the turquoise in it, it's all silver and turquoise, everyone knows that, but she loved the fucking gold and turquoise, which you can never find. Why? Because it looks like shit, that's why. And this thing on my arm? Best idea I ever had. Do you know how many girls I meet that see that tat but no wedding ring? It's amazing. They'll come up and say, 'Was Janelle your mom?' And you know what I say? 'Hell yes she was my mom, bless her goddamned soul.' They see that loyalty and it's pants-off time. Afterward we'll be laying there and they'll be stroking the fucking tattoo, and I know what they're thinking – 'This guy loves his mama. This guy's a keeper.' And what do I say? Nothing. That's what I say. You're in Elko, Dax."

Another sip.

"Shit, it's good to see you, man. I want you to talk. I'm gonna sit here and listen. You don't want to say shit, fine, just tell me, but this is your chance, my friend. You can't go on no documentary and say no one wanted to listen. I'm listening. Please. I'll listen."

"I don't know, A," Dax says. "I feel good. Weird to be out, though."

"Sure."

"I hate having to decide what to wear every day. Don't have to think about that while you're in. I thought I'd love it, but it's a pain in the ass."

"Freedom," Alston says. "Fucking overrated."

"I'm good," Dax says. "I don't know what to say."

"You a smoker now. I smell it on you. You ever have to stick the cigs in your nose like those dudes in Nam?"

"I don't know," Dax says.

Silence while Alston leans back in his chair, eyes wide, then leans forward.

"Come on, man. Give me something. Give me the best and worst. We'll clear that shit out and go lose some money."

"I'll have to think about it."

"Nowhere to be. Think, but not too much. You don't get to the stuff I'm talking about by thinking."

"Boring shit," Dax says. "There's no best or worst."

"Give them to me. I'll take them. Make it up. You got to talk about it."

"That's not true."

"That is true. It'll eat you, man."

Dax exhales and glances at the wall.

"You a deer hunter or something now?" he says. "What's up with the bucks?"

"You forget how smart I am. You're not changing the subject."

"You got all these deer on the walls, A. You're from Rutherford. Where's the mounted head? In the bedroom?"

"Stop that shit. Nobody's from anywhere. And you'll talk. I got too much beer for you not to talk."

"You're a gold miner now," Dax says. "You got one of those lights on your helmet?"

"Those are for coal miners, you dumbass. And I sure as shit ain't no gold miner. Bail bonds, man. Easy money. Dumbest fucks in forever."

"You haven't been in the army."

"Who do you think my customers are, Mormons?"

"Buddy of mine is one," Dax says. "Loved it when he said *fuck*. He got out too."

"Where?"

"Colorado."

"Same as here. All about gold. When it dries up, no more Colorado. We got gambling and water. That'll keep some folks around."

"Where we going?" asks Dax. "I saw the casino lights coming in."

"Good tables or girls?"

"Both."

"Where do you think you are?"

"Pick a place where we can win you a stuffed buck."

Four hundred up after a three-hour session at the poker table, Dax waits in the casino bar's corner booth for Alston to return with drinks. Alston promised him something "old school," and Dax senses a root root in his future.

The Eagles play from a hidden speaker and Dax stares

at a woman sitting in profile at the center of the bar. Her blond hair is cut shoulder length and her legs could reach the floor if she extended them, but she has her heels on the low rung of the stool. She's kept her jacket on, giving the impression that she could leave at any moment, but she's only two sips into her latest drink.

Near drunk, Dax wants another gulp in him before he walks over to her. He pictures his smooth approach, her eyes rising to meet his, her instant attraction. He's never gained a woman's interest with just a look, but his roll on the poker table, the drinks, the "just home from war" angle, and "Take It Easy" have him feeling good. He fantasizes that she has a place nearby, that he won't have to take her back to Alston's.

When Alston returns with the drinks, he says, "Guess what this is," but Dax grabs the tumbler and hammers his drink.

"Shit," Alston says. "You're not that big."

"Work to do," Dax says, and points at the woman.

"One-armer," Alston says.

"What?"

"See how she sits. That's on purpose. Listen, I got no issues with it, but I know you."

"What?"

"That girl has one arm. Go check her out. Can't tell from here."

Dax stays seated and examines his empty glass.

"Hey, no problem, big boy," Alston says. "Go do your thing. I've had one-armers, one-leggers."

"Shut the hell up," Dax says. "You're so full of shit."

"You kidding me? What do you want to know?"

"Nothing. Please."

"One-armers are great, because you don't have to adjust anything, but the one-leggers fuck you all up. She was cut to the hip. The whole angle in there – I don't know, man. And you don't want to stand 'em up. Jesus."

"Only you," Dax says.

"Hell no, some people like that crap. I don't like it and I don't dislike it. Doesn't matter to me. Decent face, green light."

"Got a feeling you'd take them without a head."

"I got my limits, man. No tits, no way. I've been down that road. Sad as fuck. You get the shirt off and one is missing and she's all fucked up emotional about it so you can't say anything, but I say something. Can't get past it. Happened twice. Cancer or some shit. These gals come in from the hills where they practiced the nukes back when. Beautiful chicks, but I can't touch 'em after I've seen that."

"You're cheering me up," Dax says.

"I should be. That one's got one arm. What you need two for? You got one dick, unless the war's changed you."

"Yep."

"And I've never seen her before, which is a good sign. Legs on her too. You might like it."

"Sure."

"What? The thrill gone? The root root will kick here in two seconds. Fix everything."

"It's horrible," Dax says.

"Childhood."

"Yours."

"I guess. I wouldn't go back. You better not be going. Nothing good in Rutherford. It's all gone."

"I don't know," Dax says.

"You know. There's nothing there. I can tell you're going. You're already there. It's a mistake. You don't need the city, Dax. There's nothing worth knowing. Not good for you. Don't go. You'll screw yourself."

"I'm not sixteen, A. I know what I'm doing."

"No, you think you do, but you've been away. It's not your fault. You go back, it's over. Start new."

"You're not listening."

"Far away from Rutherford."

"Travel agent now? Where's the place for me, O great one? Tell me."

"It's not home."

"I'm not you. Don't want to be you."

"Don't stall. Go talk to her."

"No, you're a travel agent and a gold miner," Dax says. "You hunt deer. You take shit from the ground."

"The drink feels good, huh?"

"I want to be as smart as you," Dax says.

"You don't want to be me."

"Smart as you," Dax says.

"You started too late."

"I should go down south, maybe?" Dax says. "The sun will be good for me."

"You're chicken shit. She's at this bar for a reason."

"She's looking for deer hunters."

"You won't go, but I will."

Alston stands and takes a step away.

"Oh, I know," says Dax. "Key fucking West."

Alston stops and turns back. He steps to the booth, grabs Dax's empty glass, lifts it a few inches off the table, and slams it down.

"Fuck, I'm glad you're here," he says, and turns and walks to the bar.

From Alston's front steps Dax stares south beyond the ridge line at the white glow in the otherwise black sky. *Digging the gold, killing the mountains.* Five minutes since his last cigarette; he leans his head back on the front door. He's always liked the black, early-morning calmness and thinks he might look for something where he can work at night and sleep during the day-lit morning.

The faintest sound of crushing rock arrives from the distant white glow, then Alston's footsteps inside the home. Dax guesses he'll have another couple minutes on his own before Alston joins him outside. He didn't expect these fifteen minutes alone, especially after they left the casino empty-handed and Alston pleaded with him on the drive home to move out west. He told Alston he'd think about it, but Dax already knows there's nothing here to connect to, nothing that excites him. There's too much space to feel close to anything. Up to this trip, Fort Carson was as far west as he'd ever been, and that was far enough. Colorado, Nevada – these were places to escape to after you'd lived a life. You could sleepwalk here and get by. There weren't enough people, wasn't enough buzz to get you to wake up.

Alston is wrong about Rutherford. Dax knows he's not returning to just his hometown. It's Rutherford and Newark, the traffic, exhaust smell; the local Pancake House, nearby skyscrapers, Madison Square Garden; taxis and cops with attitude, Connecticut pricks; airplanes everywhere, back-yard pools, everything familiar and foreign and kinetic. There, you're always awake.

But Alston's words have tweaked him enough that he questions accepting his well-intentioned stepmother's offer to crash at their place while he figures things out. His childhood bedroom might kill him at twenty-seven. She's told him the jobs are waiting for him, which he believes is shit, but even so, where to start? He knows tons of ex-army security guards, but he's done with uniforms and guns, save for the pistol he'll keep for home protection, but that one will be locked up.

Torres called him a couple days ago to let him know

about a possible speaking gig for veterans and that Ellis had hurt his foot and was coming back to Carson early. Torres had few details on Ellis. As for the job, Dax would have to travel, which seemed to suit Torres fine, but Dax isn't sure he could pull it off. He can't think of a single wartime story he'd want to tell, no matter how motivational, funny, or gut-wrenching. Besides, he struggles with the details: his memory of war is the girl in the road. Already all else blurs beside her. He knows about the patrols, laughter, showering, sweat, and boredom that filled his two tours in Afghanistan, but none of it feels real – there's no focus or faces or sounds. His war is his rifle in his hands, gunpowder in his nose, a girl in the road. How could he tell that story? Why would he want to?

The doorknob turns and Dax leans forward.

"Big guy like you," Alston says, stepping past Dax, "you'd make sixty a year collecting bonds out here. Sixty, easy. I'll wake the boss up right now. We start tomorrow. Send the rest of your shit whenever. We only have to get like a quarter of the money back to break even. You think business will ever slow down? You think this place is gonna turn into Disneyland? We'll get you a .357 or something. You'll never use it, man. Don't worry. Just shave your head and get yourself a killer tattoo. Show 'em your forearms. They'll give us more money than they owe."

"I got a tat on my back."

"You gonna walk backwards without a shirt all day?"

"I could get one of those Mike Tyson jobs on my face."

"You do whatever the hell you want."

"Yeah."

"We're goddamn brothers. You know that?"

"Yeah," Dax says.

"Hey, talk when you're ready, okay? When you're ready, let it fly."

7

Touch

ARMANDO HAS BEEN back home from Afghanistan for two weeks, and as he peers out of the restaurant's corner window he can't get over how much the mountains west of Colorado Springs differ from the cracking peaks circling Kabul. Armando's father adds sweetener to his iced tea, glances around the half-filled room, and taps the table.

"You're right, no one really cares about you. No one is thinking about you. And thank God. It'd drive us all crazy. You want to come home to an America that realizes its sins? Screw that. We want to gloat, son, and you are the proof we don't need. I don't blame you and your dudes for pissing on dead Taliban. Go for it. Piss on the live ones. Screw the Geneva Convention. Rip dicks off, hack up kids, waterboard, light that Koran on fire, baby."

"Easy. I was just saying—"

"Or treat for polio or pass out limbs like you all did. Do it. We'll forget. Don't do it. We'll forget. So yes, I guess I thank you for raising your right hand. For walking into the recruiter, clueless. And don't put this on your mother's death."

"What?"

"Seriously, who actually wants to go into the military?

Enough, I guess. Everyone wants someone to tell them what to do. That's what it was with you. Just needed someone to tell you what to do. Look, it worked. And you got it good. Someone will hire you here as soon after you sign your separation papers. They'll be called patriotic for doing it. No one is calling you baby killers these days, that's thanks enough."

"You like hearing yourself talk. That's okay."

"You said no one cares about the wars. I'm agreeing with you. You say we're at war? Where, son? Look around. Who's talking about it? Chicago isn't talking. San Fran? Memphis? We're not a nation at war. We never were. Are you serious? No one cares unless it's someone they know."

"So no one knows anyone?"

"We don't care because all of you have volunteered to die. If not in war, then when you get home all brain-fucked from an IED some illiterate planted for twenty bucks and his neck. And believe me, I think that's shit. I'm not mad at you. The VA needs to get their shit together, sure. But there are choices. You chose to be a paid rifle. You are all-volunteer."

"We volunteer to serve. We don't choose our wars. Hell, I got in before 9/11. You know that. You act like that doesn't matter. We're allowed to be pissed about where we go."

"You're wrong. You volunteer to serve at the whim of presidents and senators with no skin in the game. Holy shit, we just reelected Bush. You volunteered to let human beings like him make the call on how *you'll* die, so don't pretend you're a hero or something. Don't go strutting around."

"That's not what I said."

"Don't buy the commercials where people stand up and clap as soldiers walk through the airport. No one knows why they're clapping. Forget the bullshit parades."

"Parades? Dad."

"You really think they're for you? They're for us, son. You kill people you don't know, and they hate you the same way you hate them. That's it. I know economics. It's not just oil. I also know that no one is invading Florida."

"Would that make it easier?"

"Defending actual land, actual Americans instead of algorithms that run the stock market? Yes. That would make me feel better. Would it make you feel better?"

"No. I don't know. I used to."

"Yes you do. You want to say yes. But if you say yes, your recent trip becomes hard to swallow. And you've been told isolationism is shit, although there's no such thing as isolationism. Listen to me, there are things worth fighting for, we just can't find them. Stare into your kids' eyes and tell them about Karzai's butchers. His druggie, raping buddies."

"You know there's no honest people in the world. It's always the lesser of two evils. We're corrupt, but not as corrupt. I know economics too. You fight for a way of life."

"You're wrong. We're not as corrupt because our lie is better than their lie. And here, people know it's a lie."

"That's not true."

"Son, I like my Comcast, my fifty-five-inch plasma, and the Broncos. I want to get pissed when my cable goes out in the fourth quarter of the NBA Finals. I want it to ruin my day. I want to hate Ohio State, I want to eat blueberries year-round, pretend that Christ actually danced on water, and bang my new wife when I have a good day."

"Don't."

"I want to go ape-shit at my grandkids' soccer game when the ref makes a bad call. I tell this to your children when you're away: 'You get what you get and you don't get upset.' There you go. You want a thank-you?"

"No."

"Okay. Thanks. I love you. You know that. But your uniform means nothing. No matter what you've been told, it's only a job."

"You're wrong. Not about everything. But you're wrong about that. And people know why they're clapping as soldiers walk through the airport. They're just glad it's not them and they know that if things got bad enough it would be them. They're clapping because they know sometimes it's hopeless and we serve anyway."

"But you're getting out. Why?"

"It's not because I don't believe in what our military does."

"So let's say you were thinking of staying in. If they cut your pay and benefits in half, right now, what would you do?"

"That's bullshit."

"You don't serve. You're a paid rifle. Soon to be ex–paid rifle. I love you, son, but it's true."

"People are capable of appreciation."

"It's fear, and fear works."

The carpeted chapel seats three hundred, and three quarters of the chairs are occupied this Sunday morning. Armando's younger daughter, Mia, moans in frustration halfway through the hour-long service. Armando leans over Anna, squeezes Mia's leg, and whispers, "Don't make me." She eyes him like a stranger. She shoulders into Anna's red dress, his favorite, and quiets down.

A year away and his dark suit drapes loose on his dry, thin frame. Anna tries to calm both of their daughters as a woman with heavy eye shadow cries at the podium. She struggles through a story about how tithing has lifted her soul. She gathers herself: "It's easy to die for the Lord, but hard to live for him."

The statement settles nicely over the congregation and

all the members contemplate their lives and the things they do or do not give to him. Armando glances at Anna, and he can tell that she contemplates it all, because she has her unfocused stare on the seat in front of her. She probably considers what service to this country means, with him being away so often, or maybe just the ways she lives for the Lord. Perhaps she relives Mia's birth during his previous deployment: driving to the military hospital, only to be sent home because her body had not dilated enough; then, when it was time, waiting an hour for the anesthesiologist, giving birth, and, soon after, trying to get Armando on the phone half a world away, only to be told that he was unavailable; resting and worrying, imagining the worst, and finally writing an e-mail that she hoped he would be alive to read with nothing in the body, just the subject line: "Girl – Mia?"

Armando rubs her back and she leans into his touch, rewarding him. He's unsure if God wanted him to join the military. Armando figures God is mostly hands-off, but even so, when he prays, he does so expectantly.

The speaker now rehashes the founding-of-the-church story, centering her comments on the resiliency of Joseph Smith and his early supporters, chronicling select hardships: Smith's being tarred and feathered, the lynch mob killing him and his brother, church members dodging persecution in Illinois, Missouri, making their way to Utah in a great and difficult migration, and setting up shop near a lake of salt. Armando has heard these stories many times. There is pride there, and although the worst he has experienced is soldiers questioning his underwear, he appreciates the religious lineage of tough souls.

Mia moans again, and three people in the row in front of the Torres family turn and smirk-smile. Anna places her hand on Armando's bouncing leg to soothe him, but his mind floats in a trance, now stuck on the particulars of tarring and feathering. *Pine tar? Tar we use for the roads? Hot tar? Pour it on? Why the feathers?* Mia fusses louder and Anna whispers, "I'm taking her out" to Armando, but his leg keeps bouncing, his eyes up – *How do you get the tar off? Why tar and feather when someone can put a shirt on over it? Unless you do the face. Hot tar on the cheeks. A beard of feathers. Where do you get feathers? Chicken feathers? Who brings the feathers? Of all the choices for pain and humiliation, tar and feathers?* His head clears and he peeks over at his family, but there is only Camila, sitting silently, stuffing the eraser end of a pencil up her nose.

On their way home from church Anna balls her fists and eyes the horizon. Armando focuses on the oncoming traffic, trying to push away the thought of one of the cars abruptly turning in to them head-on. He pictures the collision, beautiful and choreographed, all of them in the sluggish lean mid-contact, a crash-test-dummy commercial. He hears "Hello" and "Hey," and Anna waves her hand at him and brushes her thighs.

Five blocks from home Anna apologizes, says, "I have to ask. Did you kill anyone this time?" She wants to understand what she is dealing with. The children wear headphones in the middle row, watching *Shrek 2*. Armando thinks of the checkpoint girl, his bucking gun, the bullet that missed everything and saved him. Then, reaching down after the Kabul bomb blast, touching the young girl's arm, grabbing the limb, pulling, her arm sliding free from her body, him holding her dangling arm by the wrist.

"No," he says.

She asks if the redeployment program on post helps at all. He opens his mouth but blanks on the answer. They have counselors, sure, but he's been through the routine before. Everyone wants to get out of there, get home, and deal

with it on their own. He has plans to leave the army anyway; no need to open up new files about stuff that they have
no clue how to diagnose or treat, if there is even something
to diagnose. He sleeps decently enough, and his dreams of
a future without bomb-planted streets arrive in comforting color. The rumor is that the VA clinic lines and the wait
time for benefits are insane, but he's not worried about
that yet. He still relishes his easy pleasures, how they are
more than just pleasures, simple spaces where he can place
hope and faith without any wounds: in his Denver Broncos,
how they win more than they lose, how Jake Plummer will
never get them to the Super Bowl; in Tiger Woods, how he
will break out of his current slump any week now; in Green
Day's new *American Idiot* album, how it plays on repeat
during his morning runs.

Armando is realistic. He doesn't expect blanket immu-
nity from his combat time. While he knows many soldiers
who deal with combat seemingly well, who move on after
their service to years of success and fulfillment, he's also familiar with the stories of good men and women, many of
them friends, who go sleepless for days, play metal music at
3 A.M., use drugs, experience perpetual sedation. Worse yet
are the many others sticking guns in their mouths and pulling the trigger, wrapping belts around their necks and tee-
tering off the chair, the unfathomable pain trapped in those
that do, the unfathomable pain left in suicide's wake.

In comparison he diagnoses himself fine, at least fine
enough. He makes love to Anna. He takes the sacrament
at church without anguish. He recognizes there are issues
with being "fine." What does it say that he's not jacked up?
Should he be different, jittery? Two deployments and he
waits for the consequences of Afghanistan, confused. In
an inexplicable way he wants the shakes for a day, an hour.

When will he feel the pain of shooting at the checkpoint girl? When will he suffer the guilt of masturbating during the prayer calls? Will his minor yearnings for the amplified voices from the minarets stop? For the Afghan streets' smell of crap, dust, and rot? Already tiny but manageable itches arise for the chaos that greeted him each morning and made him feel like he could die at any moment, and for other times, when the occasional blood moon out his window convinced him that he would live forever.

Anna's voice lifts him out of the daydream. She reaches to hold his hand over the center console.

"I want to know how I'm supposed to talk to you."

Armando hears Anna, but washed once over – a memory speaking to him – and he waits to hear how he'll reply. He grips the leather-wrapped steering wheel and stares down the blue Toyota truck approaching fast, left tires hugging the double yellow. The truck's chrome grille sparkles at him.

"I want to know how to talk to you," Anna says again.

"Be thankful I'm not hurt. I'm not limping. I can play with our children." He pauses and smiles as they turn onto their street. "And I've never been right up here." He taps his head, already aware of and disappointed by the gesture. Anna goes silent, and he sees her hands squeeze her thighs. They pull into the garage, and Armando lets Anna lift the kids out of the car.

The Torres family settles into the early Sunday afternoon, and he unknots his red tie and unbuttons the top of his dress shirt. He helps feed the girls grilled cheese and remembers that Camila no longer requires a peanut butter dollop.

Anna bought their new house while he was overseas.

The stucco rancher feels tight for their family – room walls crowd the beds on both sides. After lunch, the hallway floor creaks as his daughters skip to their rooms.

The girls nap, and Anna asks Armando what he's thinking about while he relaxes on the couch watching golf (the Tour Championship, the fairy-tale green fairways, Retief Goosen going low). He really wonders how they grow and cut the grass in diamond patterns so perfectly for the golf tournament, recalls that when he used to play the Broadmoor course with his mother the grass was cut the same way, but he can see that Anna wants something more. He notices the hope in her elbowed lean across the laminate counter, in her slightly raised eyebrows, so he tells her that he often contemplates who's going to win in the end, Allah or God. The sentence comes out a little sarcastic, but he sells the question with eye contact. He expects some ribbing or a frustrated shake of her head, but Anna glides from the kitchen to sit next to him. She turns off the television without asking.

She says that America is blowing it because there are not enough real Christians, that the Muslims have nothing against Christianity, that if Christians actually practiced their faith, were as devout as the Muslims were, most would get along fine.

"Some of the blame is ours," she says. "America's. We're strong in all the wrong ways. We call ourselves Christians, but we're something else."

"Muslims can't even get along with other Muslims. It's not that easy."

"I didn't say it was easy. Anyway, you're not going back. You're here. That's all that matters. And you weren't thinking about Allah versus God. Talk to me like you care what I think, because I worry about you. I can't help you if I don't know anything. And if you want me to leave you alone, just tell me that. But it kills me when you don't say anything or make stuff up."

"I don't want to invent things. If I need something, I'll take care of it or tell you or both. Assume I'm fine unless I tell you. I'm tired. I feel like I've just got home."

Armando takes in the living room, still new to him, the fifty-inch flat-screen too big for the room. He's disappointed he opened his mouth about the Allah-God thing. This isn't where he wanted this afternoon to go. He wants to see if Tiger can catch Goosen at the Tour Championship, wants to bask in a clear, unburdened mind, wants to consider telegenic lawn-mower patterns. He moves Anna's voice to the background and notices the crown molding where the ceiling and walls meet and follows the line across the wall.

"You've been home two weeks. You're getting out. I'm not trying to pile on here, but you're somewhere else. I'll give you space, but you have to talk to me. Your kids miss you. You're not playing with them. Be their dad."

Armando inspects a thin space between the molding and the ceiling. The work is shoddy, and the separation spells trouble elsewhere for a house this new.

"It's a big deal. I'm speaking to you," she says, and he hears her.

"Everything's always a big deal. Relax."

"Promise me that much. You'll tell me."

Armando nods along, the single physical movement he can muster, and when he doesn't respond Anna reaches out and takes his hands in hers. He looks at his wife, her hair still pinned up nicely for church. He knows she wants to heal something in him, and as they sit there together he wonders if she is disappointed that he is whole.

An hour later Armando lounges on his front porch bench, reading old Calvin and Hobbes comics. An incredibly warm day for November. He watches the Front Range of the Rockies to the west, late-afternoon thunderheads instead of snow-filled clouds cresting the peaks. He considers waking the girls from their naps and heading up to Gold Camp Road, or for an ice cream at Michelle's downtown, or maybe for a stroll around the Broadmoor's pond, but he listens to the quiet peace in the air and closes his eyes and smells the almost-rain and stays put.

He'll have to start applying for civilian jobs soon if he wants a smooth transition from military to civilian work, but he doesn't yet know what jobs to apply for, where his skills align, what he would do if he had a choice. He has an army veteran friend making good money on the motivational speaker circuit. He's told Armando there's a place for him, that you keep the speeches to smaller venues, a twenty-five-minute routine – two war stories, wear your uniform, and include the words *honor, courage,* and *sacrifice,* and you're set.

"There's no scam here," his friend tells him. "You tell the truth. The emotional truth. The World War Two, Korean, Vietnam, even Gulf War One folks want to know. They want to compare stories. People leave motivated. They appreciate service. They want to hear from someone that's been there. The story is the hero. You're just the teller. Up to a grand a speech for the truth. No one's doing this. No one. If we don't tell our stories, someone else will."

Not shy in front of crowds, Armando has thought about the offer, but when he considers which stories to dress up, he invariably returns to the checkpoint girl. But instead of a girl – it can't be a girl – it has morphed into a man, a bearded man, two bearded men in a tiny hatchback, two bearded men in a tiny hatchback yelling "Allahu akbar," and in the story he doesn't shoot, it is a story about witness, he was there but as witness to honor, courage, sacrifice. Even as he forms the new scenes, the new characters, he knows he'll never tell either story. Even in debrief that day in Afghanistan, he, Big Dax, Wintric, and the LT had different answers to the same questions: "How many times did you yell to her to stop?" "Who shot first, second, third?" "How far was she?" "Why didn't you aim for her legs?" "When did she drop the ball?" "Was it possible she was pleading for help?" "Is it true you argued among yourselves about who had hit her?"

The first droplets hit the front yard, and Armando wonders how long he'll consider himself a soldier, how long he'll want to. He's told Anna that he won't shave for a month after he gets out, but what that means he isn't yet sure. The rain is pounding now, and a crack of thunder sounds a few miles south. He sees the familiar bevy of antennas on top of Cheyenne Mountain – the nuclear war–proof mountain. *Thank you, Cheyenne Mountain.* His father's new wife used to work in the mountain, the stepmother he has come home to, unbearably kind and supportive. Disgustingly humble and already a confidant of Anna's. This woman with years in the mountain, but she can't talk about the mountain. Easy questions: "How many people do we have in there?" "Are we still tracking Russian nukes?" Armando has served at Fort Carson for years, not two miles from Cheyenne Mountain, and he knows nothing about it, save the nuclear war–proof claim, the antennas, the fact that he now knows someone who has worked there, and some unsubstantiated claims by his father. Years ago his father told him two things about the mountain: (1) that Russia's nuclear aim was so poor that living next door to it was the perfect place to be, and God help anyone around the Durango area if things started rocking, and (2) that the microwave was invented inside the mountain. Whenever Armando's father would heat up popcorn, he'd tap the microwave

door and say, "Thank you, Cheyenne Mountain." That's
what Armando hears now on his front porch, "Thank you,
Cheyenne Mountain," and the rain pounding, the antennas,
the same antennas he watched blinking at night as a child,
and he flashes back to when he was sixteen years old, popcorn popping on their Friday family movie night, each of
them arguing for a different film and Armando's mother finally deciding what to watch and all of them settling in. His
mother on the couch, his mother on the couch post-trans-
plant, saltines and 7Up, a trombone, the rain even harder
now, punishing, his father on the baseball field taking him
in his arms, the open-casket viewing the night before the
burial, his fascination with his mother's shaved face, her
funeral, singing "Because I Have Been Given Much," a
three-mile-long car procession, the bishop's promise that
they would all be together again in heaven and his father
laughing, months of his father's madness, hiding the light-
ers in his sock drawer, his sister's move to their aunt's in
Cortez, Marie to Arizona, a friend signing up for the army,
Armando going along, the papers in front of him in the recruiting office, the path forward, out, his signature, signa-
tures, his name, signing, black ink, his name.

Six minutes into the downpour Armando sees miniriv-
ers along the street's gutters and pools forming in his un-
even front yard. The Front Range is already clearing and
he guesses the rain will stop soon, and it's a good thing,
because the yard can't take much more water. Already he
knows they'll have to move from this place, maybe only
from this poorly constructed house, maybe to a whole new
city, but he's certain this isn't the place he wants to come
home to, this isn't the place he wants his kids to come home
to, and although he has no way of knowing now, he's right.

In a couple years he'll move his family about forty miles
north to Castle Rock, where they'll enjoy a better view of

the Rockies and a properly graded front yard, a home where his kids will grow and fight, where he'll watch the Broncos lose a Super Bowl, where, decades from now and wheelchair-bound, Armando will turn to hiding bottles of whiskey in boxes of Christmas decorations, a home where he'll write a letter inviting his estranged daughter Mia home and one July day, overcome with emotion, he'll welcome Mia and her daughter back into his life. But right now Armando sits and watches the shallow front-yard pond creep outward, and although the sky has now cleared above him, the rain continues to fall.

That evening Camila and Mia play in the home's fenced back yard. The moon already hugs the southeast sky, and things get heated between the girls after Camila trips Mia and tugs on her leg, pulling her around the still drying yard. Mia screams, but Camila keeps yanking.

"Easy," Armando says. He stares at his kids. They ignore him. He realizes that they're starting to look more and more like Anna.

"Do something," Anna says.

Armando is about to ask her what she thinks about a third child when she leans over, grabs his arm, and whispers, "You have to touch your children, dammit. Do you hear me?"

The words hang on him, and the shock and anger brew inside his limbs.

"What the hell did you say to me?"

This fury arrives from someplace new, and he lines up obscenities on his tongue, but before launching them he shuffles through the past two weeks of memory and comes up with a stinging recap: the girls were too shy to hug him when he came off the plane with the cameras flashing and the news teams and the Bruce Springsteen music.

He rushes past bedtime routines, feedings, a doctor's visit, walks to the park, and he realizes that he has touched them, but only in passing; he hasn't held them, not as he used to, not as he wanted to while he was away. His chest pounds and Anna's hand clutches his biceps to lead him out to the yard.

Without a word he rises. His daughters now play with the water hose, Camila half plugging the stream into a spewing water fan, and for the first time their giggles terrify him. He walks onto the wet grass, but a few steps away he shakes his head, not sure what comes next. A crushing weight stops and holds him. Does he grasp them and throw them in the air? Grab their thin arms and pull them close? Take the hose and spray them? Does he ask for permission? He wants to live for them, but it all feels wrong, and before he knows it he sits, crushing the dusk grass, and everyone pauses, even young Mia, with a puddle covering her toes. He opens his arms, but his children stand motionless.

"Please," he says.

"Girls," Anna says.

"No! I'll do it," he says. "Camila, Mia. Come to your daddy. Now."

They stand still.

"Why won't you come? Please, girls."

His arms are open. He could receive them so easily.

"Mommy," Mia says.

"No! Here, Mia. Here. With me."

"Mommy."

"Goddammit! No! Here, Mia. Camila, here."

"Armando."

"No!"

Armando slams the ground, his palms on the ground, pressing, and he closes his eyes and steadies himself. He senses Anna moving in the background. He breathes and opens his eyes, but he's still in his back yard.

"Girls," he says, his voice cracking. "Girls."

Camila takes a step forward and stops. Armando guesses that Anna is waving the girls forward, begging them with her arms to go to their father, but they stand locked in place, staring above him. He feels water on his legs, and Anna says, "Sing the ABCs." He hears her and sees his arms and hands reach out to the great expanse in front of him. He thinks of the tune and just before he begins the melody, Camila starts with the *A*, and Mia joins in by the *E*. His daughters gaze at Anna, singing slowly and softly in the air, their faces solemn. The refrain should sound elementary, but the dual-voiced letters are veneration. Armando thinks back to when he sang this same song to his daughters at bedtime, and all at once he realizes that he has taught them a beautiful prayer, one they remember. He opens his mouth and hits the right pitch on *Q*. Together they sing the building blocks to everything they will ever say to each other.

When they finish he expects a surge of something, a new resolve, or an answer awaiting him after *Z*. He wants his body to come alive, but it's near dark and the girls haven't moved and he feels the cool water beginning to cover him, then Anna's hands on his shoulders, squeezing him to life.

8

Metatarsal

FEBRUARY 2005, a moment alone in Afghanistan, and Wintric smells burning trash and shit from the other side of the post, and he hears the helicopters whipping in the dark distance, his uniform warming his body, and he walks between the rows of massive shipping containers and feels the first push in the back, and the Afghan night envelopes everything, a tackle from behind, dirt pressing his face as he struggles with strangers, but a game he knows, like all the wrestling, the UFC imitation, the bets, the boredom before battle, hearing himself, "You got me. Fine. Fuck off," then silence, instantaneously odd, no "Fuck you" or "Pussy" reply, and all at once a switch flips a separate world on and his face presses hard to the soil, knee on his neck, he's gasping now, suffocating, a heavy weight lands on his back, fumbles with his belt, then pants down, his underwear, the dizzying disbelief, his arms and legs attempt to flail, but they fail him once, and again, a will to thrash, a throaty gurgle, anus pressure and pain, pressure and pain, and ripping flesh and a grunt, and barely breathing and confusion and helpless swirling beyond, and the dirt pressing his nose and mouth, gasping, fighting, but nothing, willing his body but nothing, and pressure and pain, then silence, his slack body shedding parts of himself into the shallow night, hovering somewhere there, close.

The following days press pain and debate, thoughts of home that can't materialize, death and weakness. The dense hours crawl. Patrols like a zombie, meals he can't taste, then refuses to eat, Halo 2 for hours. A sergeant asks him if he's okay, and he hears himself say that he is, and somehow the sergeant believes him. He shits and weeps. Desperate, he sharpens his knife, considers the right spot to stab (left foot, below the smallest two toes, marked with a penned *X*), how hard to stab, swigs smuggled booze until he vomits, and straps the doomed foot down. The knife is light in his hand and he cries and wipes at his eyes, then closes them. He swings down hard. The pain rockets through him and his eyes blast open and he sees the blade lodged an inch to the right of his aim point and not deep enough to do the trick — the trick being escape. The blood starts up fast, darker than he imagined, and already he's dizzy and his arms spasm out at his sides. The tent walls around him push close, but he manages to will himself back to the knife. He pulls it from his foot and stabs himself two more times before he passes out.

At the Reno airport Wintric's mother cries and takes him in her arms. She knows her son has injured his foot badly, but that's all. They load the Ford Taurus and Wintric says, "I'm tired, Mom. Just let me look." On the drive to Chester, Wintric's mother sips at a Pepsi. Gwen Stefani, Mariah Carey, Kelly Clarkson take turns on the radio. Wintric has the passenger seat reclined and his booted foot up on the dash.

This is coming home silent: early afternoon northwest bound on Highway 395 out of Reno past Sun Valley, Bordertown, the WELCOME TO CALIFORNIA sign with a trio of golden poppies, Hallelujah Junction, high desert, sage-brushed pioneer settlements, WELCOME TO DOYLE — WORLD FAMOUS LIZARD RACES, Herlong, army munitions depot, dried-up Honey Lake, Highway 36, the supermax prison with gleaming fences, Susanville, the Sierra theater, the climb up into pine and red soil, Fredonyer Pass, green meadow, Westwood, the old dump, over Bailey Creek running at a trickle, cresting Johnson's grade, Mount Lassen holding snow against the blue sky, Lake Almanor's dark blue water, the causeway into town, the green city limits sign, POP 2200, Chester, home.

Kristen wanted to see Wintric in his uniform, but he wears sweatpants. It's been three years, and now here he is, on her couch, in her tiny living room just big enough for couch, coffee table, fern, short bookshelf, and television. Deftones play from the tiny speakers. She nudges him with her elbow. She has curled her hair and squeezed into her best Lucky jeans. Under normal circumstances she would palm the back of his head, feeling the sharp brush of his close haircut, but she's not thinking about hair. She hasn't even mentioned the package Wintric sent her from basic training that she's kept in the closet.

"Do I smell like Afghanistan?" he asks, eyeing Barry Bonds and Chris Webber posters over the bookshelf of DVDs, photos. A glance at the pictures and he finds himself in one, but it's a group photo on Mount Lassen.

Wintric's protective boot is parked on the coffee table. His unmedicated foot pains him if it dips below his heart too long. Kristen wants to see his foot, but he tells her no, at least not yet. Thirty minutes later he pulls at the Velcro on the top of the boot. He slides the boot off, then the black sock, and finally the nylon. His biggest toe is the single remaining digit, and half his foot is missing on an arc, a crescent from the base of the ankle to the single intact toe. Kristen asks to touch his foot and Wintric tells her yes, but she doesn't move. She wants to know how it happened.

"If I say someone shot it off, I'm a hero, but if I stepped on my own knife, I'm a fool. Either way, I've got a third of a foot. A scythe foot."

"A scythe foot?"

"Doc told me it's used to cut wheat down. Got a big curved blade on it. Grim Reaper carries one." He lifts his foot and swings it left. "Knocks them down for harvest."

Her eyes level up to his, and he recognizes the expression—the pity he wants and despises.

"Sometimes I think about chopping the whole thing off. Maybe then I'll deserve the fucking sympathy."

He's surprised her, and she inches back.

"Don't do this, K," he says. "Don't look at me like I've changed."

"You have half a foot. I'm not supposed to feel anything? It's enough that you're back."

"You think I'm back?"

"I'm glad you're back."

Wintric grabs his gear and hurriedly puts on the nylon and the sock and fastens the boot up. He stands up, and the spiked blood rushes down his leg. The groan brings Kristen's hand to her mouth. She locks the door dramatically.

"Sit down," she says.

She feeds him two of his pain pills, and his face flushes out. It's against the label warning, but he asks for a beer and she gets him one. He calms, says he's inquiring about work down in Sacramento in fence manufacturing, but she knows he lies.

"If you don't like it there," she says, stops. "Just because you were raised here doesn't mean anything. I'm making nine an hour at Holiday."

"We got a Subway, I see."

"There are worse places."

"I've been to Alabama. Georgia. Went up to Atlanta."

"Yeah?"

"Coca-Cola plant. The headquarters is there."

"Oh."

"The Coke secret ingredient list is locked in a vault."

"For Coke?"

"Yeah."

"But don't they have to put the ingredients on the can? It's a rule, right?"

"I think."

"Then how is it a secret if you can see it on the side?"

"All I know is that there's secret shit in there and like only two people in the world know what it is."

"Cocaine."

"That's how it started."

"Seriously?"

"That's what they said."

"Well, it's called Coke."

Wintric drinks from his beer can. Kristen thumbs the front pockets of her jeans, her chest hollow. There is no transition for what she wants to say. She was as surprised as anyone when Wintric's parents told her he was coming home, done with the army, injured, but not horribly.

"I missed you," she says. "I left you alone because you wanted me to."

"I know," he says, looking away. Barry Bonds on the wall, bat in hand.

"I would've been . . ."

"Relax. I didn't send anyone else my hair."

"I have it," she says, and rises.

"No. Don't. I believe you."

"You going to grow it out?" she asks, now reaching out

and touching the back of his scalp. "Prickly." She brings her hand down to his shoulder and squeezes the muscle.

He smells her hand, vanilla lotion, and the scent intoxicates him – *comfort, home, sex, strong, young.* Kristen's green eyes, *home.* He reaches up to her face and touches her jaw.

"It'd just get in the way, I think. We'll see."

She leans into his hand, then reaches for it, kisses it. She notices that he does smell different, but how?

He exhales and moves close and kisses her on the mouth. The warmth and fear rush at him on the couch, everything happening so fast, and he remembers standing and lifting Kristen, moving her to the wall. He pictures this muscular movement, but it seems a desire too far removed, a past fantasy, no longer a fantasy. His pulse jabs strong in his hands, but before he attempts to command his body into action a pain shoots up his leg and he winces.

Kristen remains close, hoping he can smell her.

"Stay," she says.

She stands and reaches to the bottom of her green shirt and yanks it up over her head, her curled hair lifting in the neck hole, then bouncing down. She unbuttons her pants and wiggles free. She reaches back, unfastens her bra, and slips it off. Wintric sits up on her couch, then opens his mouth.

"Stay," she says, and smiles.

She reaches to his waist and the lip of his underwear on his skin, then pulls his underwear and sweatpants down past his knees. His legs shake and he lifts his arms in front of him, but she grabs his wrists and he lets her guide them to her hips as she straddles him.

"You nervous?" she says. "It's okay. I know you."

He opens his mouth to say "Wait," but nothing comes out.

"I know you."

She feels herself weightless and she senses the tears are near, so she closes her eyes as she leans over Wintric and lets her breasts brush his face. She waits for him to say her name and he does, in a whisper, a question. She kisses his mouth and feels him kissing back, and soon she moves down and tongues his nipples, her hand running along his inner thigh – something she knows he used to love – and she hears him breathe shallowly, then her name, a question, but she doesn't answer. She kisses his stomach, his body trembling, her lips on his belly button, a mole just below, her name, and she moves her hand to his penis, half erect, and moves her head down, and she opens her mouth and feels his hands on her head, squeezing at the sides of her head, pulling her up, her name, his closed eyes.

"Kristen?"

"What?"

His eyes are closed.

"Please," he says, and he opens his eyes. He can sense her surprise when he reaches down and grabs his sweat-pants. He pulls them up to his waist and begins to stand, but stops. He looks at her silent face and reaches to her and puts his hands just below her ribs and brings her close, chest to chest, her wide-eyed face now in his hands, and he kisses her mouth hard, pushing his lips against hers, turning his cheek to her lips, feeling the pressure of her face on his, his hands now on her back, pulling her hard against him.

She places her hands on the sides of his head, fingertips pressing the base of his skull, where the neck meets. She kisses his cheek, his temple, his ear, his forehead, her hands pulling him close, his head on her chest, her arms strong and flexed, pulling him into her.

• • •

Twenty minutes later Wintric grabs a packet of cigarettes from his bag and says, "I know," before lighting one. He rests his head on the back of the couch. Kristen takes eight steps to the refrigerator, her pants still on the floor. Wintric watches her long legs and ass move and wonders where they'll live. He has already heard talk of twenty new homes out by the airport, and he sees himself on his hands and knees, his back bending at awkward angles as he nails roofing under the sun.

"Can I get you anything?" she asks.

"No."

"Are you sure?"

He still has her taste in his mouth, and he knows she'll always ask him if he is sure. She'll offer to carry things, lift things. His foot is back up on the coffee table, and he weighs the consequences of yelling to her, *I'm fucking sure. I said no,* but he eats the words. He sees his new boot on the coffee table, the scythe foot inside, and he debates cutting off the rest, making everything clean.

Marcus's coworkers wait for the day when he'll blow something up. Several of them have known him since grade school, and as long as they can remember he has worn black. This, they say, is a sign; of what, no one is certain, but they figure it can't be healthy, and he rides his bright yellow motorcycle around town, most of the time helmetless. Kristen was the one thing he had going for him, and that ended a year ago, but they can tell he still holds out hope. They know where he goes after work most nights, and they debate when to have him yanked from the heavy machinery. He's become clumsy around the saw, and it's only a matter of time before the DAYS WITHOUT AN ACCIDENT sign resets to zero, but today people up and down the line notice his newfound eagerness. He works fast, and he has all his safety gear on, a first in weeks.

Marcus lets the day's excitement brew in him. During their breakup Kristen told him that it had nothing to do with Wintric, but Marcus knows different. He's followed the two of them to the Top of the World, observed the parked car. He's watched her take Wintric into her place night after night, and watched the lights go out, but some nights they leave the lights on, and he watches their shadows move on the thin blinds. Last night he sneaked up to the bedroom window. They were arguing again, and while he hoped the fight was about him, he didn't hear his name. After Wintric left, Marcus sat underneath a tree in the dark, smoking for two hours, replaying Wintric's exit, convincing himself that the departure was final. Marcus has heard the rumors about Wintric – that there is more than the foot wrong with him – but there is little evidence now that he has lost the boot, save for Wintric putting on some weight and the fights with Kristen, which could be about anything. Marcus decides that in the end, cause doesn't matter. Already he feels more powerful and capable than Wintric, and it's this that strengthens his hopes.

After work Marcus stops by his apartment and changes into the red shirt Kristen gave him. He checks for Wintric's Bronco before approaching Kristen's door. She answers in a torn shirt, her eyes glossy.

"Where is he?" Marcus asks, already shaking.

She shoulders the door frame.

"Jesus, Marcus. What are you doing here? Shouldn't you be hiding under a tree?"

"Tell me where he is and I'll take care of it."

Kristen feels a pain inside her and senses Marcus awaiting her command. She pinches the bridge of her nose. It's already dark, and she considers for a moment whether

Wintric would be jealous if she invited Marcus in, if the simple action of Marcus crossing her home's threshold would shake Wintric back into reality, or at least shake him enough for him to be willing to talk to her. She wants to hurt Wintric for last night, for months' worth of nights that have left her worn — for leaving for the army and sending only his hair — and she sizes up Marcus, desperate and lost in his red shirt. His mouth is open and he smells like cigarettes and sawdust.

"Go away."

"He did that to you?" Marcus says, reaching out to touch the torn fabric of Kristen's shirt. She lets him caress the material and brush her skin.

"Does it matter who did it?" she asks.

But Marcus has stopped listening. He focuses on his index finger, how his finger reaches between the ripped fabric of her shirt, the way his skin feels on the smooth skin above her collarbone. He takes a step closer, resting his foot on the threshold.

"I bet he's at the Top of the World," she says. She doesn't know what will happen, but as the words leave her mouth she's as excited and fearful as she's ever been. The past two months have racked her — Wintric's insomnia and apathy mixed with moments of energy and resolve. Yesterday she arrived home from work to find Wintric in an overflowing bath, fully clothed, a blue Sierra Nevada Brewery hoodie pulled over his head, submerged jeans and Nike basketball shoes.

She lifts Marcus's hand off her, and his face whitens as he steps backward.

"Is he alone?" he says.

Kristen turns and slams the door behind her. She's unsure whether Marcus can figure out all the roads to get there, but that's not her problem. She stands in her living room, just inside the door, on a welcome mat still damp from Wintric's dripping clothes, where he stood and yelled before leaving last night. Her hand on the arm of her couch, where Wintric plays Halo 2 and pops OxyContin while she works, where he tells her he loves her, begs her to stay with him, tells her that he is her folded American flag, only alive. She walks to the kitchen, to the stove, and turns on a burner without any intention of cooking. She watches the burner brighten orange, feels the subtle heat in the air. Next to the stove, on the side of the refrigerator, hangs a calendar, stuck in June even though a mid-October day is ending. Tired, confused, and guilty, she finds her phone and calls Wintric. She tells him that Marcus is angry, unreasonable. She hears his drunken voice.

"Thank you," he says. "I'm here. Still here."

She hangs up, turns off the burner, and calls the cops.

The lit plume of smoke pours upward from the mill, dissipating into the stars. Wintric has been coming to the Top of the World for years, but lately he's come alone. It's where he goes to return Torres's phone calls and avoids answering his questions. Wintric prefers to listen while Torres practices his speeches on him, but they never include the checkpoint girl, a fact not lost on Wintric. For him, the girl has submerged just below the pain of his rape and his injured foot, but she's there, potent each time she surfaces.

Tonight Wintric forgoes a fire, slumps in a cheap nylon folding chair, and steadies his bad foot on a block of wood.

The night is cool, and he sips at a fifteen-year Scotch his neighbor gave him when he came home in the boot. The streetlights on Main Street spread out in front of him like a runway. Eight minutes since Kristen's call, and a lone motorcycle speeds across the dark expanse well below him. Although he knows there's a causeway underneath the tires, it seems as though the bike zips along the top of the water. The velocity is amazing, the oval headlight beaming the black away at full throttle. The bugs are thick, and Wintric guesses that Marcus's helmet is covered with flattened bug bodies.

Marcus can't hear the tiny pings that come fast and fill up his visor. This is the first time he has pushed the bike past sixty, and he can barely see. He dreads removing one of his hands, because the bike shakes. Marcus knows that if Wintric is at the Top of the World, Wintric could spot him, but is he watching? Does Wintric have his pistol with him? Marcus has heard the betting stories, and he's scared but wired. His vision slowly disappears behind the crushed flies and gnats and mosquitoes.

The bow his mother gave him for his eighteenth birthday wraps around his chest and squeezes him. He has put an arrow down the back of his shirt, tip up, rubbing against his helmet. He has no plan, and he struggles to organize his thoughts, but somewhere among the whirling emotions and projections he feels Kristen's hands on him once again. He knows he's being used in a way he doesn't fully understand, but she almost invited him in. The road is empty and black, and Marcus wrenches the accelerator and squints.

Wintric hears the bike. The throttle sound varies depending on the ridge, the turn, and the grade. Even though he sips at the Scotch slowly, he has refilled his glass twice before the bike's gravely throat is on him, the bike's light swinging around the final turn.

Wintric was shocked when Kristen told him about the relationship with Marcus — the shy soda fountain kid in all black, a half-capable wrestler. He didn't believe her at first, could not understand how she could go for Marcus, even if their families were close. As time went on Wintric came to believe that her choice was more a comment on him, that he and Marcus were somehow equals, he and the kid who dished out ice cream and dreamed of the mill. This thought has cornered Wintric, and since his return he's watched Marcus around town; watched as he rides his rundown motorcycle back and forth to work, as he shops at the market where Kristen works. Wintric has spied him jogging in the street and wondered if Marcus purposely runs by the El-lises' place. Wintric's parents' house is out of the way, but once or twice a week Marcus jogs by with his jerking, elongated steps, his elbows pinned. The stride is outrageous and pitiful, and Wintric envies every whole-body step. He realizes they might not even be equals.

The motorcycle pulls in twenty yards from Wintric's chair, and the bike's headlight shines at his feet. Marcus removes his helmet and unfurls the weapon over his head. Wintric remains seated, bypasses his glass, and lifts the bottle to his lips. Marcus fumbles badly in his attempt to place an arrow on the string, and Wintric knows that he has never used the bow before.

"Hey, can you take the other half of this foot off for me?"

Marcus draws the bow.

"You're drunk."

"You're not?"

"I'll kill you here."

"Lower. There, I know it's dark. I don't know you."

"Don't believe me, you son of a bitch?"

"I believe you, Marcus. But right now, tonight, it doesn't matter. Go, buddy. Take the town. I'm leaving here."

"You're not leaving."

"I don't even know you, Marcus."

"You know me. Stop saying that."

"Seriously, pull up a seat. Tell me."

"Shut the fuck up."

"I don't know you."

"Shut up."

"Have her, man. She won't help. She's nice, though, right? Goddamn. If she was from somewhere else, she'd be a catch."

"You know me."

"I see you running your marathon, stud. What you training for? You training for the mill? You running the Fourth of July Fun Run? Marcus, you badass. You should join the army, man. They'll love you. You can serve ice cream all day long."

"I'll shoot you. You hit her, I hit you."

Wintric squints. "Hey, you wearing red instead of black? Mixing it up, hero?"

The sharp whipping sound of the arrow cuts the air above Wintric's head.

"There you go! Come on, Marcus." Wintric drops his leg off the log, yells out in pain, and tumbles off his chair to the ground. He rolls, clutching his foot, stops on his back, and pulls his left knee to his chest.

"Fuck, fuck, fuck."

Marcus has frozen in place, holding the bow away from his body. Wintric braces himself on his elbows, breathing hard, the pain mixing fast with the Scotch.

"You brought one arrow?" Wintric says. He waits, and when Marcus says nothing, Wintric laughs. "Fucking Robin Hood."

Marcus lowers himself to the ground.

"Her shirt is torn," he says.

On the causeway below, two patrol cars scream out. The red and blue lights play in the dim landscape.

"We've got five minutes," Wintric says. "What you want to do?"

"Kristen called the cops," Marcus says. The words arrive as a question and a statement and he tries to paste them together. He feels himself fingering the tear in her shirt.

"She called me," Wintric says.

Marcus pauses for a few seconds, jumps to his feet, and rushes to the bike, but before he gets there he stops and lifts his bow. In one fluid motion he spins and hurls it toward town, launching it high in the air with a grunt.

The cops disappear, negotiating the twenty-three switchbacks, two road changes, and a navigable stream. Wintric pulls himself back into his seat. The town lights flicker.

"I'm pressing charges, asshole," Wintric says. "You better run, boy. Run. I know you, Marcus. I know you, man. County jail, bitch."

Marcus jumps on his bike, starts it up, and speeds off.

Wintric listens to the sound of the departing motorcycle and the incoming sirens as they mesh together for a while before the rising sirens take over. He will recognize the cops who arrive. Everyone in town knows all the cops – there are only eight – and these guys will be pissed that they had to come out to the Top of the World, but everything should be fine as long as he doesn't give them any hell. Wintric brushes at his arms, knocking off pine needles he picked up from the fall. He reaches for his glass but finds the bottle first and uncorks, then drinks. The cops are close and he anticipates a spotlight in his eyes, but he has a few seconds, and he looks out over the town's lights below, a pocket of amber glow in the California blackness.

Kristen has her brown pants on and reaches for her white work shirt in her closet. Last night Wintric called her after the cops pulled up to the Top of the World. She forgets much of what he said, but in the end the cops said they would talk to her later and Wintric said he would stop by sometime. Apparently the warning call was enough for him, but he was drunk, and she's unsure if he'll remember or if anything will change. She'll answer a couple more questions after work, but she guesses everything will blow over in a week and find a comfortable place in the local gossip. No one has heard from Marcus, but Kristen expects to see him in the store.

She buttons up her shirt and eyes the box at the top of her closet, the one with Wintric's hair. She's running late, but she grabs her footstool and brings the box down. Narrow and long, like a box for a sword. It has a layer of gray dust over its white cover. Kristen sits on the side of her bed with the box in her lap. She thinks about blowing the dust off the top. She thinks about writing a word with her finger, but no words come to her.

9

Redwoods

S EVEN WEEKS PREGNANT and nauseated enough to search for the women's bathroom, Kristen sweats in the "Express – twenty items or less" line at the Susanville Walmart and tries to calm her stomach and mind; she regrets the Jack in the Box tacos she had for lunch, and her mind replays her answer to Wintric's question about an abortion: "I don't know."

Married for two weeks, she wears a solitaire diamond ring and a silver wedding band, and while she hasn't asked him, she guesses Wintric purchased the set from the same store where she now stands and vises down on the shopping cart's handle. She's still acclimating to the minor weight of the set and the protruding diamond, and the inside of her left-hand middle and pinkie fingers are sore from the new rub.

She swallows and fingers the sweat away from her face. She reaches into her purse and grabs the small plastic baggie of saltines she totes around, selects a cracker, and places it on her tongue.

Unloading her cart onto the conveyer belt, she surveys her soon-to-be purchases: a whistle, a gray T-shirt, a new

sports bra, dry-erase markers, a dry-erase board with basketball court markings, an iron-on *Coach* logo, the Dead
Rising video game, the latest *People* magazine, three gallons
of milk, tortillas, instant coffee, deodorant, toothpaste, and
athletic socks.

She guesses the Walmart checkout man is new, exhausted, or stupid, because he struggles to locate the bar-
code on everything he attempts to scan, and while she
counts out her sixteen items before the plastic bar that separates her things from the cowboy-hatted man's stuff in
front of her, she realizes that the conveyer belt isn't moving,
that everything is taking too long for her trembling stomach and esophagus. After another cracker and two more
minutes of nervous gulping, the cowboy has his total, and
he reaches into his front jeans pocket and brandishes a
leather-bound checkbook, then asks for a pen. These acts
will delay her bathroom entrance by a minute, probably
more.

Miraculously, the second saltine has helped, offering a
sliver of reprieve—enough, she thinks, to get her through
the check writing. She glances left, to the inviting stand
of magazines and candy, and catches a photo of a sultry-
grinned Fergie, light blue *Cosmopolitan* at the top, deep red
"THE SEX HE WANTS" below. Next to *Cosmopolitan*, *Time*
magazine, "LIFE IN HELL: A BAGHDAD DIARY." Next to
Time, *GQ* and a flirty-grinned Justin Timberlake, "THE PRI-
VATE LIFE OF JUSTIN TIMBERLAKE."

Kristen pops another cracker. Her esophagus and stomach downshift from tremble to sway.

The checkout man offers an enthusiastic "Hi there,"
smiles, and fumbles with the sports bra, turning the gar-
ment in his hands although the barcoded tag dangles near
the clasp. *Brand new,* she thinks. *Why in the world would
they give him the express line?*

When he fists the first gallon of milk, Kristen says, "It's on the front."

"Thanks," he says, smirking with a hint of newfound annoyance. "What team?" he says, holding up the *Coach* logo.

"Basketball," she says, swallowing a cracker. "Girl's JV. Over in Chester."

"The Chester Volcanoes," he says. "Cool mascot."

It's then that she spots Marcus twenty feet from her, pushing a cart full of groceries toward the exit with his girlfriend, Stacey. Kristen lowers her head, then peeks back up. There's no desire or longing, just a nervous wish to avoid eye contact. She's heard that Marcus got on with Caltrans and is making good union money working on the paving crew, and there's a town rumor that Stacey did time for simple assault on a girl over in Greenville who called her a drunk Indian, which, as far as Kristen knows, is a fairly accurate description.

Occasionally Kristen sees Marcus's blue Chevy truck rolling down Main Street in Chester, heading south to the aging, valley-bound highways, but he no longer shops at the Holiday market, where she still works, preferring, she'd guessed correctly, to make the forty-five-minute drive to this Walmart. Kristen watches them walk away, Stacey's hand on Marcus's back, her long black hair hanging down to the top of her jeans.

Kristen pays with cash and moves toward the exit, but pauses by stacks of on-sale bottled water, Lucky Charms, binders, and dog food. She doesn't want to run into Marcus or Stacey returning their cart or discover that they've parked next to her, so she glances over at the bathroom entrance and grabs another saltine from her purse and peeks at a clock on the wall. She watches the second hand and decides to wait three minutes. She hears the old-man greeter welcoming people to the store, and she digs out her phone and sees the background photo of Wintric and her at a San Francisco Giants game.

Her father had given them the tickets for her birthday, five rows up from the Giants' dugout. The Pirates intentionally walked Barry Bonds three times, but the afternoon was sunny and the stadium was even better than she had imagined, with the bay right there, the eastbound ocean breeze in her hair, and she and Wintric each downing two overpriced hot dogs before the fifth inning. In the phone's background picture Wintric has his arm around her and she's tucked into him, smiling under her black-and-orange-brimmed Giants hat. It was that night in an Oakland Holiday Inn Express, sunburned and exhausted and happy, that she became pregnant.

Kristen stands near the Walmart exit, one minute into her allotted three. She texts Wintric that she's about to head home, that maybe they should order pizza for dinner. She knows he won't see the text right away, as he'll be finishing up splitting the pile of wood he hauled home yesterday. It was another example of his four-month roll of energy and optimism, which Kristen wants to believe can last forever, even if she talks herself into taking everything a day at a time.

When she took his last name it seemed like something she had known would always happen, something inescapable but comfortable. Already her new name sounds familiar: *Kristen Ellis*. She thinks of Wintric splitting the wood into fireplace-sized pieces, and she believes the war won't live in him forever – at least not as it has – that there are too many things that happen in a life for the past always to live downstage. She believes that people are always someone different the next day. Already she sees Wintric anew as they laugh together watching *Arrested Development,* or as he hums while they walk along the boggy shore of Willow Lake, or as he takes in the Chester Fourth of July parade, which she hopes one day he'll walk in with the rest of the veterans.

Recently Wintric has replaced all the ceiling fans in their place, dropped down to two OxyContins a day, with plans to kick them altogether, and surprised Kristen with lunch – freshly made turkey sandwiches – a few times at work. She trusts these things are not signs, they aren't teasers; this is who he is. Still, she understands days rarely pass by easily, regardless of his motivation. She navigates this world and lives through the days just as he does. In the past week she's put in five thirteen-hour days at the Holiday supermarket, changed the oil in their car, and finished the sixth Harry Potter book, all under the stress of work as a new assistant manager at Holiday and the pressing debate of whether to keep this child.

Kristen swallows, her dry throat constricts, and she feels slightly dizzy. She walks over to the drinking fountain and sips, then tracks the clock's second hand. At three minutes she makes her move outside, playfully scolding herself for her cowardice. She surveys the parking lot for Marcus's truck, then watches the Chevy depart from the back of the lot by the Jack in the Box.

The sun is hot on her body as she loads the items into her car's empty back seat. She starts the car and turns onto the highway that will take her back to Chester. She rolls down Susanville's main thoroughfare, aware that Marcus and Stacey are a few minutes in front of her, driving the same route home, and she can't help but glance ahead to see if they've caught a red light, but there's nothing.

During the drive home – up over Fredonyer Pass and down into the valleys outside Westwood – Kristen sips on a Coke, apprehensive that she's catching up to them, so she keeps it at 50 mph and studies the road for a blue Chevy truck. Her nausea simmers and her right leg aches, and she turns off the one local radio station that plays top 40.

Up ahead she spots a dirt turnout she's passed a hundred times on her way back and forth to Susanville and Reno, a turnout big enough for one of the few diesels that take this route. She grabs her right quad and steers her car to the turnoff. She gets out, stretches her leg, lifting her right ankle back toward her butt.

On the far edge of the turnout stands an old brick fireplace and chimney, the remnants of what Kristen guesses used to be a pioneer home. The ruin has always been a welcome sight for her, marking twenty minutes' driving time left to Chester, but she's never stopped here before, and she studies the old fireplace, clean from a recent rain, wondering why it was left intact. She looks south, across the valley, past grazing cattle, to the distant ridge line there, then to a hill in the otherwise flat meadow. She camped at the base of this hill once when she was twelve. Her father took her and one of her friends there and told them ghost stories and brought out kids' bows and let them shoot arrows at the blackbirds that sat on the rotting fence posts. Kristen considers the outing: the absurdity of shooting arrows at birds that would leap away, then return to the same fence posts; losing all the arrows; the meandering cows; her earnest father and his ghost stories that scared no one. Her father, his gentle demeanor, his Sunday trips to the local Methodist church alone; her father, surprising Wintric and her with Giants tickets and a hotel in Oakland. When Kristen told her parents about her pregnancy a few nights ago, he begged her to keep the child, even though she hadn't voiced any other plan.

Kristen stares at the hill and thinks of Marcus and Stacey hitting the Plumas County line, Wintric running the wood splitter in the back-yard heat, and this minuscule baby inside her – the only proof of its existence being two home pregnancy test results and nausea. She stares at the hill and hears the cows' calls in the distance. Just before her cell phone rings, her father's words return to her: "Keep the baby. Keep the baby."

Wintric's name appears on her phone, and she answers with "Hey, babe." When he says, "You get Dead Rising?" she hears his drunk-drugged voice. Her feet and hands sting, and again she sees him at the controls of the wood splitter, the iron wedge driving through the large round, his sweat, his dirty shirt, pine chunks falling to the yard.

"Win. Tric."

She says the two syllables hushed, detached, and a new vision arrives: Wintric on the couch, Halo 2 on the screen, a narcotic, lazy smile as he sips a fourth Coors Light under a spinning ceiling fan. "Oh my God."

"Baby, you on your way here? You on your way?"

Kristen bends over at the waist.

"Wintric," she says. "What have you done? God. Shit. What–"

"I'm sitting here. Where you?"

"Outside Westwood."

"What?"

"What have you done?"

"Where you at, baby?"

She hears another "Baby?" and the hand holding the phone drops from her ear to her side. She sees herself in the doorway of their home, crossing the room to intoxicated Wintric, her arm reaching out to him, handing him the new video game, returning to the kitchen; she's opening the refrigerator, placing the milk gallons on the center shelf. She's leaning over the counter, watching Wintric's joy as he picks up the game controller and hits Start.

At the turnout a waft of manure hits Kristen and she

walks over to the fireplace and reaches out and touches the bricks, pressing her left palm against the chimney. She glances at the square diamond in her ring and moves her ring finger. The bottom of her ring taps the bricks.

Kristen drafts ultimatums in her head—*no more alcohol, no video games, rehab, time to cut out the drugs*—but she can't conjure a threat. She wouldn't leave, it hasn't gotten that bad, and really, has it been bad at all? It's the first relapse in over four months. And what's a relapse? Drunk at 2 P.M. on a Saturday? He's not soaking in the tub fully dressed. He's not running away or locking himself in the bedroom or pulling a gun or driving drunk. What is she worried about? Maybe his foot is killing him from the wood splitting. Maybe he split all the wood and threw back a couple waiting for her. She is later than she said she'd be.

After Kristen and Wintric's engagement, her father took her aside and told her that she should never ask Wintric about the war, that there were no answers that would make sense, and besides, there was only one way to gauge if someone was ready for marriage: if he would still love his spouse after one of them had starting shitting their pants in old age. "I'm just waiting on your mother to start," he said, with a raise of his eyebrows. The comment had made her laugh at the time, and though she couldn't visualize an aged, pants-shitting Wintric or explain why she felt like he was the only one for her, she yearned to be with him and to care for him—she had as far back as she could remember. It was not a curse or a blessing or a surprise.

Kristen clutches her phone and the questions and guilt and rage invade. What if she hung up too soon? Wintric installed the ceiling fans and painted their bedroom a light blue for her. He danced at their back-yard wedding reception without a whisper of pain.

What makes it worse is that he won't be upset with her.

He's never upset with her. He never asks her to do anything for him. *Calm down,* she says to herself. The cattle graze in the meadow. The yellow grass. The ridge line in the distance. Almost home. This is the world she knows, but most of it she's only driven through, and at the moment she's not sure what she knows or wants or expects. The threat of beginnings gnaws at her. Is this the first in a series of drunken phone calls she'll get from Wintric? What is her fault? What does he need to recover from? Will she always overreact? Has she now? What does she want?

She climbs back into the car and her chest tightens and the nausea expands someplace inside. She peers out the windshield and notices a new chip in the glass that will run on her come winter. Her eyes close, and she promises herself that when she opens them everything will still be there. In past moments of stress she's always heard her mother's motto that the only folks who experience real anxiety are the ones who don't know when they'll eat next. The perspective has always helped, but nausea isn't just a state of mind. Her stomach clenches and opens, and she leans out of the car and throws up.

Kristen washes her mouth out with lukewarm Coke and spits. A minivan pulls into the turnout. In her rearview mirror she watches a boy jump out, look around, and scramble behind the fireplace. Soon a stream of pee appears from behind the bricks. She wants to look away, but the scene is fantastically bizarre, this fireplace springing a leak, cows in the background, her little hill and those damn blackbirds. She hears her laugh before she feels it, and she lets herself go and her laughter fills the car and she wipes at her eyes and tastes the Coke film. Soon the pee stream stops and the boy runs back to the van and hops in, and the van pulls back onto the road.

Kristen's nerves ease momentarily, but she sits in the silent car and the worry creeps back in. She knows what she wants – she wants nothing else to change today. She wants no news or answers, big or small. Wintric hasn't called back or texted, and she guesses that he's already forgotten about her hang-up, is now fully reinvested in Halo 2, another half a beer down. She remembers that she gassed up in Susanville before heading to Walmart and she wonders how far she can drive on a tank. Where could she go where there's no news?

When she hits Chester, Kristen keeps her foot on the gas, down Main Street, past her home two streets over, past the airport and the Forest Service station. By the time she reaches Mineral she's guilt-ridden but exhilarated. She knows where she wants to go, just not exactly how to get there, so when she pulls into Red Bluff she asks a 7-Eleven checkout woman the way to the redwoods after paying for two Mountain Dews and a cylinder of Pringles. In the parking lot she debates calling Wintric, but she doesn't want to hear his voice, so she thumbs out a text: *I'm fine. Need alone time. Drove west to clear head. Home tomorrow or next.* She considers typing *Don't worry* or *I love you,* and while she means both, she stops herself and presses Send, then turns her phone off and slides it into the glove box.

At Redding she turns west, singing first to Coldplay, then to the Killers through Weaverville, then parallels the Trinity River under the setting sun. In McKinleyville she smells the salt air and buys a turkey sandwich at the Safeway. She eats the sandwich while a man in a Portland Trail Blazers hat tells her he's pretty sure there's a redwood up near Klamath that cars can drive through. A woman with a shaved head seconds that, so Kristen heads north, pulling into Klamath's Hinkle Motel a little after ten, where the smiling man at the desk tells her she's in the right spot, that the Klamath Tour Thru Tree is only a mile away, that he'd be happy to show her the way in the morning.

With room key in hand, Kristen decides to ditch two of the gallons of milk, but she squeezes one into the tiny refrigerator in her room. Exhausted, she lies on the bed and stretches her body. She observes the room's reflection in the turned-off television screen and begs herself not to think about Wintric, but she wonders if he's already called her parents. If he shares her text with them, all will be okay. If he plays it up, there could be issues, but it's only been a few hours. It's warm, and she closes her eyes and kicks off her shoes and lets the silence of the room come to her.

A knock at her door jolts her awake and she looks around, dazed. A lit lamp. A television. Brown curtains. White walls. This is her room. She's in Klamath.

Kristen searches for a clock and finds one on the nightstand: 11:15 P.M. She's not sure what that means. When did she get in? Another knock. A double tap. Kristen stands and steps to the door, not thinking to glance for a peephole. She pauses for a moment. Klamath.

Through the door, a voice.

"It's Dennis, from the front desk."

Kristen inspects the room, unaware of what she seeks. She remembers there's no suitcase to find. The bed appears huge. Her purse on the bathroom counter. The clothes she wears. She turns the door's handle and cracks the door enough to expose her head.

"It's Dennis. You know. From the desk. Just wanted to make sure everything was okay in here." He smiles. His hands are behind him and he rocks back and forth.

"Yeah. Everything's fine. Thanks."

"Good," he says. "Good."

He rocks in place, and Kristen comes to. *Eleven-fifteen,* she thinks. The motel's lights cast a blue shade onto the parking lot.

"Yep," she says.

"So the drive-through tree is down the road here. Hell, you could walk to it. You know, there's three redwoods you can drive through in California. Two of them are down south a bit."

"Oh."

"I haven't been there to those two, but . . ." He pauses and Kristen waits for him to continue, but there's only silence. He rocks in place.

Kristen thinks Dennis may be wearing a different shirt, and she gets a whiff of his cologne. She notices that he's combed his now wet hair. He's tall and overweight, and his large hands appear at his sides, then slide into his front pockets. She cases the parking lot for someone, but there are only two cars parked in front of dark rooms on the far side of the place.

"Yeah," she says. "Well. I'm fine with this one. Thanks." She moves her left hand to the door's edge and grips, pointing her ring set at him, but his eyes don't leave hers. At the far side of the parking lot someone appears and walks a few steps in their direction, then pauses and lights a cigarette. Dennis glances at the smoker, then turns back to Kristen.

"I'm glad the room works," he says. "There's not much going on, but we got a bar across the street." He points.

"I'm not really —"

"I know Rick, the bartender. It's the one game in town." He gulps. "No pressure, of course."

The parking-lot smoker has moved a few steps closer to them and stopped. Kristen eyes Dennis's boots, a couple feet from the doorjamb. She breathes his cologne.

"I'm married," she says. "I mean, he's here . . ."

"Wow," he says, and laughs. "Married. You the only one?"

"I'm sorry?"

Dennis lifts his hands and presses his palms to his chest. Kristen decides to shut the door, to slam it, but her hands don't move. She flexes her arms and the muscles tighten.

"I mean I'm just being nice, telling you about the bar," Dennis says. "That's what we got here. You from some big city looking for the drive-through tree. That's what I'm saying. I'm not asking if you're married. Just being nice. You seemed a little out of sorts, that's all. Just being nice."

"I know," she says. "I'm sorry. Long day." She hears her words and this repeated apology.

"So?"

"Sorry?"

She tells herself to close the door. Why is she asking questions?

"So you agree about nice people? That there are nice people?"

"Sure."

"That's all I'm saying. Why does everyone have to be scared all the time? You're scared and I don't know why. I know your husband isn't here. That's fine. I'm checking on a guest. I live here, ma'am."

"I know," she says. "Sorry."

"You know?"

"No. Please."

"Please?" he says. He lifts his hands to his face. He covers his eyes. "My God. I'm sorry." He leans back and takes a step away. The smoker sits on the pavement.

"Okay."

"Have a great night," he says, shaking his head as he

starts his walk away. "There's a deadbolt on the door if you have issues."

Kristen closes the door and presses her body against it. She finds the deadbolt and twists it locked and backs up against the door. Her mind whirls and she grabs her purse and sits on the bed. She turns off the lamp and reaches into her purse for her phone, but remembers she's left it in the car's glove box and says, "Fuck." Narrow strips of blue light leak from the bottom of the curtains onto the AC/heater unit. She picks up the room's phone and hears the dial tone, then puts the receiver down. She stands and walks to the curtains and draws them back and peers out. She sees her car and the unmoving parking lot. Near her knees the AC kicks on, and she jumps back. Quickly she reaches into her purse and grabs her car keys, steps to the door, unlocks the deadbolt and handle lock, opens the door, and looks around. Nothing. In the distance the sound of brakes from Highway 101, and in front of her a deserted parking lot.

From her car's glove box Kristen snatches her phone and a bottle of pepper spray. Back in the locked room, she sits in the darkness, surprised to find herself here, on this bed, in this room, confused that she isn't bound for another place. She sets the pepper spray on the bed next to her and turns on her phone and studies the background photo while the phone searches for reception. Three missed calls and five texts from Wintric, two texts from her mother. She places the phone on her chest and tries to relax.

The cool air from the AC reaches her legs and she hears a car door shut outside. She grabs the pepper spray and stands.

From outside, a woman's voice: "One seventeen. No, one seventeen."

Kristen tries to remember her room number, but nothing comes to her. She edges to the curtains and stares out. Outside, a woman stands near a car holding a sleeping child. She enters the room next to Kristen's. Kristen hears the woman's movements through the shared wall. A man waits for a moment in the parking lot, then reaches into the back seat and brings out a baby in a car seat and a large bag and follows the woman into the room. Before she closes the curtains, Kristen hears the short beep and sees the headlights flash as the car locks.

Back on the bed, Kristen listens to the family settle in the room next to hers. She retrieves her phone and opens the first text from her mother: *Okay? Worried. Call ASAP. Love you.* From the next room, the rising cries of the baby and the muffled reaction of the parents. The infant unleashes a full-blown wail as Kristen types a text to her mother: *Drove to coast. Need deep breath. I know weird. All okay. Home soon. Help with Wintric. All okay. Love.* The baby screams, then quiets, then screams, and Kristen realizes that Dennis may have put the family next to her as some sort of punishment, but tonight the noisy family and thin walls comfort her. They'd hear if someone knocked on her door. They'd hear her if she called out. Kristen rereads her text to her mother — *All okay.* She hits Send and keeps her phone on but in silent mode. The AC kicks off, and though she's still hot, she stays on the bed, guessing it will turn on again soon. The baby cries, and Kristen wonders how young the child is, if it's a boy or a girl. She grabs the pillow that Wintric would use if he were here and clutches it to her chest.

In the morning, about half a mile from the motel, Kristen slides five dollars into a slot in a yellow shack beneath a handwritten sign that reads $5 FOR CARLOAD. PUT MONEY IN THE SLOT. WE TRUST YOU. Guiding her car up a steep road just behind the shack, she comes upon the Tour Thru

Tree so fast that the scene instantly surprises and disappoints her. A green car is parked halfway through the massive tree and two teenagers stand nearby, taking photos with their phones. Kristen stops and glances around, but there's only this small clearing with the massive, holed tree and a thin paved road looping through. Somehow she's already here. She rolls down her window and hears a group of Harleys on 101 and one of the teenagers saying, "Humboldt."

Kristen searches amid her building frustration for preconceived images of this place, but there's only a residue of expected wonderment. Whatever it was, what she hoped this moment would bring, it was never this tourist trap, this huge redwood practically on the highway, these two teenagers posing in front of her. It wasn't Dennis or a crying baby or a glass-of-milk-and-potato-chip breakfast or two days in the same clothes. It wasn't alone.

She doesn't want to curse herself for driving here. What if she'd driven home and handed Wintric Dead Rising? She leans her head back on the headrest and watches the young men move around the tree to the back of their car and snap more photos. One jumps up on the trunk of the car and gives two thumbs-up to the other. After several more photos, their show is over and they pull away, circling back the way they came in, waving to Kristen, who ignores them.

Kristen eases forward, and by the time the nose of the car enters the tree she's almost numb. The car fits comfortably, engulfed in the redwood. The tree's darkened innards sport horizontal scratches and carvings from side mirrors and knives. Scattered graffiti dot the upper reaches of the cutout. Kristen looks to her left and reads some of the inked messages: "Amy and Brett 98," "alien tree," "Calvin Hobbes Me." She wonders if the other drive-through trees are marked up like this, and she lets herself think they are

in fact worse – spray-painted inside, with long lines of cars
and a ten-dollar entrance fee. Outside the tree a light rain
begins, and she stares right and reads "CA sucks." Suddenly
she understands she'll learn nothing here.

She reaches for her bottled water in the front cup holder
and drinks. In her rearview mirror a truck with a thick deer
guard pulls in behind her. She peeks at the windshield and
thinks she sees Dennis at the wheel. She squeezes the water bottle and turns around to get a better view, but the rain
beading on the truck's windshield distorts the man's image. Blood rushing, Kristen waits for the wipers to wipe,
but they don't move. She presses the lock button, but the
doors are already locked and all she gets is a weak reminder
click. She's kept the car in drive, and she lets off the brake.
The car moves, slowly at first, emerging from the tree into
the rain. She circles around and tells herself not to look, to
drive away from this place, back to somewhere she knows.
Still, she glances at the truck, hoping for a view of the driver,
but the truck has already entered the tree, so all she sees as
she exits is the bed and rear tires and the illuminated brake
lights.

Kristen isn't sure what caused her to swerve off 101 only
an hour into the trip home – maybe the funny name on
the sign, *Lady Bird;* maybe the lure of a final choice and
the hope of not walking through her front door in Chester
empty-handed – but here she stands in a dripping redwood
forest halfway into the 1.3-mile Lady Bird Johnson Grove
Trail outside Orick.

Alone on the dirt path, she hugs herself and takes in this
other world: the trees monstrous and time-warped, the li-
chen fluorescent and the moss dark green, the forest floor
covered in flattened ferns, billions of needles and insects

seeping into the dark soil. She's lived within Lassen National Forest her entire life, but it's nothing like this, this place where there's no medium growth, only the world-aged giant redwoods, a few pines, and the ground cover.

Her shirt is soaked through along her shoulder line, and she closes her eyes and inhales the thick air. All around her the light impact of things falling – water, leaves, feathers. She opens her eyes and the immensity of the woods rushes at her, but there's no fear, only a sense that she's finally discovered a place worth finding.

Kristen walks the trail, and the spreading wetness trickles down her shoulders to her arms. She considers what she'll tell Wintric when she gets home. The lines she rehearses all have *redwoods* and *I needed* in them, and these words, so absurd and amazing, repeat in her mind. She moves down this trail, and then, without warning, off to her right she spots an enormous mound, a circular darkness just past the first line of forest. Surprised, she stops and raises her hands and focuses on this mass. She takes a couple more steps and studies it, this felled redwood. The tree exposes its huge base, a twenty-foot tentacled wall of roots and dark earth. The stunning displacement has cratered the ground.

Moving off the trail and ducking under a few damp branches, she stands on the edge of the bowled-out earth. She checks the area, but there's no sign of violence: no other felled trees, no signs of wind or fire. And before her, on this tree, no lightning or chainsaw marks. Up the trunk green needles flare from the branches and she knows this is recent, that this tree is not dead but dying.

Kristen looks up to the circle of sky that was once blotted out by this tree, then reaches out and touches one of the gnarly roots. She closes her eyes and smells the damp soil.

This place is real. She is here. Everything seems so slow around her, the scattered and patient dripping, the turning earth.

When she opens her eyes, she's leaning on the tree, unaware how long she's been gone. Above her the gray sky, and somewhere down the trail voices calling out and, closer, the low bark of a dog. Kristen hurries back to the trail and glances around her. In the next moment she finds herself running, striding out long and fast, unable to recognize the force that propels her forward. Her heart pounds in her ears and her arms swing wildly; she runs and leans into turns, now outside herself, beside herself; the forest speeds by, the straining legs and heartbeat someone else's.

She arrives back at her car and the deserted parking lot faster than she guessed she would, and she bends over, hands on her knees, gasping. She waits for her mind to return to this body.

Inside the car she removes her sandals and leans back and feels her drenched shirt on her skin. She takes it off, drapes it over the passenger seat, and starts the car. Her right quad starts to twist and she rubs at the pain. The insteps of her right and left feet are rubbed raw, and she knows that she'll suffer blisters. Breathing through her nose and out her mouth, she waits until she can no longer hear her heartbeat.

She turns on the stereo, puts on Modest Mouse, softly at first, then cranks the volume and sings. It's then, among the thrashing thoughts of driving home, of this mad dash, of her wet and blistering body, as she breathes in to attack the chorus of track two, that she realizes she's not nauseated.

Inside the idling car Kristen turns off the stereo, reclines her seat, and slides her drying hands inside her shorts and over her lower belly. She pushes her belly out and feels the pressure against her hands. She wishes now that she hadn't told her parents so soon, at least not until she figures out what she wants. If she has the child, it'll have a March birthday. It seems so far away: 2007. Spring. There's still snow in March.

Kristen sits up and levers the seat upright. She punches the stereo button and track two comes alive. She runs her fingers through her hair and looks up past the nick in the windshield and sees the way home.

10

Safety

NICHOLLE, DAX'S NEWLY MINTED serious girl-friend, hails from southern Alabama. The first time he meets her family, her brother, Sim, chauffeurs him to his swimming hole. They hike on a narrow path from the car through a blanket of kudzu and pockets of honey-suckle, dodging large bees. Moments before they splash in the muddy stream, Sim slaps Dax's back and says, "Watch for moccasins and snappers." Soon they're neck-deep under the hazy summer sky, and just as Dax's body relaxes he spots a black snake slithering down the bank and entering the water. Dax isn't sure what a moccasin looks like, and he throws up his arms and calls to Sim, who appears unfazed.

"Army didn't teach you 'bout snakes?"

"Just to stay away."

Birds sound above them and something rustles in the branches.

"Sim, I don't see it. Sim?"

"Splash a little."

Dax tries to go onto his toes, but he sinks into the soft stream floor. An echo from his army training: *Never get caught in the water. You're helpless in the water.* He examines the slowly moving water along an imaginary line between the snake's entry point and his half-submerged stomach, then splashes the water in front of him.

"I was kidding about the splashing," Sim says. "Jesus, stay still."

"Shit. Shit."

"If you see white in its mouth, that means it's a moccasin. Everything else is okay. You're a big guy. They don't want to mess with you."

Dax doesn't hear the last sentence. He imagines the possible biting scenarios—*a big guy,* so much surface area to choose from: the moccasin attached to his face (*can it jump?*), the moccasin attached to his dick (*can it submerge?*), the moccasin still attached to his blackening arm at the ER (*do they let go?*), and he pleads with himself to stay calm, but the mash of all these possibilities overtakes him. *Helpless in the water.* He hurls himself toward the bank with lumbering steps, his thick legs sluggish through the stream. With yards to go to dry land he peeks back, and every ripple grows a tail and fangs. He hears a high-pitched whine coming from his mouth and, somewhere beyond, Sim's laughter.

On the bank, Dax stands and surveys the ground around his feet. The birds have quieted and Sim floats on his back.

"I don't see it," Dax says.

"Well, damn," says Sim. "It lives here. Where else you want it to go?"

On the drive back to Andalusia, Sim puts on some Jim Croce and sings along. His hair is cut at varying lengths, and a scar runs from his left ear across his cheek. Dax's knees and shins are pressed against the Honda Civic's dash; an empty Monster Energy can and a dog-track receipt are on the floorboard. Dax stares out the window at the greenery flying by. Lush and overgrown. Nowhere can he see bare earth. He recalls Alston's fear of sharks, relayed during one of his high school root root diatribes – "I'll fight a lion or a bear, man. Forget sharks. Fuck hippos. It isn't fair. You're drowning and bleeding and you can't even move. At least I feel the dirt under me against a lion." Dax replays the effortless motion of the snake entering the water, the silent shift from land to liquid. An unexpected gust of memory: high school English, *My Ántonia,* bored out of his mind, then the teacher reading out loud, a child hacking a huge rattler with a spade, the nerve to get close enough to kill with a spade; now his black snake, closing in somewhere in the water. He shakes his hands, and as he comes to, hearing Sim's singing voice, an in-tune tenor, Dax transitions from daydream fear to real-time marvel. He listens as Sim matches Croce's falsetto, even harmonizes on "I Got a Name."

Sim stops midchorus and starts up about Andalusia even though Dax hasn't asked.

"We got a porn star, a Miss Alabama, and Robert Horry. Hank Williams got married here. I'm eighteen and I know more about this area than most. Besides that, I don't know what to tell you. Cole won't move back here, but you know that. What hasn't she told you? What you want to know?"

"Not sure," Dax says, recognizing the slim chances of anything good coming from this conversation.

"Dad isn't thrilled you all are living together."

"Okay."

"Cole is smarter than she lets on. She went to Vanderbilt, you know? No one goes there from here."

"Yep."

"She tell you she hates northerners? I'm just shitting. I'm surprised she picked up an army dude. She's not exactly thrilled with guns."

"I'm not in the army anymore."

"No. Yeah, that's what I meant. That you were. I mean, once you've been in. Whatever."

Sim slows down for a tractor in the road, and the car shakes. "Bad, Bad Leroy Brown" through the speakers and Sim hitting the chorus hard, then shaking his head.

"Croce was in the army. You know that, right?"

"Nope."

"A pecan tree got him. You know that?"

"No."

"Plane hit a tree and crashed. Louisiana."

"Jesus."

"Every time I have pie I think of 'Time in a Bottle.' It's true, man. Everything about time."

Dax spoons mashed potatoes onto his plate at the dinner table with Nicholle, Sim, and their parents, and he wonders if there is anything in his New Jersey upbringing that would scare Sim. Although he searches hard, all he recalls is a harmless bluegill attached to his pinkie when he was eight. He peeks across the table at Nicholle's mother, a cheerful, plump lady who, if he unfocuses his eyes enough, could be Nicholle in thirty years. Nicholle's father smiles approvingly.

After dinner Sim and Dax smoke on the front porch. Sim asks him if he was ever waterboarded. Dax tells him no.

"Me either," Sim says, "but I beat up a homeless guy. Dumbass didn't even fight back, just laid there."

"Thanks for that, Sim."

"You seen some shit, I know. What's the worst thing? Kids hacked up? Damn Taliban."

"Not my favorite thing."

"I hear they like the little boys," Sim says. "Will tie them up and hump 'em. Crazy shit like that, but chicks can't show their faces. That's dumb, covering up their bodies makes the dudes want to hump even more. Hell, even Jesus knew that. Taliban got it backwards. Show everything and the mystery is gone. No one cares. In Jesus' time women were running around naked and there weren't the issues we got now. Well, you should know, I've seen some shit around here. Cole don't know this, but I can count cards. I act broke, but there's ten thou in my room. Swear. I got a buddy working at the Venetian, man. Got one at Bally's. Vegas."

"Okay," Dax says while fingering his chin. "Cool."

Dax has no idea why he says *cool*, a word not normally in his go-to reaction vocabulary, and even Sim stares at him, curious.

"You count cards?" he asks.

Dax does, but he isn't interested in where the conversation will go or what he'll be invited to do.

"You mean, like gambling?" Dax says, and puts his cigarette out on his forearm.

"Damn," Sim says, laughing. He shakes his head. "Gambling."

What Sim doesn't know, and what Dax plans on telling Nicholle later on, is that he does gamble. It's not bad. Local games with friends. He brings what he can lose and that's it. Even so, something warns him that Nicholle won't approve, and it's the one minor thrill he allows himself. If it came out now, there might be an argument, but nothing more than a night on the couch and an animated call from Nicholle to her sympathetic mother. On Dax's scale of guarded secrets, the card games barely register. The one that still stalks him, the one he doesn't know how to talk about, is his Afghanistan girl; how she walked toward him with a soccer ball, how the day ate her up; how for a few minutes he let the power overtake and fuel him, and later, how surprised he was that only one bullet was found, how intensely he argued with Wintric about who had actually shot her; how he had had to wait for EOD to arrive to detonate the vest she wore, still attached to her body; how the hour passed and the men saw her block the road, dying, then dead. And later, the doubts: *Was she forced to wear the vest? Would she have stopped?* The hope now that the bullet was Wintric's after all.

Dax doesn't know where his belief in a just universe comes from, but it exists, godless but real, and one day, be it snake or other ailment, he knows there will be retribution for the girl, no matter what she wore that day, no matter the situation. In the end he made a choice to shoot at a child. He can't get it out of his head. *Retribution.* The worst part is the waiting game, and so he waits and senses the possibility of harm hovering over him, pausing until the time is right.

Two weeks before the Obama-McCain presidential election, Dax calls Nicholle's father to ask for his daughter's hand in marriage. Her father cries. "I couldn't be happier," he says. "I'll let you talk to Karen." Silence over the line while he passes the phone, but his voice comes through again. "Two things, son." It's the first time he has called Dax son. "One. I'll only loan you money if Nicholle asks. Two. All I care about is her happiness." Silence over the line again. "Two and a half. You're a Tide fan when you visit. Good luck."

A week later, after Dax asks Nicholle to marry him under a flowering dogwood, she makes him call Sim.

"Know where I been?" Sim says, after telling Dax good job on the proposal. Dax says no. "Riverboats, man. Rivers are international waters. No rules, buddy. State, government can't touch 'em."

"Okay," Dax says.

"Should get married on a riverboat. There's one called the *Gypsy*. I can sing."

"We'll consider it, Sim."

"Love you, Dax," he says.

Dax passes the phone to Nicholle, who's all smiles. "The *Gypsy*?" she says. Dax stares at the floor. "You want to sing at the wedding?" She gives Dax a look – Sim is off-limits.

During their engagement Nicholle and Dax pick up books about successful marriages. They open their favorite one, *The Questions You Should Ask Before "I Do,"* whenever they Sunday-drive around Knoxville, where they live. Dax learns that Nicholle would never adopt, is pro-choice, thinks sex twice a week is enough, hates cats, wants three kids, doesn't mind if he has to travel for work, doesn't want Dax's childhood friend Alston at the wedding, is scared of getting her mother's cheeks, thinks Dax should remove the eel tattoo on his back, and doesn't like it when Dax says "You know what I'm saying?" when trying to prove a point.

She learns a lot about Dax as well, at least the stuff he wants her to know – sex three times a week is about right, every person should know how to shoot a gun, kids should never have to answer the "Which parent?" question during a divorce, he hates snakes, he hasn't determined his dream job, Rutherford and New Mexico are his dream retirement spots – but her face goes to stone when he tells her that his number-one pet peeve is when people praise God only for the good things in life.

"What the hell is up with cancer and dropped touchdown passes?" he says. "No one points to the sky and pounds their chest during chemo or when a pass slips through their fingers."

They go at it pretty good on this topic – she invokes C. S. Lewis – and near the end he warns himself, *If you're smart, you'll never say these things again.*

All this learning about each other is fine, but the intense material comes out as they pull in their chairs at a restaurant in a white, stuccoed courtyard on their honeymoon in

Savannah. They wait for their food, sipping on red wine, when Nicholle asks Dax the worst thing he has considered doing to someone else, even if just for a split second. He wonders if she's fishing for something from his deployments and he considers the checkpoint, but all that comes to him is a mongoose darting across the road, then the girl, far away, waving. He pushes the image away. He searches his mental catalogue for relief, and it doesn't take him long to sift through the many momentary revenge wishes to a wooded lot outside Rutherford.

Dax starts talking and the memory materializes – he was twelve, cutting down a dead pine with his father. He had taken a break and rested against the old red Dodge truck, and in a bizarre mental pulse he thought of taking the chainsaw and hacking his father. He imagined the roaring saw, the blood and limbs mixing with the sawdust, the dumbfounded look in his father's eyes before the spinning hot teeth bit. He remembers even in that moment being ashamed and thrilled at the same time.

Now, in the Italian restaurant courtyard, he holds the saltshaker in his hand and avoids Nicholle's brown eyes. Dax is unsure if the words have come out right.

"It's crazy," he says. He places his hands in his lap. "I don't know what I'm saying. You know what I'm saying?"

She wears his favorite sundress, a white number with red and yellow flowers. She's tanned and has her hair pulled back, her arms toned from years of swimming laps. A large party two tables over clink wineglasses. They're all visitors.

"Stealing a baby," Nicholle says. "I don't know where it comes from, but there it is. I'd planned names, escape routes from the local hospital, everything. I didn't care if it looked like me. I even thought it might be easier to take a one-year-old, not a newborn. She'd be eating solids. And it's always a girl. I remember very clearly thinking that I could pull it off. I was fifteen, maybe. I'd keep her in my room, not eat all my food and sneak the rest to her. Her name was Jodi. I've always loved that name. Jodi."

"Almost like Jedi."

"That's not why."

"Yeah."

The food arrives. Dax cuts the veal with his knife. He takes a bite and watches Nicholle move her bare arms as she negotiates her utensils into her pasta, then grabs her wine-glass and gulps. They should laugh. He considers laughing.

"So," he says. "I'm glad we're the normal ones."

After their honeymoon, Dax and Nicholle move into a roll-ing subdivision in Knoxville called Hawks Nest. About a month into their stay, the two hawks they were told about as they debated buying the home make their nest in a giant pine in their front yard.

The place is spacious and they have privacy on almost an acre – dogwoods, a pear tree, a tall row of hedges run-ning the property lines. The neighbors are fine, but a guy who lives around the corner lets his retriever shit in their yard. One Sunday morning, Dax trims the flowering bushes in the front yard, and the neighbor comes around with the dog and waves friendly to Dax before the dog scampers ten feet onto Dax's front yard and poops. Dax lacks the courage to say anything. He's out-of-shape heavy and he has come to believe a fistfight hovers in every confrontation, no mat-ter how minor. This neighbor is a large guy, like Dax, but it seems like he wouldn't mind a fight, win or lose. Sometimes Dax sees both the neighbor and his dog rolling around on the guy's front yard when Dax comes home from work.

Other than the shitting dog, life is good: Dax works for a local collection agency and lies to his Nashville boss most days about where he is, the hours he puts in, but he works hard enough that his boss never questions him, so he gets in a round of golf at the local course on Thursday mornings. The money is okay, and Nicholle does well at a local consulting firm, well enough for them to come out ahead a little each month. Dax is a converted Tennessee fan, but Nicholle is Alabama all the way, so they sport "house divided" license plates, half orange, half crimson. They join a coed softball league, help clean up the local park, and make the HOA meetings about a third of the time. He enjoys the routine, and for the first time he assesses himself an adult, living a regular life. Even so, they break up their regular life enough to keep everything interesting. Nicholle begins highlighting her blond hair with bright colors – she switches from pink to orange every couple of months – "Because I can," she tells Dax. One day, after the linoleum warps in their master bathroom, Nicholle suffers the long lines at a local hardware store before deciding to bypass the registers altogether, and she walks out with four hundred dollars' worth of beige tile on a large cart and loads the lot into their truck and drives home.

Sim phones one night and talks to Nicholle for an hour. When Dax pokes his head into the room, Nicholle waves him away.

She descends the stairs and Dax turns off the Tennessee game, expectant.

"He needs money," Nicholle says. Dax's head is already in his hands. "Five thousand." They don't have an extra $5,000 anywhere. "Let's give him what we have. It's serious and he'll pay us back. He says he'll pay us back. I know what you're going to say. It's not Vegas. Please. He wouldn't ask unless he needed it. I know. He can't go to Dad. I know."

Dax has prepared – the phone call had to be about money, and he has decided not to say a thing.

"He's desperate, and we can cash bonds if we have to. Say something. We need to be together on this."

Dax knows she's near tears. The pleading hurts her, but Dax remains parked on the couch. He leans back into the cushion. He wants this to sting a bit, and his reclining works. He guesses what is going through her mind — *we'll never see a penny back, we can't afford it, you despise me for asking* — and yet here she is. Sim, her brother. Dax tells her he wants Sim to drive up so Dax can see him face-to-face when he hands him the check. Everyone agrees, but two weeks later Nicholle puts the money in the mail and talks to Dax about the price of gasoline.

Although they understand that there's never a perfect time to start a family, Nicholle and Dax have thought about it for some time, and agree on a Tuesday night in April to make love without protection for the first time. After he comes she raises her legs, grabs the backs of her knees, and pulls them to her chest. "Gravity," she says.

Years of teenage warnings and general fear of accidental pregnancy trump the stats that tell them it will take time to get pregnant, and for the first three months they approach the pregnancy test with expectant glee. They're both healthy, but after six months Nicholle is not pregnant. Their conversations about sex lead to arguments, so they decide to lie to the doctors, tell them they've been trying for a year so they can get an appointment to figure out the issue. One of the first things the doctor has Dax do is provide a semen sample. He complies with the request in a specially furnished hospital room with clear plastic on the couch and recliner and drawers full of oddly titled pornography (*Brick, Lemon People*).

Soon they learn that his sperm have "square heads," that this could be an issue going forward. When they get the news, he pictures mini hammerhead sharks swimming around in his testicles. He says, "Like mini hammerhead sharks?" but the doc shakes his head and Nicholle cries into her palms so he shuts up. It's in this moment that he realizes Nicholle wants this more than he does, or at least is more serious about everything. He wants to be a dad, but he isn't sure why, outside of the fact that he thinks he would be a good father. He visualizes Little League games and bike rides, skinned knees and good-night stories, but this optimistic collage is all he has, and he worries that it may not be good enough.

Dax reaches over and rubs Nicholle's back underneath a painting of cherry trees in bloom. The doctor lets her cry for a while before telling Dax to avoid saunas and hot tubs and to eat more fruit and test again in six months.

Nicholle and Dax fight and stress, and making love morphs into an exercise of forced monthly routine over the next year. In that time he takes a job as a rep in a pharmaceutical company – a favor called in by Nicholle's dad – selling various pieces of medical equipment. The company wanted veterans and the money is better than at the collection agency, but he travels frequently.

Dax is sitting down to eat inside a Taco Bell in Jacksonville when Nicholle calls. He shifts the greasy bag to his right hand and answers the phone.

"You're going to be a father," she says.

"Okay," he manages. "What the hell? My God, Nicholle. I wish I was there. I'm coming home."

She cries over the line and he wants to, but contrary to all things he thought he might feel when they eventually received the news, he imagines the future drive home from the hospital with their newborn child in the back seat. He thinks of all the new drivers, the drunk drivers, the red-light racers. He relives the painful surprise of talking to

Torres after his accident, hearing his words, "I never saw the car."

"We need a car seat," he says.

"I love you," Nicholle says.

He loves her too, but he says, "Does this mean we don't have to steal a baby?"

Five weeks later he's standing on the sidewalk outside the VA hospital in Charlotte when Nicholle phones and lets him know there's trouble. He hears the words *ectopic pregnancy*, not sure what that means. Mid-July and dust swirls in the sky, and as she explains, he thinks of their growing child in her right fallopian tube, budding bigger and bigger, slowly killing his wife. She says the doctors are going to take care of everything the next day, and they do. He flies home and he and Nicholle rest in their living room, Nicholle's head in his lap, and he rubs her back, then reaches down and strokes her legs. She hasn't shaved them in eight days and he feels the bristles on his fingertips. He can think of nothing to say.

"We have to wait three months," she says. "We'll try three months from now."

The ceiling fan spins above them, but the rushing air does little to help the thick humidity. He studies her body from her head down to her hips and bent knees and tucked feet. Slowly she uncoils. She has yet to tell her parents — which surprised Dax — but as she heads upstairs and closes their bedroom door, he knows she'll reach for the phone. He hears Nicholle's muffled voice through the ceiling. There's nothing her mother can do from that distance, but he knows there's a safety in that bond that he'll never be able to join.

Downstairs and alone, he turns on the television, then

turns the set off. He sees his reflection in the blank screen. He waves at himself and stares at the reflection of his living room furniture. Nicholle's building cries travel through the ceiling and he considers the disproportionate pain of their situation, how he does hurt but mainly by proxy, how Nicholle bears the brunt of everything. *Is all this part of my penance? I don't have to bear the pain full on. A life for a life? Am I even with the universe?* The pain of losing something sight unseen seems a reduced sentence somehow, losing something not even named. *Is this just the beginning?* The ceiling fan turns overhead and Dax stands. The room has an eight-foot ceiling, and the fan's blades whip inches above the top of his head, the cool air on his shoulders. *A person in a fallopian tube.* Replaying the Afghanistan checkpoint, he sees the shawled girl curled up, an embryo. His girl. Her bare heels digging into the dirt. He named her long ago, and tonight he hears it in his ears: Courtney. It's a lie, an impossibility, an American name, but he doesn't care. He hasn't met a Courtney since. She's the only one.

After a second miscarriage, Nicholle becomes pregnant again. Seven months along, with a big, beautiful belly and a dark line bisecting her bulge, she and Dax ride in a city bus on the way to a Tennessee Volunteers' game in Neyland Stadium. Dax can't stop touching her, his fingers on her thigh, his palm on her belly.

Across from them sit four men in turbans and orange shirts with capital *T*'s on them. Logically Dax knows that these men aren't terrorists, they're probably not even Muslim, but he's nervous. The men speak a mix of English and a language Dax can't decipher and appear to be joking with one another, but one of them gazes over at Nicholle, at her belly, and stares. His brown face goes slack, trancelike. Dax wonders if this is the moment: This man will make a move toward them. The friends will hold him down while the man struggles with Nicholle. Dax may survive the attack, alone. When that flurry of images passes, he imagines the man flying a plane, a single-prop Cessna, over their neighborhood. The front-yard hawks are up and circling high in the sky. The man brings the plane into a dive, tears up the birds, heads straight for their shingled roof, but before Dax can complete the daydream, Nicholle reaches for his clenched hand, unfolds it, and intertwines hers. The man stares unflinchingly.

"Soon," Nicholle says to the man, tilting her chin up. "Two months left." It takes a second for him to realize that she spoke to him. The man breaks his stare. Nods. Grins. "Soon," Nicholle repeats. She smirks. "Go, Vols," she says.

The man taps his orange shirt above his heart, taps his forehead, and circles his hand toward them.

"I think girl or boy," he says, and laughs. "One hundred percent correct."

The magnolias Dax planted bloom large white blossoms. He stares at them with a cup of coffee one Saturday morning when the neighborhood man brings his retriever by. Nicholle's parents are in town, and her father stands next to him, and the dog unloads one on their driveway. Dax is near his limit, with no plan. He tries to talk himself down, but it's been too long now, and he is tired of being on the road, tired of coming home and running over shit on his driveway, stepping on shit when he mows, smelling shit even when he avoids direct contact. Nicholle's father gives him enough time to say something, and when he doesn't, he asks, "How often?"

"I only see them on the weekends," Dax says.

"That's not what I asked."

Later in the week Nicholle's dad informs Dax that the dog-walking jerk works the graveyard shift, that he must walk the dog after he gets home in the morning. Dax doesn't ask how he's come by this information. Nicholle's father steps into the den and calls Sim on his cell phone. When he returns he says, "You'll have to help."

He asks Dax to wait in the parking lot of the local Walmart, and he comes out with a plastic bottle of antifreeze. Before he lowers himself into the car, Dax assigns the guilt to Nicholle's father: *his idea, his purchase.* He has decided that he won't say no as long as Nicholle's father pours the concoction into the dog bowl himself. Nicholle's father plops down with a heavy exhalation.

"Sim's done this a couple times," he says. "Says to mix in a cup of vinegar, a little honey, helps it go down."

"Vinegar?"

"That's what he says. Said he'd do it himself if he was here. Sends his love. Wanted me to tell you."

Late that night Dax and Nicholle's father walk down the street with a jug of antifreeze, honey, vinegar. Dax has downed five Heinekens in the past hour and a half, but they haven't loosened him as he had hoped.

Before they arrive at the targeted street, Nicholle's father slows.

"I need a smoke, and I think you do too," he says.

"Yes."

They veer over to a nearby pocket park and sit on a wide bench. Dax lights Nicholle's father's cigarette, then his own. He takes a drag.

"I've promised Nicholle I'll try to stop once the kid is born," Dax says. "They say heroin is easier to kick."

"That's probably not true."

"Maybe. The president smokes. Good enough endorsement for me."

"Obama can do what he wants. You see those before-and-after photos? Those guys age like twenty years in office, and that's got nothing to do with cigarettes. Obama wants to snort coke, go ahead. Anyone who wants to be president deserves what he gets."

Crickets everywhere and a diesel's air brakes on Middlebrook Pike, the air humid, bats darting. Dax knows they won't go through with their dog-killing plan; perhaps he knew it as they left, even before then. This pocket park, this new direction for the night, and the gathering nicotine soothe his body.

"Tell me what you thought when you first met me," Nicholle's father says. "I've never asked."

"First time?"

"First time you came down to Alabama."

"That you would kill me if I did anything to Nicholle," Dax says. "I'm serious. I thought that you would do it."

"More."

"Then you have to answer."

"Sure. Keep on."

"Alabama hick, but nice as hell," Dax says. "That you worried about me. Your girl was too good for an army vet. I think I heard *Vanderbilt* ten times in forty-eight hours. I wondered why anyone would choose to live where you live. You know, there are other options. But overall I thought, *Don't blow it. Everyone here seems sane, relatively.* Maybe that's pushing it with Sim, but really, that's it. It's been good. No BS."

"Your arms," Nicholle's father says, and Dax realizes that he hasn't listened to his minor confession, only that he wanted to get to this point, right now. "Your arms. I've always wanted to know about that. That's the first thing. I'm no doctor. Disease? Your doing? Father? I've never had the courage to ask. War thing?"

Dax keeps his cigarette in his mouth and runs his right fingertips over his left forearm, the small bumps there. He looks down, but it's dark, and he wonders if anyone could identify his own forearm if all he had to go on was touch. He remembers the first time he pushed the lit cigarette into his skin. Fort Benning, near the end of basic training: the searing but fleeting pain; the faint flesh-smoke smell; the silent admiration of a few nearby soldiers. He hasn't put out a cigarette on his arms in some time – *last time with Sim?* – and he's about to speak, although he doesn't know what will arrive in the night, but he hears Nicholle's father's voice.

"You know I skipped Vietnam. Or didn't volunteer. I didn't go. I'm sure Cole has told you. I don't regret it, but there's something there. Not guilt. Just ... I'm not sure. If there was a word that meant guilt but wasn't guilt, that would be it. I pass by it easily, but it's there."

A car drives by and they watch it pull into a driveway.

"They had these draft lottery drawings, you know. On television. They'd reach down and pick a birthday on a slip of paper and post it to a big board, and damn, you didn't want to hear your birthday being read. It's the one time in my life that I feared my birthday. It's a shit thing to do to someone. It's then you realize that the day you were born has nothing to do with you. You'd give it up in a second."

He takes a drag, and Dax, still feeling his forearm, stares at the orange glow of the cigarette draw.

"Anyway, here we are. Your arms."

Dax has had enough time to think about his answer, but he was focused on the lottery, the exact opposite meaning of that word as he understands it – winning the big one – and still no answer about his arms.

"Is it too difficult?" Nicholle's father asks. "I understand, son."

"My arms," Dax says, hearing himself. "I've done this."

The doctor invites Dax to grab one of Nicholle's legs before he instructs Nicholle to start pushing, and before he can say no, Dax finds himself holding Nicholle's right leg, staring above her head, repeating *Don't look down, don't look down,* but he does. Emma arrives a little early; six pounds, three ounces.

Dax knows no man could endure Nicholle's schedule of no sleep, all-go patience, and worry. Emma has Dax's blue eyes, and even though many children are born with blue eyes, hers are his deep shade. He sees them under the oxygen mask she has to wear for several hours to keep her lungs full. A few days later he drives Nicholle and Emma home, his foot hovering over the brake, eyes scanning for sixteen- and ninety-year-olds.

Eight weeks later Emma has some neck control and Dax starts out on the road again. He returns from an Indianapolis-Louisville-Lexington trip exhausted. His back kills him, and he's noticed a new red mole on the side of his rib cage. Emma rests on his chest and Nicholle sips half a glass of cheap Shiraz.

Dax had stopped by another VA hospital on this latest trip, and he tells Nicholle that if they play the percentages, he will probably die before her, most likely from some kind of cancer caused by the crap he breathed in while deployed—the jacked-up cells have probably already started multiplying somewhere far inside his slippery body.

"Great, Dax," she says. "Welcome home. Shut up and hold your girl. She missed you."

Sometimes he worries that Nicholle might die first. When she's late getting home from a mom's night out and he gets her voicemail – her gentle voice, as if everything is okay – his mind allows about a thirty-minute cushion and then begins the murmurs of what-ifs. The whole scene flashes by: the dreaded call – auto accident, funeral, insurance money, his baby girl growing, him dating or not, the guilt of either, moving, different career, Emma's wedding – but then, as always, the garage door rumbles open and Nicholle saunters in, because in the end, nothing is wrong.

Dax travels more now: outside the local rounds, he's gone a week every month. When away, he calls home at 6:30 Knoxville time every night. Emma has normally finished her bath, and Nicholle puts the phone up to her ear so she hears her daddy's voice. Emma is eight months old and already she plays with her first steps.

Whenever he's in Memphis he plays cards a couple blocks off the strip in a brick basement where there's a password. This is his trivial thrill. He recognizes most of the participants. They aren't thugs, at least in his opinion – when they lose money, it hurts. They have polo shirts and middle-class mortgages.

One day after he negotiates the sale of ten new blood-sugar monitors at St. Jude Hospital, he showers and heads to the card game. The password is *sycamore,* but Dax says *live oak,* last week's password. They let him in anyway.

Five hands in and Dax spies his flush and a story starts up around the table about a guy who had his dick put in a vise. The poor genital-squeezed guy owed money to the wrong people. There is laughter. Dax stares at his spades, organized and lethal. He reaches for chips.

"Named Sim," says Brent, the organizer of the game.

"Sim?" someone says. "Deserved it."

Jordan, a banker with nervous hands, asks if people can die from that – a dick in a vise.

A new guy, Ian, quiets everyone with his monotone.

"Yes," he says. "If you leave 'em there, eventually they die of hunger."

"You could rip your dick off," Jordan says.

"I guess you always have a choice."

Dax thinks of what he'll say to Nicholle. *How many Sims can there be? What do I ask? Water moccasin Sim, snapping turtle Sim. Torture.* Dax remembers Sim laughing in the muddy water as Dax dried off on the bank, unable to get his knees to stop shaking. *Where else do you want it to go? This is where it lives.*

Dax waits until the next day, 7 P.M., to call home. He has spoken to Emma, and Nicholle explains how she is considering going back to work, just part-time, over the summer, then how she's struggling to lose the last ten pounds of pregnancy weight.

"I need something to do," she says, "outside the house."

"When's Sim going to come visit his niece?" Dax asks. It's the easiest lead-in.

"I don't know," she says. "He's not coming with money, if that's what you're asking. He called last night. Said he was in international waters. Probably the Mississippi."

Sim rolls his truck four times outside Mobile on a Monday at 3 A.M. He's drunk and his face and chest bruise up good. Nicholle's parents call—her mother asks for their prayers. Nicholle prays and Sim stays in critical condition for eighteen hours, but he pulls through. Nicholle's mother praises God and his mercy and his comfort. Glory and grace is all she talks about for a month. Sim drank a bottle of Jack and got behind the wheel; he forgot to put his seat belt on; he was ejected from his rolling vehicle and landed on his back in a patch of grass, looking up at the stars. Dax wants to ask Nicholle's mother whether sobriety or buckling in is the devil's work. *Do we praise Jesus if Sim impales himself on a mile marker?* He doesn't say any of this. When he finally talks to Sim, he says, "I'm glad you're with us."

Two months later Sim shows up at the house twenty pounds lighter, hands shaking. He smells like cabbage and urine. He says he's been in the same clothes for a week, sleeping during the day, driving at night. He's out of money and in trouble. He says this is the kind of trouble you don't wake up from.

"Got to stay out of 'bama," he says.

Before Dax can wrap his head around the situation, Nicholle has invited Sim in and shown him to the guest room. He showers upstairs while Nicholle and Dax cuss and stomp. Before the shower water turns off they've reached a compromise. Sim has two weeks; he doesn't leave the house, his truck stays in the garage, he gets no calls, and he's gone, cops called with any weird stuff. After that he's on his own. Dax knows Nicholle won't kick her brother out at the deadline, but he'll let himself be surprised.

For two weeks Dax finds himself in pleasant shock as Sim sleeps for two days, then cleans up and helps around the house. Gently enthusiastic and outwardly caring, he plays dolls with Emma, plays horse with Emma, helps feed her, bathe her. Just finding her walking legs, Emma trails Sim around the house, almost pronouncing his easy name, and he, nervous of possible falls, protects her from the brick fireplace, a backward tumble from the stairs, three inches of bathwater. His unexpected involvement frees Nicholle to extend her work hours, Dax to make a few more phone calls without a screaming child in the background. On the last night of Sim's allotted live-in time, Dax and Nicholle crawl into bed with each other. No one has talked about Sim leaving the next day. They both know it's his agreed-to

time to depart, but he's volunteered to wake up early with
Emma, to take her to the park if they need some quiet time
at the house. Dax leans over and kisses Nicholle, and for the
first time in two months they make love.

A week later Dax makes the morning hospital rounds in
Little Rock. He isn't scheduled to leave until the following
day, but he considers changing his flight to get back to the
girls and Sim that night. He hustles back to the hotel and
picks up the ringing hotel room phone just before he leaves
for the airport. Nicholle's nervous voice. She asks why Dax
isn't answering his cell phone, but before he can answer,
she says that there are two men, a tall one at the front door,
the other standing at the side of the house. She's ignored
them, but the man at the front door has stopped knocking
and is peering into the long, narrow window to the left of
the door. Emma sleeps.

"Am I crazy?" she asks.

"Wait a minute," he says. "Are they in uniform?"

"No," she says. "Why? Did you schedule something?"
But she doesn't let him answer. "Because it's been far too
long. They've been here five minutes."

She tells him that she can see the one at the front door
glancing around, not into the house, but around at the other
houses in the neighborhood. He hears Sim in the background.

"Put Sim on." Dax waits for Sim's voice, and the pause
stretches. Dax forces himself to breathe.

"Not lying. There's some shit," Sim says. "Damn. Damn.
Nothing is gonna happen, man. Trust me."

"You son of a bitch. Handle this, Sim." No reply.

"Hello?" It's Nicholle. "The one on the side moved into
the back yard," she says. Dax pictures the spacious yard and
medium dogwoods. It's 3:15 his time, 4:15 there. "Sim pulled

the damn truck out into the driveway a few days ago. Listen to me. Something's not right here."

Dax stands in the hotel room, packed suitcase at his feet. "Go get Emma," he says.

Nicholle breathes heavily into the phone and says, "My God."

Dax traces her path in his head, down the long second-floor hallway, through the white door into the baby's yellow bedroom with block pink letters above the crib: EMMA.

"We're back in our room. Emma's — they're in," she says, interrupting herself. "The other one's in the screened porch and the man at the front door, he's knocking again."

"Lock the bedroom door and call 911," Dax says. "Do it now."

"But Sim —" she says.

"Lock it now. Call 911."

"Don't hang up, damn you."

"I don't hear Emma."

"She's here."

"Where's Sim?"

"He's down there. They're screaming."

It was twenty bucks a month for the alarm whose wires probably dangle unconnected. Dax pictures its white box under the stairs. Then the blue safe under their bed.

"Get the gun," he says.

"I'm putting the phone on the bed." Over the line Dax hears Emma's labored breathing. It sounds like she's trying to put the receiver in her mouth.

"I have it," Nicholle says. "Okay." A pause. "They're fighting. God, they're fighting."

"Like we practiced. Put the magazine in. It should have rounds in it."

"Crashing downstairs."

"Pull the hammer back," Dax says.

"What? What's the hammer?"

"I mean the slide. Shit, the slide. We've practiced this. The top part, throw the slide back."

"It's sticking. On the stairs now." She whispers. "Up. The. Stairs."

"Yell out to them, 'I have a gun.'" She does.

"And again," he says.

She says it again, and "I will shoot you." He hears her say the words, and she says "motherfuckers." Emma cries.

"It's sticking," she says to Dax.

"Do you remember?"

"Yes," she says. "I know what to do, but it's sticking." Her pitch rises. No one is on their way to them.

"Got it," Nicholle says. "They're talking on the stairs." Her voice lowers even more. "They said Sim. My God, they know us."

"Say it again."

"What?"

"The gun," he says.

"I've got a gun," she yells.

"If they open the door, you shoot until the gun stops firing and then load the next magazine."

She hears the finality in his voice, because she says, "No. No." Dax hears her right before he hangs up and dials 911. He slings information as fast as he can to the operator and pictures the safety tab on the gun Nicholle holds, turned down, the red fire dot hidden. His sight goes wavy, the ceiling lowers on him, and he thinks of the locked trigger. He hangs up, calls his home phone, and the metallic tone pulses off and on until the answer machine engages. It's her morning voice: "You've reached Nicholle and Dax Bailey," and his voice in the background, "and Emma," she squeaks. "We're not in right now, but please leave a message and we'll get back with you. Thank you." He listens to the entire thing, thinks about leaving a message, his voice loud on the machine, but hangs up. She won't be able to hear him, no matter what he says into the phone. He calls her cell phone, and when he gets her cell-phone message — just her voice — he hangs up immediately. He stares at a dark stain on the hotel carpet. *Someone's on the way. Someone's on the way.* He calls the home line again. This time he lets the whole message play and stands with the phone in his hand, a beam of light from the hotel window now shining through. Dax closes his eyes. The muffled near-silence records him listening, and he thinks there's a chance, if he's loud enough, Nicholle might be able to pick up one word, through the drywall and beams and carpet, past Sim's body, past the men knocking on the locked bedroom door. He breathes in through his mouth and nose and screams "Safety," over and over and over, until there are no more words, just his machine now recording his empty lungs.

11

Resurrecting a Body Half

I N   H I S   H O T E L   E L E V A T O R   Armando fingers the exec-
utive-level key card and stares up from his wheelchair
at the four-inch screen showing the Israeli prime minister
at a podium with the red breaking news headline "Israel
Prepares for War with Iran." The screen flashes to a police sketch of someone Chicago authorities search for. Armando wonders how one slides into the position of sketch
artist. His local police department – where he volunteered
briefly – lacked the money, so when necessary they would
bring in the high school art teacher, Trent Kellogg. He
would show up with his charcoal set and pound the paper.
He wasn't an accomplished artist, and most of the time the
department would be embarrassed to put the sketches out,
but what Armando remembers in detail is Kellogg's face
while he drew, the bundled forehead and contorted mouth,
saliva leaking out.

This sketched suspect on the elevator screen is a white
or Hispanic male, twenty-five to thirty years old, five-foot-
eight to six-foot-one. A moment passes before Armando
recognizes the absurd range of people who fit this description, but when he does, he recalls the details he slung at

Kellogg: a red-haired female in a blue sweatshirt. At least he could describe the car, the brown Buick LeSabre that ran the stop sign on his early-morning jog and smashed him. A day after his spinal surgery Kellogg came in and they walked through it – the thin nose, the haircut, the chin – and Armando realized he didn't know as much as he thought, but he overheard himself dealing out a description that barely registered, and before he knew it, he and Kellogg had created someone. Kellogg was into it big-time, shaking and groaning, using the side of his hand and fingertips, whipping the charcoal lump like a madman. He finished and Armando sat up in the hospital bed and studied the bust of a woman he half recognized, so he nodded and sent Kellogg on his way and returned to the dreaded wheelchair catalogue.

In this elevator, on the small screen, the artist has conveyed an androgyny and universality that denote everyone and no one. Armando considers his own features, and someone softly touches his shoulder, then his neck. He twists around awkwardly, and a smiling, attractive woman brushes his cheek with her hand. She leans back and settles comfortably against another woman. The space is packed, and Armando turns back to face the front, trying to neutralize the confusion that erupts. *What just happened?* In his dreams he has neared this experience and he always has something witty to say, but here, in the moment, he freezes. *Pity? Desire? My cheek?* His fingers throb, and in what appears to be a miracle, he feels a twinge in his groin for the first time since his accident. He tries to summon the courage to acknowledge the feeling, to turn back to them, but what would he say? *Thank you? Let's go? I'm married, but she's lost interest?* The problem is, he wants everything to be easy: no stories. He wants one of them to invite him to her room, where they'll undress him and lick each other before they take control and use him, but as he imagines the scene he has already lost their faces. There was a time when this squeeze and cheek brush was all his body needed to respond with an uncontrollable erection, but tonight a twinge means more than anything in his past. He smiles and a surprise desire fills him. He's uncertain where to reach or how to breathe. Chatter fills the elevator: a feminine voice murmurs of a bad back to a friend, two teenagers about Derrick Rose and the upcoming season for the Bulls. He has three floors to go, with no plan, no idea of what he's capable of, and then he's at his floor. The doors open. He takes one look back to get the faces and they look right back, and seconds before the doors close on his healers, one of them nods and smiles. The elevator doors close, and he turns to watch the numbers scroll upward, noting the pauses (23, 27), until the elevator starts back down.

Two months after the accident, at the official lineup, he saw her, the woman in Trent Kellogg's drawing. He knew that there was no such thing as closure or justice, not when you lose your legs and spine to a person driving and texting. He picked her out, said, "That's her." In the end his eyewitness testimony was important, but less critical than the woman's dented LeSabre, previous driving convictions, and eventual confession.

On the way home, Anna drove — has, from the moment of his accident, always driven — and held his hand in the car.

"May she rot in hell for what she did to us," she said. "Fuck her. They should cut her hands off." Armando didn't say anything when the obscenity left her mouth, but the word *us* haunted him instantly. *What she did to me,* he thought. *What she did to* me.

· · ·

The hotel's handicapped-accessible room is smoke-free, but Armando smells the dirty cigarette smell in the walls. He sits in his wheelchair, naked, the shower warming up, television tuned to the first presidential debate:

MODERATOR: But if I hear the two of you correctly, neither one of you is suggesting any major changes in what you want to do as president as a result of the financial bailout. Is that what you're saying?

OBAMA: No. As I said before, Jim, there are going to be things that end up having to be —

MODERATOR: Like what?

OBAMA: — deferred and delayed. Well, look, I want to make sure that we are investing in energy in order to free ourselves from the dependence on foreign oil. That is a big project. That is a multiyear project.

MODERATOR: Not willing to give that up?

OBAMA: Not willing to give up the need to do it, but there may —

Armando turns away. *Poor McCain,* he thinks. *No matter what Obama says, you got no shot.*

In the spacious hotel shower Armando turns the temperature way up and lets the steaming water drench him, and he sits on the specially equipped shower seat and touches his wet body. He feels his chest and face and hair. He rubs at his eyes. He pinches the skin at the elbow without nerve endings. He thinks of how his spoiled body retains his healthy name.

He soaps his arm and touches his biceps scar, then reaches down and soaps and rinses his feet, a raised scar on his left foot. He recalls a photo taken two days before that jog. In it he stands in their living room in a bathrobe he hates. He poses for Anna, sticking his belly out in between the crossing flanks of cotton, patting it. After she took the photo Mia screamed from her bedroom, and in his rush to her he cut his foot on the doorstop to her room before calming her down from a nightmare. All of that action he has to create from a photo where he stands frowning at his body. He considers sliding out of the shower, but the hot water keeps coming and he feels like he breaks even with the pricey room when he drains an extra five minutes from a steaming cleanse.

Armando scoots to the edge of the plastic seat and caresses his testicles and fingers the space beneath them, pressing hard. He searches for the twinge that receded after he returned to his room. He tries to convince himself of the miracle in the elevator, that it actually occurred, and he knows that the only proof is to feel it once again. Once is a mirage. Although he has washed himself already, he again soaps his penis, testicles, groin, inside his ass and he dreams up images of the women's mouths on him.

Once Armando feels lightheaded he turns off the water, but he stays seated while the steam escapes through the slightly open window. He grabs at his narrow quadriceps and pushes down, running his hands to his knees. After he and Anna were married they would routinely make love in the shower, everything slippery and smooth. He'd crouch down to a half squat to enter her, and after, he'd always let her get out first to dry. They'd lie on the bed and he'd silently curse his aching knees and knotted legs before falling asleep. In the long hotel mirror he considers his rehabilitation in the elevator, debates the consequences of sex without his wife, whether there must be morality in miracles.

He dries as best he can and squirts cologne on his neck, buttons up a tailored shirt and squirms into slacks, then finds his fifth of Wild Turkey. He unscrews the top and sniffs the bottle before taking a few biting gulps and hearing talk of war on the television.

OBAMA: And so John likes – John, you like to pretend like the war started in 2007. You talk about the surge. The war started in 2003, and at the time when the war started, you said it was going to be quick and easy. You said we knew where the weapons of mass destruction were. You were wrong. You said that we were going to be greeted as liberators. You were wrong. You said that there was no history of violence between Shia and Sunni. And you were wrong. And so my question is –

MODERATOR: Senator Obama –

OBAMA: – of judgment, of whether or not – of whether or not – if the question is who is best equipped as the next president to make good decisions about how we use our military, how we make sure that we are prepared and ready for the next conflict, then I think we can take a look at our judgment.

MODERATOR: I have got a lot on the plate here . . .

MCCAIN: I'm afraid Senator Obama doesn't understand the difference between a tactic and a strategy. But the important – I'd like to tell you, two Fourths of July ago I was in Baghdad. General Petraeus invited Senator Lindsey Graham and me to attend a ceremony where 688 brave young Americans, whose enlistment had expired, were reenlisting to stay and fight for Iraqi freedom and American freedom. I was honored to be there. I was honored to speak to those troops. And you know, afterwards, we spent a lot of time with them. And you know what they said to us? They said, let us win. They said, let us win. We don't want our kids coming back here. And this strategy, and this general, they are winning. Senator Obama refuses to acknowledge that we are winning in Iraq.

Armando runs his fingers along his jaw, his short, well-kept beard. He mutes the television. *Oh, McCain,* he thinks. Then, out loud to the television, to a close-up of McCain's face, mocking, "Let us win, they said. Please John, let us stay here forever and win. We love it here! We're winners! Fuck you."

He runs the channels on the muted television: *Sports-Center,* a *Friends* rerun, news, *Mr. and Mrs. Smith.* Brad Pitt and Angelina Jolie trading punches.

Six months ago, a Tuesday night marked the three-year anniversary of the hit-and-run accident, but no one said anything, and Mia threw a fit over dinner in her purple overalls, screaming and pushing. She knocked her chicken enchilada on the floor and told Anna to shut up. At five years old, Mia knew it was spanking time, but she darted away and taunted Armando. He put down his tumbler of whiskey, but he couldn't catch her in their white kitchen, and he could see the confidence in her young eyes. *Catch me, cripple.* With a rush Anna snatched Mia's shoulder and spun her. Armando wanted Anna to bring Mia to him so he could teach her a lesson she wouldn't forget, but before he knew it Anna wound up and delivered a fist to their daughter's lower back. This adult-world punch cut the wind from her and she fell to the kitchen tiles. Anna grabbed the bottom of her straps and yank-lifted her up and slapped her temple, picked her up again and slapped her red cheek. Armando saw Mia's eyes, vacant and disbelieving. Anna said something, but he couldn't hear the words above Camila's screeching. Anna looked up at the ceiling and screamed and somehow Mia slipped away and bounded to him, crashed into his chest, shaking and choking him. Anna moved toward them, leaning into the stride with her shoulders, and for the first time in his life Armando feared her and realized there was little he could do, so he lifted his arm in defense, heard himself, in a voice unfamiliar and weak, begging his wife to stop.

Armando senses the energy and whispers of opportunity in the city night, so he wheels around the hotel lobby, trying everything he knows to appear as if he isn't waiting for someone. He may luck into a chance encounter with the women, but the odds aren't good. He's willing to wait awhile before he asks the doorman if he's seen the women. On a normal travel night, he'd do some mind fucking, because when you're married it's the best self-preservation, even for the guilt seekers. A few minutes before eleven and he debates the strength of his whiskey breath. He pops a mint, and because this is his night, the women emerge from the elevator and one of them has a late-night sway Armando recognizes. She is younger and plumper than he remembers from the elevator, in a red skirt that shows her meaty legs. She says something from a distance that he doesn't catch, and her friend wraps her hand around the swayer's biceps and gently pulls. Armando waves and they walk toward him.

"It's Courtney," she says with a southern accent, and takes a breath as if she's run out. Before he can reply with his name, she comes close to him. "Okay, tell me."

"Motivational speaker," he says. "That's what I'm doing here."

"We could talk around it, but I want to know, because she says" – pointing over to her friend – "that by the look of you, all of this is new."

She smells like strawberries, and her cross necklace

dangles close to his face. The faintest twinge returns to his lower body, and a biting sensation at a toe. Armando senses gathering emotion, but he holds himself together and runs through a catalogue of stories and picks one that answers Courtney's lazy eyes.

"Come close, because it's embarrassing," he says softly. She does, her ear inches from his mouth, head bobbing. "Have you heard of Kabul? Of course you have. So you know the battles and bombings. The bottom line is, I was caught in the middle, doing what I could. There's no easy way to say it. The Taliban were closing on our position outside the city, but we managed to save most of the children. We had them lie down at our feet while we fired back. The fighting was brutal, but we hung in there. In many ways I'm lucky, even with all of this."

His lie sounds magnificent. He slows the story down now, varies the intonation, and remembers to include her name.

"Well, Courtney, I was in the wrong place, doing the right thing. Courtney, I remember the sting, the fire tearing through my back. I remember running away, then crashing down with my blood on me. But I was hit in the back, so I didn't see the blood leaving me. That's a crazy thing, to feel your blood leaving you but you only have your hands to tell you how much. You can't see it. It's not easy to see what's supposed to be inside your body on the outside. I fell in a soccer field, as my fellow soldiers and children gathered around. I don't talk about it often, but I want you to know. Courtney, I can tell you'll understand."

He needs her to touch him, even a brush, or at least look at him. More sensation. Another toe. He touches his legs and senses the slight pressure.

"So you weren't born with it," she drawls.

"No, Courtney. In Afghanistan . . ."

She pops upright, somehow satisfied, and strides toward the bathroom. Her friend, leaning against the wall with her arms crossed, lets her go.

"Wait," he says. "Just wait."

At the door Courtney stalls.

"Coming?" she asks the door.

Armando moves to the middle of the marble corridor and stops as she enters the women's bathroom.

"Hey, buddy. You go in there . . . ," says a voice behind him. It's her friend, still facing away. "You go in there, you walk out with something. I'm not judging." The statement confuses him, but she puts her right index finger to her nose and shakes her head. He wheels to the bathroom door and places his hand on the door's dull brass push-plate. It's warm, and a whiff of cleaner stench hits him. The fake mahogany door is an inch thick, on hinges, but he can't bring himself to push. He imagines Courtney on the other side, leaning back against the black marble counter, the top three buttons unfastened, waiting, and as he rolls back from the door he wonders how long she'll wait for him there. Heart and mind racing, he's frantic, time leaping ahead, and he glances at the friend, now leaning at the intersection of two walls, and nods. He hears Courtney emerge, speak over him. She flicks her nostrils with a newfound awareness in her eyes.

He guesses: *Cocaine?*

"Should have come, hero."

"Courtney," he says, but she passes him with no hint of recognition and walks to her friend, puts her arm around her, and they exit through the heavy front doors of the hotel.

He follows, hoping for a glance back, a beckoning, a

tease. The doorman, quick on his feet, gives him a chance to catch up, but he has no clue what to say or do. He hears their laughter as they disappear behind a row of taxis.

After the accident Anna waited months before asking him what he wanted from her. He knew this meant that she needed something, anything, even if the offer was to him, so he took down the sheets and kissed her mouth, breasts, lower stomach, and moved down while he held her hips in his hands and tongue-searched her to hit her spot — the spot he used to know, but it had been so long — and he searched for the accompanying pressure that always arrived in him but felt nothing, not even as she moaned and jerked and pushed his head away. He watched her flail in the lamp-light. She smiled and helped him to his back. She hovered over him, serious and tender.

"Do you want me to try? Do you want me to touch you?"

Armando wheels to the side of the entrance to the hotel, purgatory for all smokers on windy nights — just warm enough to make the buzz worth it but too cold to enjoy the burn. The space is abandoned except for the bass from the club down the street. Across the street, Grant Park, then Lake Michigan and clear skies.

Twenty minutes later a woman in a wheelchair wheels up and stops, puffing smoke from her extra-long cigarette into the night air. He's just finished his cigarillo, and to start a conversation he pulls a new one out and asks for a light. *Midthirties,* he guesses. Her delicate jaw slides into a petite chin, a seemingly reconstructed nose odd-fitting with the rest of her face. No wedding ring.

"You know what I hate?" she asks after lighting him. The question sounds rhetorical, but he thinks of guesses, still shaking off his encounter outside the bathroom: *Paralysis? Wheelchairs? Life?*

"Stars," she says. "What a crock. Most are dead, yet here they are, shining away with all their fake-ass light."

Armando winces. He guesses there could be bad poetry coming his way, but he nods to project interest. She smiles at him as if she's let him in on a secret.

"I don't think *most* of them are dead," he says. "Maybe a couple."

He needs to keep the momentum going, so he pulls out the fifth and tilts the bottle. Ms. Starlight sits in a fading light the color of weak iced tea.

"No. All of them are dead," she says, in a confident, near-preachy voice. "It takes their light a million years to get here. I know this stuff. Nothing we see in the sky is actually still there except the other planets. It's all a mirage except shooting stars, which aren't stars at all, just lunar dust particles floating around. But you know this. You can't trust your eyes."

Armando is fairly sure she spouts flawed astronomy, but she rides in a wheelchair, and although he understands that makes them equals in a way, he still registers a healthy dose of sympathy as the woman puffs on her cigarette. Her chair is a power model, glistening blue. Her right hand clutches the joystick, tenderly fingering the top. He can tell she wants him to understand all this celestial babble as she leans over her armrest toward him. Her blouse lifts up over the collarbone, revealing a red bra strap. He considers for a moment what they would look like on the bed together.

"Sure, all of them are kaput," he says, but his voice sounds tired and dismissive.

"You don't believe me. Fine. Not important to you."

"Yep," he says, and she leans back.

"You, at the fancy hotel. You, searching for someone your type. You, a damn believer."

The shift to awkward accusation surprises Armando, and before he realizes that he won't understand any answer, he asks the question.

"You're not staying here?"

"Doesn't matter."

"What?"

"I know a broken vet when I see one."

"What?"

"You're a war man. You care about nothing because you think you've been through everything. I got a cousin like you."

"You don't know me."

"I'm good at guessing. Let's see, a war hero, back to a country that doesn't take care of you. VA sucking the life out of you with long lines and doctors that, let me guess, just don't care. Married, broken dick, so kids are out of the question, war hero wears off, and you cry when you drive by fucking pick-up basketball games."

"I have kids," he says faintly, before the adrenaline hits and pours out over everything. "Okay," he says, then takes a drag, holds the smoke in his mouth, and thinks. The chemicals burn his tongue and cheeks.

"Since you're a bitch that can fit into a dress, I figure a dud in high school, but an athlete, cheerleader maybe, doing the big boys, flunking science. Had the looks before you were T-boned. Couldn't have been your fault. New nose, but Johnny Ballplayer walks away after four weeks, and thank God he never used the ring sitting in his drawer. Nice settlement, but it doesn't help the old back, and you'd climb on anyone if they'd only offer you a compliment. Let's see here. You're not so bad in the shadows."

He knows he has her, because she swivels the chair to face him and reaches up to touch her ear, making sure it's still there. She grins with a hint of defeat, and he figures he'll forgive her in the coming minutes. The pause stretches, and he questions whether he got all of it right.

"You think I can't walk, don't you? You think this isn't a choice?"

Armando goes mute. He's at the end of a tunnel. No matter what has happened, this is a line, one he would fight over – *faking it?* – but this insane question scampers away and he can't bring himself to answer. His mind spins and the muscles in his back tighten; he's tired now and conscious of the last seventeen waking hours. His cigarillo is a nub.

He's about to give up and respond, flick his smoke away, and head up to his room. He's decided on "I'm tired," but before he gets the two words out, Ms. Starlight stretches both legs outward, holding them parallel to the ground.

Armando's vision flexes and blurs. His anger forms from somewhere deep. The doorman nods off, and the pounding bass from the club has disappeared. Legs still extended, she scowls at him and laughs.

"All of this," she says, "just a temporary thing. Nothing but a fall and three weeks while the bruise heals. You, on the other hand –" She stops midsentence. Her forehead crinkles in frustration. After a few seconds he's convinced she's said everything, so he turns back to the doors, but before he gets to the entrance she clears her throat.

"You sorry fuck," she says.

Alone in the elevator. The screen displays the police sketch again, a full-body sketch, and Armando realizes that the accused always stand in the police lineups. His head aches while he replays his lobby story to Courtney, Ms. Starlight's parting words, and now, unsolicited, a dark and shifting memory materializes – this time the M4 bucks on his shoulder and the Afghan girl runs at him barefoot before exploding from the chest out, and when he reaches her she is somehow whole again, but dead, and Armando raises her shawl, but there is no vest, no bomb, nothing but her shirt and ribs and chest.

The elevator screen shows forty degrees and foggy at the airport, which is never good. His 7 A.M. flight will be delayed. He tries to think of the plane, tries to hold the image, envision its angle upward into the early morning, but the late night engulfs him and he thinks of Anna at home and he wonders if she's ever had another man over while he is away. What kills and saves him is that the answer is very likely no. More likely Anna wallows nightly in the crushing guilt of the "for better or for worse." He imagines her greeting him tomorrow in the driveway, taking his suitcase from his lap. He hears her yelling to the kids that Daddy's home, and the girls rushing out, arguing about who gets to push him up the ramp. He can taste his wife's kiss the first time they tried to make love after the accident.

They had waited months, her floating over him.

"Do you want me to try? Do you want me to touch you?"

"Yes," he said, and being so scared of the silence that followed, scared to look down, scared to count the seconds pass as he sank into himself, feeling Anna's hand on his chest, stomach, then nothing, only empty, numb, nothing below, and later, with shaking hands and an upper body on fire with anger, wheeling to the kitchen and pulling out a bread knife. The serrated edges of the knife pulling against the sharpener, taking his boxers down and gripping his genitals in his left hand. He felt the knife's weight in his right hand but nothing when he pressed the sharp edge to the base of his penis. He saw the skin open slightly and blood began to run down the blade and onto the floor. He heard one of his daughters rise and use the restroom down the hall, heard the toilet flush, the tap run and stop, soft footsteps, and the closing bedroom door. The house quieted and he heard night insects outside and he stopped the bleeding with paper towels and cleaned the floor and cleaned the knife and put it back in the drawer he could reach. He turned off the lights and sat alone in the dark room.

The elevator doors open to his floor and he starts out, but something in his arms fails him and he pauses in between the closing doors. They close and open, close and open around him – chewing. He ponders the worst thing that could happen if he gets back in the elevator, but before the doors close for the third time he's back in, pressing the 23 button. Something in his working bones tells him that Courtney's room is on the twenty-third floor.

He rolls off the elevator and takes his place beside two fake leather chairs and a granite console table with a gold-faced lamp. He stares at the two elevator displays, digital red numbers stuck on L. One of them moves to 4 and down again. Another begins its ascent, and he's stuck in this miracle lottery. The number climbs above 17, stops, and starts up again. His seat creaks as he adjusts. He isn't sure how long he can last, if he has enough resolve to stick this out, but as he looks down at his bent legs in his wrinkle-free slacks, he feels a warming in his gut and begs it to lower. He understands the astronomical odds, but he has faith that the elevator doors will open to him and for the first time in years he'll feel his pants slide down over his knees before they fall to the floor. Ms. Starlight was right, he's a believer, he has to be, and tonight there will be a reckoning, a savagery, enough passion and blood and faith to resurrect the universe at one in the morning, but as the elevator doors open and he sees Courtney's smeared makeup, he wonders if he has enough of anything.

12

No Doorbell

Two hours before showtime in his army dress uniform at the Fourth of July parade, Wintric lounges on his living room couch, fingering a recently purchased pocketknife as his three-year-old son, Daniel, tries to balance on one leg. Daniel teeters on his right foot for three seconds before losing his balance.

"Put your arms out," says Wintric, miming the arm movement from the couch.

Daniel glances at his father and raises his arms out to his sides. He lifts his left foot a couple inches off the living room floor and wobbles, then stomps the foot down. He tries again.

Wintric's left foot rests on the carpet. His only remaining toe on the foot—his big one—brushes at the light-pink remnants of an old cranberry juice stain he recently gave up on. His big toe has done this minor back-and-forth dance as long as he can recall, but the involuntary movement has become even more noticeable since the other digits disappeared.

Five years since he last wore his uniform. Wintric steals a mental picture of the green army getup in his closet, sucks in his belly, and wonders if the few extra pounds he carries will be problematic come zipper and button time. The parade organizers have asked him to walk in the patriot group each year since his return to Chester, but this is the first year he has agreed, largely to appease Kristen's pleading, her insistence that their son would be proud to see his father walk down Main Street with the other veterans who have returned to their California mountain town.

Wintric ignored her requests for years, claiming that he was no longer a soldier, that he had despised his time in the army, that the single reason he kept his uniform was to remind himself of what he so gladly gave up, but the truth is harder for him to reconcile – the rage at his uniform, at hearing the words *army, sacrifice, honor,* the anger and pride he feels when someone thanks him for his past service or when he sees a map of Afghanistan or photos of flag-draped caskets or White House Medal of Honor receptions on the Internet. He can't list all the reasons that he said he would wear the uniform this year, and his son may be one of those reasons, but he knows that if he can get it on and walk through the fury and the Main Street chaos, he may just snuff out some of his attacking memories.

The living room smells like bacon from their earlier breakfast, and Wintric hears Kristen's shower singing from the back bathroom of their two-bedroom home.

On television Rafael Nadal is in the athletic throes of destroying Tomáš Berdych in the 2010 Wimbledon men's final. NBC's sports announcers talk over the action, belaboring the fact that England's queen personally graced the tennis event earlier in the week for the first time in thirty-three years, but what gains Wintric's full attention – as a man who has never watched or even considered watching tennis – is a point-winning roar from the muscled, animalistic Nadal.

Wintric focuses now on the Spaniard as he moves angrily across the court, stomping, hurling his sculpted body at every shot. There is little grace, but Nadal's ferocity has Wintric entranced. The ball shoots off Nadal's racket as if stunned into velocity, into impossible angles that ride the white out-of-bounds lines. After each winner Nadal flexes his bricklike biceps and stares into the stands. During volleys Berdych can only guess where to move next, and when he guesses correctly, his luck prolongs the point a mere few more seconds. Even when he wins a game, only minor fanfare arrives. The battle seems more like boxing than tennis, and although the match just started, Wintric knows it's over, and he can tell Berdych knows it's over. Wintric understands that one of the most difficult things is to finish the fights you're supposed to win, and this is ultimately why he falls for Nadal. Because although the Spaniard is heavily favored, he appears not to realize just how good his odds are, so all of this will end quickly.

After one of the commercial breaks, the commentators interview Monica Seles, a player Wintric has never heard of, and a moment before he changes the channel the television screen cuts to a video: *1993* in the lower left-hand corner, a young Seles, an orange clay court, and a man walks onto the court, then chaos as security grabs the man, and Seles, now curled on the clay, reaches to her back, wincing in pain. Wintric turns the volume up and the words jumble: *stabbing, nine-inch boning knife, two years before she came back, never the same player.* Wintric thinks of how easy it is to hurt — just walk out of the stands with a knife, simply veer your car a couple feet to either side; he exhales and a memory arrives, his childhood bedroom.

Wintric was twelve, asleep in the room he had wallpapered with posters of NBA basketball players, when his father shook him awake, handed him a revolver, and snap-whispered, "If something happens, shoot for the body."

He was all nerves in their narrow, predawn hallway and
scooted forward, left hand on his father's back, right hand
gripping a heavy gun – a loaded gun – and as they glided
past his infant sister's bedroom, Wintric heard knocking.
The whole scene cluttered within him: *shoot for the body,
murderer, knocking, Are we shooting through the door? What
criminal knocks? I don't have shoes on, How big is a bullet?*
His father disappeared, so he crouched down on the floor
in a flood of fear and closed his eyes, then opened them, but
there was no difference in the darkness, and still that feverish knocking. He waited for the shot, for his name in the
night, and the carpet was cool on his feet. The standoff was
taking too long, and then a slurring voice filtered through
the door; the voice hurled his father's name – John – and
then lights on, door open, and their drunk neighbor spit
out, "Your back yard's on fire."

Then dawn, and Wintric watched his father direct the
water stream from their garden hose onto a smoking pile of
leaves they had left for Glad bags later that day. They would
never discover what lit them, and he didn't know why, but
his father still gripped his gun, and so did Wintric. He in-
spected the silver gun, the bullets' brass backings. He was
unsure whether the revolver's safety was on, and that was
something he should've known. It was the kind of thing his
father expected him to know when he gave him the combination to the safe in the bedroom. Wintric performed a
slight tug on the trigger and watched the revolver's hammer start its backward ride, but he stopped early and everything slid back into potential. Another tiny tug, and the
minuscule movement of the hammer shocked him. His father shook the morning cold out in his shorts, nightshirt,
and old slippers and stared mesmerized at the water flow,
and Wintric realized then that he could shoot him. Not that
he wanted to, only that he could, with minimal effort. He

could kill him if he aimed straight enough. Without prompt he stroked this strange charge of power and alarm that people must feel when they realize they can do absolutely anything they want if they have the nerve.

Wintric turns the tennis match off, runs his fingers through his shoulder-length hair, and watches Daniel – the one-legged balancing act now over – bang his fist on the wooden coffee table.

Daniel, short for three, wears a 49ers shirt and Lightning McQueen underwear. His son smiles at him, and the genuine expression wrenches Wintric and the familiar pit inside him opens, the competing hate and desperation and care for this child, an accident, an "orgasm gone wrong" he told Kristen upon hearing the news of her pregnancy. On the days he feels something for the boy it angers him that his son resembles Kristen more than him. Especially lately, Daniel's large nose and brown eyes feel like a cruel betrayal. Wintric has had a harder time lately fighting off the days that circle in upon him, the logging town he swore he would escape, the girl he thought he was leaving forever as he headed off to basic training, the half a foot that slices him with shame.

Wintric stares at his left foot, and even after all these years, it seems more a sad prop than part of his body. He taps into the hate, how in his entire life he has really wanted to kill only one person – even counting the war, just one – how he has failed to act on that constant desire, how each day he continues to fail, how the girl he did kill has nothing to do with this focused resentment.

The man Wintric wishes dead is Derek Nelson, once Sergeant Derek Nelson, one of the men Wintric believes assaulted him. There was another person, perhaps two, but Nelson is the one name that pierces and haunts him. Wintric has no proof, save for an incredible moment before being airlifted out of Bagram Airfield. He sat off in a corner of the rudimentary passenger terminal with his carved foot elevated when a solider he'd never met approached him and said, "It was Nelson," nodded, and walked away.

Wintric knows that Nelson lives in Green River, Wyoming, in a yellow mobile home on Davy Crockett Drive. He has a black Lab and a beat-down Tacoma missing a tailgate. He leaves for work with the gas company around 7:30 A.M. and gets home around 5 P.M. Wintric knows this because he has sat in his car on Davy Crockett Drive with a loaded .44 and watched Nelson leave and arrive at his home multiple times. The closest he ever came to fulfilling his revenge wish was in the middle of June two years ago, his second trip to Green River. Deftones blasted from the speakers, and Wintric opened the car's door and walked halfway across the street before turning back, closing the driver's door, sobbing, then pointing the car back west, all the way home to California.

"I'll get it," Daniel says, and leaves the room. He returns gripping a Nerf dart gun that Wintric bought him for his birthday. Daniel has recently got the hang of the play weapon: pushing one of the thin suction-cupped darts down the muzzle, pulling hard on the rear plastic tether until it locks back in place, now ready with enough pressure-build to launch the dart on a line across the room. Daniel has been taught not to aim at people, but Wintric has told him that he can shoot his daddy every now and then for practice, an act that draws Kristen's complaints and an encouraging "Nice shot" from Wintric.

Wintric thumbs the pocketknife in his hand. He opens up the three-inch blade, locks it into place, places the knife on the coffee table, and leans back. His big toe digs into the carpet, and he thinks about the upcoming parade, meeting up with other vets, the hot day, thousands lining the street, gawking. His neck tightens. Daniel stops pounding the table and points the gun at the blank television and shoots a dart at the screen.

"Nice," Wintric says.

"I shoot it," Daniel says.

Wintric glances at the ceiling – an intricate corner cobweb – and back down to the coffee table.

Through three walls, Kristen sings a Whitney Houston ballad in the shower.

"Knife," Daniel says, pointing.

Wintric watches Daniel's hands. One stays at his side with the toy, the other points at the knife.

"Knife," Daniel says, staring at Wintric. Daniel lowers his hand to the table a few inches away from the knife. Wintric's body warms, and he sees his son's eyes widen and his back straighten, and Wintric gives his son a nod and watches Daniel's hand slide the last three inches to the black handle and grip down.

"Know what you have there?" Wintric asks.

"Knife," Daniel says, eyes down.

"Whose knife?"

"Daddy's."

"That's right."

Daniel releases his grip on the knife and stands quietly. He searches for another dart, but none are nearby.

"You can play with it," Wintric says, then nods. "Play with it."

Daniel considers the knife, then Wintric, and pauses. He steps toward the coffee table, places his hand on the knife's handle, and glances back up at Wintric.

Wintric sees his son's small fingers on the black handle. He inhales and holds the air in. The room comes alive, brighter, the same peripheral illumination Wintric encountered once while bathing Daniel as a newborn. He let Daniel slip under the water, and for a few seconds he left his helpless son there, submerged and floundering, while the air lit up around him. He struggled to name the rush he felt that day in the moments before he saw his hands reach down into the sink and lift his son upright. Now, with Daniel's grip on the knife, no words arrive, only this tragic high.

Wintric's temples pound and his eyes lose focus. He envisions his son picking up the knife and digging the blade into his own hand, the blood there, *holes in hands, crucifixion, nails, roofing, falling from the McIntires' roof last fall,* how he had time to think before crashing down onto the cinderblock fence, how the back brace pressed him tight. He had to explain to people that the brace wasn't from his time overseas but his foot was.

Daniel holds the knife straight out now, a miniature sword. He stabs a half foot of air and looks at Wintric.

"Walk around," Wintric says.

Daniel strides to the window and surveys the street, then turns and points the sharp blade at the television, then the rocking chair—he grins—then at a honeymoon photo of Wintric and Kristen at Lake Tahoe, then back at the wooden coffee table. Daniel sticks the knife's point into the wood, enough to catch, then pushes down, leaning with his small shoulder, and abruptly loses balance; his hand slips forward, running down the knife's handle and the blade's safe backside.

"You slipped there, son. Watch. You're learning the wrong thing."

Wintric picks up the knife and holds the blade toward his son.

"This is sharp. Sharp means hurt."

Daniel turns away.

"You don't care."

Daniel turns back, blinks, and Wintric grabs his son by

the back of the neck, yanks him forward, lifts his chin up, and forces the blade to the front of his son's neck.

"Daa," Daniel moans, stiffening.

Wintric moves the blade over to the flesh above his son's collarbone and places the tip's razorlike half inch over his son's carotid. He closes his eyes and tries to ignore the white light filling in around him, attempts to feel his son's pulse through the blade and handle. Nothing. Daniel gasps, and the slight jerk of his body wakes Wintric, now opening his eyes and repositioning the knife where Daniel's Adam's apple will grow in, now guiding the blade up and down, shaving at the thin skin there.

"Sharp," Wintric says, then nabs his son's left wrist and flips his hand over. "Sharp," he says, and he pushes the tip of the blade into his son's palm. Daniel falls to the floor, crying.

"Calm down," Wintric says, and he rises, strides to the kitchen, and returns with a Band-Aid. The rush of guilt assails him, then backs off, and his hands shake. "Daddy loves you," he says to his son, and he licks the small drop of blood away and attaches the Band-Aid. "Play with knives, but be careful. Understand?"

Daniel looks away.

"Say yes," Wintric says, tightening his grip. He grabs his son's ears and squeezes.

"Daa."

"Say yes," Wintric says, nodding up and down. "Yes?"

Daniel nods.

"Good."

The seven veterans stand and spit and scratch in their military uniforms at the Collins Pine lumberyard parking lot, waiting for the Fourth of July parade to begin. They touch and straighten their pressed uniforms, and after a truck backfires one veteran successfully fights off a flashback to the past by imagining a nude Angelina Jolie. Here in this northern California small-town haven, there are no mortars, no IEDs, no bullshit commander, no Arabic. Those days are long gone for them, passed to others crouched on the other side of the world, waiting for someone to say stop, to come home, and to walk in their own parades.

One young soldier is missing both arms, her sleeves hanging flat and pinned to her sides. She nods at her new boyfriend and he swigs a Coors Light and tosses the silver can to the ground. Wintric and an airman in the group will soon showcase their limps as they stroll along the straight avenue.

Each of the seven is a recent veteran, not long back from Afghanistan or Iraq, save one Vietnam-era graybeard who hasn't missed a Chester independence parade in twenty years. Their group is sandwiched in front by a flatbed truck carrying the high school's small jazz band and behind by a dozen 4-H kids holding photos of fattened-up cows, goats, pigs. The sky is clear, except for a single line of clouds that could pass for a contrail. Douglas firs and cedars surround the paved lot, and a paramedic kneels off to the side in the summer grass. He rubs his face, then squints.

A pair of old, smiling women wearing T-shirts with a cursive *Lake Almanor* on the front walk up to the group and pause.

"When do you go back?"

"We're all veterans."

"So you have to go back?"

"No. We're not in the military anymore."

"Oh."

"We used to be."

"You get to wear uniforms?"

"Sometimes."

"Okay. Thank you, all of you," one of them says, then points at the armless solider. "Especially you." The soldier nods, glances down at the parking lot asphalt, and shakes her head.

The women start to walk away and she cough-speaks: "Bitches." It gets a laugh. "Esssspecially you," she mocks.

The parade is starting late owing to several locals finishing up the nearby 5K Fun Run at a breathless walk. Fire trucks, clowns, Shriners' hats, classic cars, and decent floats for Boy Scouts, the Elks Club, the Plumas County beauty queen, the county commissioner, the community chorus, and the Little League All-Stars mix together and form a bunched half-mile line leading from the parking lot. Wintric guesses that all the floats will get applause but that the crowds lining the street will rise from their cheap foldout chairs for his group and the American flag that accompanies them. Some will put their hands on their hearts, some will chant "USA," and more than a couple will point at them, directing their children's attention to the uniformed few and whisper well-meaning half-truths into their kids' ears.

In the parking lot, the high school jazz band in front of the seven starts to warm up, then launches into a barebones version of Glen Miller's "A String of Pearls." One of the soldiers shakes her head at the out-of-tune mash coming from the trumpet-trombone-tuba-saxophone-clarinet combo.

"Shit," she says.

"Convoy or parade," says one. "Not an easy choice."

"Screw you."

"Chester, baby."

"This is a movie. A wonderful movie," the graybeard says. "And this is our anthem."

"Play Metallica, damn!"

Then some movement. The seven straighten up and six instinctively run their hands down their chests and stomachs, smoothing their uniforms and feeling themselves underneath, but it proves a false alarm and everyone stops and exhales.

"Hurry up and wait."

"It's okay to be happy, everyone," the graybeard says. "You'll get that after a few years."

"That's some Yoda shit," Wintric says.

"It's a choice, my young friends. It's not an easy choice, but it's a choice."

Soon, after another false start, it's go time, and they walk the double yellow lines on the street and wave and soak in the day like their uniformed siblings across the country, past the salutes, the swelling communal pride, the repeating three jazz songs that get worse, then somehow better, as they all stop and go, stop and go.

The sweat begins in earnest when the seven hit the parade's half-mile point. There has not been a lot of chatting between them since the parade started. It's hot out, and most of them prefer not to rehash what they have in common. They learned long ago that you never want to appear as if you're having a good time in uniform. It sends the wrong message.

The Chester High School band in front of them has moved from a too-slow "String of Pearls" to a squeaky "Take Five," and already Wintric is near his breaking point.

The crowd, three to five deep on each side of the road, points, whispers — most smiling. Happy, sunburning fat people are everywhere, locals mixing with the tourists. The parade's pace picks up, and Wintric's good foot begins to cramp. He glances over at the armless soldier walking next to him and wonders why she didn't wear prosthetics for the parade.

A sweat stream flows down Wintric's leg and runs into the holster strapped to his shin. Something about the .380 hugging his right leg comforts him, even though it's the one of his eight guns he hasn't fired in the last six months.

The crowds have grown considerably since he was a kid watching a similar procession, and he uses the thick multitude as an excuse to give up searching for Kristen and Daniel. He wonders if they're packing up their things at that very moment. He imagines Daniel tattling – "Daddy stuck me with his knife" – and Kristen leaving for Chico or her parents' place or heading off to get the sheriff, who would be hard to find on account of the parade. Maybe Daniel won't say anything; maybe it was just an accident with a kid playing with his dad's knife.

Up ahead a fire truck blasts its horn for the twenty-second time. Wintric wipes his brow and concentrates on his protective boot and minimizing his limp as much as possible as he walks his town: past the Beacon gas station, past the road leading to the elementary school, past the dirty tire shop, past the dentist's office, past a shallow stream where he used to catch crawdads with his friends, past the Holiday supermarket. He searches for a cloud, but they've disappeared, and his good foot revs up the ache again.

The heat and the collective stares close in, and for the first time he notices how tightly his uniform hugs him. It's all too much to bear, and he decides to ditch this whole thing midwalk and flee through the supermarket's parking lot back home, but the band conductor says "Star-Spangled Banner" and the parade slows to a halt.

"Here we go. For God and country," the graybeard says.

"Hope they do the Hendrix version," someone whispers.

The seven come to attention and the crowd rises and quiets.

"One. Two. Three," says the conductor, counting the band in, and the players all take a breath together, ready to exhale into their instruments, and in that moment before sound someone shouts "Peace!"

The first few bars of the song roll over Wintric and he closes his eyes. He avoids the things that normally come to his mind during the anthem: army events, the flag, Washington, D.C., the Olympics, San Francisco Giants games. He feels the gun on his leg, thinks about its shape, how his hand fits around it just right, the clean silver finish, the gorgeous oily smell when he holds it close to his nose.

The crowd starts singing with a purpose when they hit "rockets' red glare," but Wintric is still lost in contemplation when his left foot zips him with pain. He shuts his eyes tighter and his insides turn. He wishes he had popped four pain pills instead of two and hears "flag was still there," but it's distant background noise now as he focuses on the pain, how his bright nerves throb with his pulse, how the electric pinging travels from his foot all the way up to his scalp — *this cut foot, this big toe digging, the living room cranberry stain, falling from McIntire's roof, the cramped plane ride to Reno, my discharge, Afghanistan, the knife lodged in my foot after the first strike, shitting blood, face-down in the dirt, the first push to my back, the smell of burning trash, a moment alone.*

Wintric sits in his car on a Saturday morning across Davy Crockett Drive from Nelson's yellow house with a .357 revolver in his lap. It's his third trip to Wyoming, and the light fog is beginning to burn away under the rising sun. Nelson's black Lab yaps at a crow that has perched on a new doghouse. His Tacoma has been replaced by a new Jeep Wrangler with *AFG* and *Wyoming Cowboys* window stickers. The squat homes on the street are lined up close, and Wintric searches the road to see if the dog's barking has anyone's attention, but there's nothing.

Wintric sips at his coffee and considers the fifth of whiskey in his glove box, but decides against a pour. His roofing kneepads rest on the passenger-side floor by Audioslave, the Tragically Hip, and Deftones CDs and a Burger King bag. The dog has exhausted herself, and the only noise is the idling car's engine and the AC on low. Wintric reaches down on his right side where his ass and hip meet and pushes and rubs at the soreness. In his head he repeats the slogan he's been repeating across the Great Basin – *It's easy if you want it.*

This time he thought he'd drive to the house and walk up to the door without hesitation, but he's been stuck in the car for fifteen minutes. A garbage truck drives by with no one on the back, and Wintric sips at his coffee and spills a couple drops on his Sacramento Kings T-shirt.

Nelson's front door appears freshly painted and clean against the fading yellow siding. For a moment Wintric thinks he sees the door move, but nothing happens. *Easy if you want it.*

Wintric's phone vibrates and he peeks at the number – Kristen.

Two years ago Kristen placed her *People* magazine down on her bedroom nightstand and asked him if he was having an affair. Does he love her? Does he like anything in his life? Is he going to leave her? Her hair was down, and he saw the despair in her face. Her yearning broke him, and he described the assault out loud for the first time. He expected tears, but the story arrived emotionless, straight: the dark night, the helplessness, not knowing who it was, the whispered "Nelson," the silence out of fear and pride, living with it all. At the end he heard himself repeating the lie he keeps safe: "And then I step on the fucking knife." It's her face that he sees now: mouth slightly open, eyes narrowed, one large crease that he had never seen before stretching across her forehead. It's her words that he hears: "Just tell me what you want. What do you want to happen?"

Wintric answers the phone.

"Baby? Where you at?" Kristen asks.

"Here," he says.

"I'll go."

"No. Talk to me. Just for a second."

"Dammit, Wintric. Get out of the car and do it. Right now. Keep me on. Walk up to the front door. If you wait, it's over."

"Yes."

"Do something. Please."

"Yes."

"Got your gun?"

"No."

"Good. Get out right now. Open the door. I love you."

"Okay."

"Go now."

"Talk later."

Wintric glances in the rearview mirror, runs his hands down his cheeks, exhales three times, slips the gun into his waistband, opens the driver's door, stands up, and closes the door. A motorcycle rounds the corner, and he lets it pass. He leads with his bad foot and crosses the road. When he hits the first step of the home he pauses, and the dog trots over to him. No bark. Four more stairs and Wintric stands in front of the door, and through the chaos he notices that the door isn't freshly painted; it's unlike any door he's seen, plasticky and shiny. He searches for a doorbell, but there isn't one. He cocks his arm back to knock but pauses for a few seconds, waiting, listening. The smell of dog shit wafts over him. He moves his body and his knuckles strike the soft surface and he hears the weak sound of his fist knocking on the flimsy door. Wintric steps back from the door and moves his hands behind his back and sticks his chest out. The dog yaps, but Wintric refuses to turn. Ten seconds. Twenty. He steps forward and accidentally kicks the threshold with his right foot before knocking again. He steps back, and the dog is at his side. He swats at the Lab, but the dog jumps back, then forward again. Ten seconds. Twenty. No answer. Nelson's absence isn't something he had considered, and he stands there on the landing in momentary paralysis.

Wintric turns around and surveys the neighbors' homes, but nothing moves. He runs his fingers through his hair. A Harley rumbles in the distance and the black Lab walks to his side, nuzzles.

"Get," he says, his voice cracking. "Get, fucker."

Wintric places his open hand on the door. He pushes and the door flexes. A whimper from the dog, and he feels the gun in his waistband.

"Get."

The sound of his voice turns something in him, and he rolls his hands over and sees the sweat. He steps forward once more and knocks on the door, the sound this time three strong strikes, the noise coming to him as rapture. From somewhere behind his jaw Wintric finds emotion near, and he tries to calm by breathing through his nose, but his chin begins to move from side to side, and he realizes he has seconds. He pushes the dog aside, walks to his car, and gets in. He starts the car and punches it down the street, through another neighborhood, past two churches, out to the highway, where he rides the bumper of a gray Buick. His sobs come with guttural moans, and he uses his forearm to wipe at his face. He drives over the Green River and pulls into the back of a McDonald's parking lot and turns off the car. He lifts his shirt over his head, bunches it up, and presses it hard to his face, over his nose and mouth. He screams into the cotton and lowers the shirt and sees his eyes in the rearview mirror and it's him, alive, in Green River, Wyoming. Behind him the drive-through line in the mirror inches forward. He watches the vehicles stop and go, stop and go. Wintric grabs the gun from his pants, empties the bullets, and slides the gun into the center console, bullets into the glove box. He looks at his gas gauge, although he knows the tank is nearly full. He rolls down the driver's-side window and listens to the people ordering and the metallic voice reading their orders back.

Although he's attempted the emotional exorcism before, Wintric tries again; he decides he isn't looking for Derek Nelson. He reinvents the past twenty minutes. He closes his eyes, calls up the vision, comfort, the story he'll tell Kristen. *I met Nelson. He was there at the door. I saw him and I asked him and he looked at me like I was crazy and he invited me in, but no, just passing through, Go Army, Go Army, best of luck, brother.* It's not sticking. *Go Army. Brother.* The vision isn't sticking. *Nelson at the door.* He's not there. Wintric can't see it. He sees the door, only the door. *The white door. Fist knocking. The door. No doorbell.*

"Come home," Kristen says. "We're here."

"Don't put him on. I can't handle it right now," Wintric says.

"Come home." Aside, in a whisper, "To Daddy, honey."

"Don't put him on."

"Where are you?"

"Through Elko."

"We miss you. Things are going to be better now. You know that. You faced him."

"Yeah."

"You never have to tell me what he said. It's for you."

Midday and fighting sleep thirty miles outside of Winnemucca, Wintric single-lane drives behind a diesel doing forty-five on an eight-mile stretch of construction in the middle of nowhere I-80. The diesel has a pair of old mud flaps with a busty, long-haired, reclining woman relaxing in chrome. Every now and then the sun strikes it right and she throws a bright flash. Desert hot, and the AC pushes out cool air and the car's temperature gauge flirts with the yellow zone. A Circus Circus Casino billboard arrives and races by to his right, followed by a billboard for reverse vasectomies. Wintric takes in the miles and miles of beige rock intersected by a slit of blacktop.

Already halfway through Nevada, he fights himself about his decision to leave Green River, not to wait it out. This mental manipulation along this same strip of land is nothing new. He's called Torres on the way home after each of his failed attempts and lied about where he was and his reason for phoning, and each time Torres has listened to the made-up stories and offered advice that Wintric can't use. Even so, Torres's soothing voice has helped get him home. Wintric looks at his cell phone, at the default blue background, but there's no service.

Coming into Imlay he spots a bizarre, bony structure south of the interstate that he's never noticed. He pulls off into the almost ghost town to stretch in the post office parking lot. He's never stopped here; normally he presses on to Fernley or Reno. A new American flag flies over the double-wide tan building. His sweaty shirt smells like his chicken sandwich lunch, and the early afternoon sun hits hard. He wipes at his eyes, then pops four pills and gulps a swig of warm water. A woman and her daughter exit the post office and squint. Wintric walks over to the building, to a map of the local area. He runs his finger to the *X* that marks the spot where he stands. Surprised, he studies what appears to be a large lake nearby. Rye Patch Reservoir. He scans the distance, but all he sees is desert scrub, fences, and the hazy outline of cracking mountains. He thinks, *Water somewhere.*

Later, he stands on a rocky peninsula and the blue water appears to be a misplaced fantasy, a geological mistake. No trees with all this water. Far west, two small boats. Overhead, blue sky and crisscrossing contrails. A darting white bird descends to the water and lands near him. A subtle crosswind blows across the great, shallow bowl of land.

The cool water offers some reprieve from the hot day and Wintric lowers himself to the shore. He presses his middle fingers to his temples, then inhales and holds the air until his body forces him to take another breath. He inhales and holds the air again, feeling his neck and eyes pressurize before his forced exhalation.

A gust of wind races across Wintric's face, and he digs up a white rock that catches his eye and tosses it out near the bird. He yawns and follows the bird's ascent into the air and his eyes stop on an unusual gray balloon in the far distance. The scene takes him a minute to process. Deep in the landscape, the large, slender balloon floats high in the air. He guesses that the ruler-shaped object is three or four stories tall, but gaining any perspective is impossible. Wintric watches it for a minute, peering for a tether or movement, but the balloon appears to float, motionless.

He reclines on a smooth spot of shore and brings his hands to his face. An orangey light filters through his joined fingers. Fanning his fingers open, he sees the balloon through the gap between his left hand pinkie and ring finger. Closed, orangey light. Open, balloon. Closed. Open. Closed.

Wintric wakes, dreamless. The wind brushes his face and something crawls across his hand. Above him a large black bird circles in the heat. He peers west, but the boats are gone. In the distance the gray balloon hovers. He stands and brushes himself off. He finds and crushes two ants crawling up his forearm.

In the car, he turns the key in the ignition and the engine turns over. His foot on the brake, he shifts the car into drive, feels the slight lurch, and glances at the horizon, the balloon. *Three miles away? Ten?* He shifts the car back to park and reaches for his gun, grabs it and some ammunition, and gets out.

Back at the shoreline, Wintric digs his big toe inside his boot and he thumbs the hammer back, then raises the revolver. *Hundred to one? A thousand?* He keeps both eyes open and places the balloon in the sights, then raises the gun higher and aims there. Blue sky in the sights, and he visualizes the bullet's trajectory all the way to the balloon, the gigantic drop of the bullet over the miles. A gentle exhalation and trigger pull. The blast sound echoes out and he lowers the revolver. He studies the remaining bullets' brass backings. He raises the revolver and smells the gunpowder in the air. A trigger-pull blast sound. Another. Then quiet, except for the ringing in his ears, sirens circling his head. He stands listening to the sirens circle and circle and circle before slowly leaving him. He stands staring at the balloon, stands for minutes, searching for movement, but the balloon floats in the air, miles away.

In Lovelock, Wintric stops at a convenience store and buys a Coke, a bag of jerky, a package of Lightning McQueen stickers, a postcard with a picture of the Pershing County Courthouse, and a stamp. In the parking lot he finds a pen in his glove box among the unused bullets and owner's manual. He addresses the card to Nelson without a return address. He writes, "I was there," then scribbles over it. He thinks for a minute, then writes "AFG" and "my revenge." Below that, "your house" and "no doorbell." He stops and looks up and wonders if that's enough. *If it's him, will he know? If it's not, does it matter?* He places the card on his lap and picks up his phone. He wonders if he and Torres are in the same time zone. His phone has service, but he puts it back down in the cup holder.

Wintric looks at his postcard. He places the tip of the pen on the card to write his full name, but in the time that it takes him to begin the first letter he decides to write just "Wintric." He sees the pen's tip on the white surface. He starts the *W,* but stops at a *V.* He lifts the pen and holds it in the air.

Thirteen Steps

LATER FAHRAN'S FATHER will meet Fahran at the door with a scratch lottery ticket worth five hundred dollars. He'll thank the stars and embrace his boy before he notices Fahran's defeated face and slumped body and hears that his son has watched a man die. But right now Fahran is a skinny thirteen-year-old at the packed Farmington, New Mexico, community swimming pool on July 3, 2013. The day is sunny, and it's the part of the hour when everyone has to take a five-minute break. Whistles blow, and two lifeguards jump in the water from their elevated chairs, relief spilling over their faces when they crest the surface and slick back their hair.

Fahran's diabetic mother wears her dry red swimsuit with her insulin pump hanging off her left hip. She reclines in her green-and-yellow plastic folding lounge chair near the three-foot end, sunning herself. Fahran has been swimming for an hour. He rests on the slatted wood bench near the shaded fence within reach of his mother, his fingers feeling at his waterlogged palms. She works at the hardware store, and Fahran figures she's about as happy as she can be on one of her few days off, gently falling asleep amid the laughter, chlorine smell, and frequent shouts to walk, not run. She rarely accompanies him the four blocks to the pool, but earlier in the day she appeared in the hallway with her long towel and cheap sunglasses. She wrapped her gray insulin pump in a plastic bag but still reminds him that she has to keep it dry.

Now, she rests her head on her forearm, the straps on her bathing suit crisscrossing her brown back, which is scattered with tiny moles. Fahran sees the same skin on his belly, and already a few moles of his own. One, just south of his belly button, bothers him enough that he's tried to pinch it off with nail clippers, but it bled all over. He peels back his shorts and glimpses the lighter brown skin beneath them. It's enough of a contrast to the bronzed upper and lower halves of his exposed body that his mother calls him Oreo, but only at home. Fahran takes in his midsection and he checks on the gangly dark hairs that protrude around his genitals and up toward his belly button. He's proud he won't be the last one to show.

Fahran is mostly scared of his body. He has started to wake up with damp circles on his shorts and the bed sheets. His dad has told him about wet dreams; in fact he's pretty open about all the sex stuff. It's just that Fahran doesn't know the right questions to ask when his father says, "Ask anything."

All around the edge of the pool kids begin to line up for the lifeguards, who climb up their perches. One lifeguard, Kylie, a thin brunette with brown eyes, places the whistle in her lips and blows. A dozen kids leave the ground simultaneously. Her one-piece suit dips just low enough, presses just close enough to her breasts, for Fahran to fantasize about the lower, covered two thirds. She's a couple years older and sits with her knees a few inches apart. Normally Fahran would be one of the first back in the water, but he's decided to let all his sliding droplets dry on the bench while his body calms down. He leans forward, placing his elbows on his knees. His mother shifts to rest on her back.

Fahran swats at a yellow jacket that sniffs around his feet and ankles. To his left a large man talks through the fence to a woman. They smile and their fingers meet through the Cyclone diamonds. Fahran attempts to hear what they say over the collective splashing. The man appears to be his dad's age, but this guy's belly hangs over the top part of his swimming trunks, and little dots of scarred skin speckle his forearms. On his back a peculiar snakelike tattoo winds up his spinal column. The woman has dyed pink into her blond hair and wears a sleeveless purple dress like the ones he's seen on women in the bank. They stand close to each other and kiss. Fahran tilts his head so he can spy on their joined faces. They press their bodies against the fence, and after a few seconds Fahran glances around to see if anyone else notices, but no one looks their way, so he turns back to see.

The woman goes up on her toes, and still they kiss, all through one narrow gap. Finally they pull away, just their faces, and stare at each other. The woman says, "I'll pick Emma up at four," and turns away. The man shakes the fence before spinning around, his eyes catching Fahran's on their swing toward the water. He strides six steps, past Fahran and his sunbathing mother, before launching his body into the air.

Fahran's world stops. He doesn't know what awaits, but something is already off: the angle the man's legs form with his diving torso, the listing ash trees in the background, the wind, the smell of urine and sunscreen—everything mysteriously shifts and blurs. The water absorbs the man's body up to his waist, but a halting, spastic jolt snaps his lower legs, calves, and feet concave. The tension squeezes Fahran's face, and he waits for ten seconds for the man to emerge, until a woman in jeans and a white button-up shirt across the pool leaps into the water. In the hazy moments that follow, kids jump off the diving board and more carefree laughs enter the air. The dressed woman struggles through the three feet of water, and her labored stride grinds to slow motion.

In an eerie crescendo the screams arrive as a red blood-cloud blossoms out into the blue water. Fahran stands at the edge, gazing down into the gathering maroon. Help is still ten feet away, pulsing out waves in her mad, sluggish dash. One of the waves spreads the flowing blood enough for him to see the man's submerged back. Fahran's mother kneels beside him, leaning over the edge, her arms elbow-deep in the murk.

Whistles join the shrieking, and the lifeguards scramble. The clothed woman arrives and lifts the huge man up in a heap of water and blood and skin.

Fahran's mother grabs his shoulder and spins him around, pushes him to the bench, but before he sits, he turns and sees the woman in the purple dress. She stands motionless in the middle of the sidewalk, then turns back toward the pool as if someone called her name, eyebrows up, curious. Her tangible happiness careens into alarm the moment her eyes focus. She stares right at Fahran, and yet somehow she knows everything. She pivots in her high heels, and her right arm flies up like a dagger into the air, starting her sprint. Her eyes and mouth open wide, and she covers the distance quickly, crashing into the fence, bellowing vowel sounds.

The lifeguards reach them and one boy bends down to start CPR, but when he takes the man's chin in his hands the neck moves like jelly, and the lifeguard lets go. Kylie says, "Listen for breathing," but the other lifeguard just kneels, eyeing his own hands. Fahran stands across the rattling fence from the woman, and for a minute no one touches the man. An amazed space settles around his body, a force field of nerves and fear and oddity. Already the body has lost its vitality, is now wet, unmoving muscle. Kylie bends down and edges her ear to the man's mouth. She shakes her head, then clasps her hands, places them on the man's chest, and pumps up and down.

Soon the paramedics arrive and take over and Kylie steps back. Someone asks, "Dead? He's dead?"

As the paramedics press on the man, Fahran tries to understand how this body could be the same mass that dominated the afternoon five minutes ago. Later, when he reflects back on his life, he'll understand that this was the moment when he began to believe in souls.

Eventually the paramedics slow the compressions. A stretcher arrives and more sirens fill the air. One of the EMTs turns his attention to clearing the area, save for the witnesses. Fahran's mom tries to get Fahran out of there, but the manager says they need to stay to be interviewed.

The EMTs let the hysterical woman in the purple dress ride with the body to the hospital, and as they load the stretchered man into the ambulance Fahran notices that no one pumps on the man's chest. The pool complex empties except for Fahran, his mom, the woman who jumped in the pool, and the lifeguards.

Everyone is quiet, waiting for the cops to show. The woman who jumped in the pool leans against the fence. They've given her a pair of oversized trunks and a Farmington High Scorpions T-shirt too large for her. She stands with her arms crossed, staring at the sparse hill and plateaus west of town. Her wet clothes hang over two chairs. Fahran's mother approaches the woman, but she says,

"Please, no," and moves away from the rest of the group, to the other side of the pool.

The lifeguards gather near the entrance, and Kylie holds one of the boys in her arms. He touches his own face. They're the same age, but she cradles his head against her chest and runs her fingers through his dark hair. She talks to him, and while Fahran can't hear Kylie's words, he imagines she's saying, "It's okay. I'm here. I'm here." She might be singing to him, even, but whatever nurturing it is, Fahran hates the boy, hates his weakness, hates that he himself is not the one.

Fahran doesn't want his mother to hug him or comfort him in front of Kylie, and she abstains, but her complete passivity surprises Fahran. When the cops show up, they speak with everyone else first. The woman who jumped into the pool exits under the late-afternoon sun, dazed, her drying clothes over her left shoulder. The lifeguards stroll out one at a time. Kylie, now wearing a towel, keeps her head down.

A short, plump cop talks to his mother, then walks over and takes a seat by Fahran.

"Okay, buddy," he says. "This is important. Did someone push the man?"

"No," he says. "He jumped."

"Thanks," he says, and starts to rise.

"Ask him another," his mother says. "Please."

Fahran is embarrassed; he understands his standing in the world, but the cop sits back down with a grunt. He has nothing to ask, he knows the drill, has all the answers he needs, so he sizes up the sky for a few seconds, searching.

"Um," he says, "how far away from the fence do you think the woman was when the accident took place?"

The question surprises Fahran. He isn't ready. He thinks

about the man's dive, the neck angle, the bag of limp limbs thrown on the no-diving picture.

"How far?" he repeats. He glances at his mother, who nods her head. "In feet?"

"Whatever, son."

Fahran has no idea what the answer is, but he wants to say something.

"Thirteen," he says, "steps. He had a snake tattoo." The cop jots it down and leaves without a word.

On the walk home, Fahran's mother, usually prone to lectures, hums a song Fahran doesn't know. The day is still hot, and they pass through the shadows of the overhanging trees. Fahran's tired mind negotiates the thousands of images still spiraling through him. When they near their home his mother stops short and says, "Ice cream."

When they reach the porch the door flies open, and Fahran's father, before taking them in, wraps his arms around them and thanks the stars for the five hundred dollars he won by scratching the correct four hearts on Hearts Are Wild!

Fahran and his father are off for ice cream in his father's car. His mother couldn't take any more of the day and drew herself a bath, put on some Norah Jones, and told them to go celebrate.

Eight at night, the cooling air, and from the car's radio news of Egypt's coup and a U.S. drone attack in Pakistan before Fahran's father taps the radio off. Although he appreciates what his son has experienced, he's feverish about the five hundred, how he can get new tires on the truck, take Fahran to K-Mart for new clothes, maybe even install a basketball hoop over the garage. They'll have to wait until after the Fourth, after the parade over in Aztec and the night's fireworks, but that's okay, his father says, on the fifth they'll go and spend it all. Fahran doesn't dare interrupt him. He's never seen his father this happy.

They drive down Butler Avenue over to East Main and Fahran rolls his window down. They pass a Wendy's and a McDonald's, and the dry night wind blows through Fahran's hair and over his right forearm. The city lights appear new and clean, and Fahran's father is now up to a new television with a remote control, a leather couch, a motorcycle.

Fahran waits anxiously, eager to switch the conversation. He wants to get to the point where his father says, "Ask anything," because he's ready now. He imagines himself in Kylie's arms in a dark place, alone, and her voice, "I'm here. I'm here," the smell of chlorine on her summer body, and he wants to know what he must do to get there, to that place where you finally get what you want.

14

Two Things from a Burning House

SIXTEEN-YEAR-OLD MIA IS hung-over from her older sister's going-away party the night before, so she pops her birth control pill with two aspirins and pours herself Lucky Charms and stares out the square kitchen window at the first swells of the Rocky Mountains. Late July, the time of year when the Torres house needs the air conditioning it lacks, but the high-country mornings are cool enough for her sweatpants and a faded orange Broncos shirt. Her parents sleep in the back bedroom, and Mia figures her sister is screwing her boyfriend, Elliot, one last time before saying goodbye. Unsure of what time the army recruiter is due at their house, Mia figures she has a couple hours before she waves Camila off to basic training.

Mia understands why Camila would enlist. Their father served for a number of years and used the G.I. Bill to obtain a college degree and a job as a motivational speaker. Maybe it's the perfect time to join — hit the end of the downturn of America's Middle East adventure and slide into a pocket of peace for twenty years and train your way to medals and rank and a nice rancher outside Castle Rock. Mia's father smiled when Camila strolled home with the "I enlisted" news, patting her on the back with "It's your call, honey."

Mia sits on a worn barstool and spoons her cereal up to her mouth as her mind works, weaving together the previous night's party. She expects to field questions, and most likely consequences. Her parents hit the tequila hard, and Mia perked up when her mother handed her a Bud Light. It's not Mia's favorite, but the cold drink felt good in the party heat of their basement. Five beers later she let a boy with black fingernails fondle her breasts in a downstairs closet next to a broken-down pinball machine. When she opened her eyes at the sound of the closet door, her sweating mother appeared, already in midpunch. Her mother had finished the bottle of Cuervo and missed the ducking boy, hitting a wall stud instead. Within seconds her fist began to swell. In the morning silence Mia considers the irony of her mother swinging at the preservation of a virginity that had been lost two years before on a school trip to Yellowstone.

Camila is halfway down the hall when Mia spots her and shoots a nod, but Camila refuses a return glance and glides past Mia and slips into their mother's blue Colorado Avalanche jacket.

"Big day," Mia says. "Could all be downhill from here."

Camila opens the door and walks out into the clear morning.

Mia rinses her bowl and hears the floor creak. She prays it's her father. He'll laugh last night off, but her mother is a different monster, alternately dishing out cruelty to try to save her daughters from themselves and ignoring both of them altogether, as if she's given up hope. Mia isn't ready to talk about the boy in the closet – his name is Raul – and if the encounter goes the day without being addressed, it might never be, but when she turns to the sound, her mother approaches with the stern face Mia knows bodes a lecture.

"You don't know where your sister is," she says, blowing a toothpaste-Tequila exhalation.

"She went outside."

"You don't know where she is."

"You're asking me?" Mia says, confused. Her mother leans in.

"I'm not asking. You don't know where she is. No matter who comes calling. You don't know."

"Okay. I don't know where she is. Fine. She's lost."

Mia turns away, but her face tilts back toward her mother.

"Is this about the recruiter?" she asks.

Her mother hasn't hit her in years, but Mia thinks she might. Her neck veins throb and she grabs Mia's shoulder, hard at first, but she eases the grip. Her mouth draws tight. She has seized Mia with the injured hand.

"Your sister is an adult," she says, flexing her fingers in and out. "She makes her own moves." A breath. "And this is the most important part. She's not a whore."

In the future, during rounds of drunken remembrance, Mia will recall this moment and practice strongly worded, clever retorts, but in real time the air leaves her body and she steps back. Her mother stands, morning sober, in front of her. Her eyes lack their usual redness, her body having given up the fight against the hard stuff.

"Is this when we talk about Yellowstone?" Her father's voice. Camila was the only person Mia told, so her father's words float in the room a bit before Mia sucks them in. The air thickens around her mouth and nose, and her feet disappear beneath her.

"Yellowstone," he says, wheeling into the room. "Bears and moose and boys." He grins. He bleeds through torn touches of Kleenex along his jawline. His hands grip the gray wheelchair wheels.

"I told him the night Camila told me," her mother says, placing her hand on her husband's shoulder. "You should know that. It's what parents do. He didn't believe it until last night, when I caught you jacking off that freak in the closet."

The room slants and Mia visualizes the shotgun in her parents' closet, but she blanks on the case combination. She flashes to the neighborhood park where she told Camila – they were swinging in winter, and Camila playfully placed her ear on Mia's belly; to her first period, reaching down into her pants in a Safeway bathroom.

"Have you screwed boys in my home?" her mother asks.

Mia has, twice. She stares at the beige tile floor and thinks about Camila and Elliot, the dozens of sexual sessions they've had in this very house, on Camila's pink comforter under the boy-band posters, and then she wonders why she cares if her parents know – she has no moral pretense, no angel reputation, no great grades or letters of recommendation headed her way. Losing her virginity at fourteen doesn't seem that unusual to her. She knows girls eleven and twelve years old who let the word get out. Mia senses her body folding in on itself, and she angers because she cares what her parents think, and because she still can't think of the gun-safe combination or anything to say. Again the mental image, the surprise of brownish blood on her fingertips, of the Safeway around the corner, the area next to the checkout where her mother sniffed at a green bottle of Brut aftershave and Mia stepped out of the restroom and ran to her mother to tell her the news, and her mother, near tears, taking Mia in her arms, repeating, "My girl, my big girl," before they walked together to the maxi pads and Mia pointed to the ones she'd seen commercials for. *Was that the last time she was proud of me?*

Then, back to the kitchen, to her parents, to the morning hangover. Mia has forgotten the question, but she hears herself say, "My body was ready."

Her father's mouth opens, and Mia senses a surge of excitement when nothing comes out. "My body was ready," she says a little louder. Silence. Neither her mother nor her father appears ready to argue. Her father touches one of the tiny circles of bloodied Kleenex on his chin, then folds his arms.

"Damn," he says, and turns away; surprisingly, so does her mother. They move down the hallway and her mother stops and looks back, but not at Mia. She scans the living room and then locks her eyes on the oak front door, as if it's been moved slightly and she wants to remember its location when she comes back.

Mia is unsure how old her mother was when she lost her virginity, and she realizes that they've never had the sex talk, or really any talk of substance for some time. Mia thinks, *When I have a child, she'll know everything,* and much later Mia will tell her daughter everything, she will talk to her about sex and blood and regret, she will drive her daughter to the clinic for her abortion and stroke her hair while the drugs wear off. But today Mia tugs her sweatpants down below her hip bones and her mother shakes her head, kisses her fingers, and touches Mia's third-grade photo hanging in the hallway.

Mia moves her hands in a ray of dusty sunlight that beams through the crack in the living room drapes. She visualizes taking her blue baseball bat to Camila's healthy knees. *That traitor bitch.* She envisions Camila's lifelong limp and grins, but the dream evaporates as her parents move down the hallway with luggage.

"We're going to Estes Park," her mother says. "Don't

call. You're a big shot. You and your sister can do what the hell you want." She disappears into the garage.

Before her father leaves he grabs a bottle of Johnnie Walker and tucks it into his duffel bag. Rashlike bumps of dried blood dot his jaw.

"Yellowstone?" he says. Then, in a drawn-out, mocking falsetto, "My body is ready." He shakes his head. "Good luck with that," and out he wheels.

The maroon sedan backs out of the garage, and for a few seconds Mia sees her mother laugh and her father's mouth move, and she wonders if he retells his parting words to her. After they disappear Mia slides her vision over to their neighbors' house: the Burtons' red-brick home, the aspen, hedge, and prairie grass landscaping, a Toyota truck in the driveway with an *I'm proud of my Eagle Scout* bumper sticker. She guesses this is Camila's hideout. Not one to question, or even consider, the morality of adult-level commitment, Mia wonders if everyone has gone crazy. *How is she able to walk just feet away from her army obligation, and no one blinks an eye? Not our army dad, not our freaking Eagle Scout neighbors?* She places Camila in the Burtons' basement, probably already comfortable and confident, and nosy Mrs. Burton eyeing the roadway, ready to prevent the big bad military from taking their innocent neighbor. Never mind that Camila signed up herself. And then the answer comes to her. Mia brushes away the bat-to-the-knee revenge and frames a new, more enticing proposition. She turns the television on and gets comfortable, with an eye on the driveway. Screw her mother; she knows exactly where Camila is, and when the time is right, so will the recruiter.

Four reruns of *The Vampire Diaries* and a full fruit juicer infomercial later, the green-and-white army Ford Taurus pulls up to the front of their home. Before the uniformed man can leave the vehicle, Mia stands in her front yard, grinning. The recruiter is younger and shorter than she imagined, with a narrow face and a limp.

"Camila's next door," she says when he reaches their driveway.

"Okay."

"She's hiding, but she's over there. It's the Burtons' place."

Mia steps toward their neighbors', but the man doesn't follow.

"Your folks here?"

"No."

The recruiter removes his hat and clicks his tongue. He has picked up all types. He scratches his neck.

"Why don't you go get Camila so we can talk?" he says, lowering his voice a half octave. "I'll wait here."

"She won't come if it's me. That's the point." Mia overhears her own eagerness and tries to dial it back. Unknowingly, she plays with the drawstrings of her sweats. "Besides, doesn't she have to go?"

"You want her to go?"

She knows the answer, but she waits for the right words. Before she can comment he asks, "How old are you?"

His eyes dart to her torso.

"I'm in high school. How old are you?"

"Okay."

He gazes up at the sky and taps his foot. "Listen. I'm happy to talk to your sister, but I'm here for pickup, not deliberation. If you want to get her, great. If not, she can give me a call, but there are consequences." He hands Mia a card. "I have other stops today." When Mia stays in place, he nods his head, limps around to the driver's side, gets in, and drives off.

• • •

When Mia wakes, she rubs at her sweaty neck and pulls herself up from the leather couch. As she comes to she recalls her morning anger, and the fury rises in her again – a complicated rush of anxiety and the impulse for revenge.

Raul arrives at her house ten minutes after she calls him. She can hear the old Ford truck from around the corner, and when he pulls into her driveway she notices the purple driver's-side fender on an otherwise faded red truck. He wears a bright orange hunting vest over a black shirt, and cargo shorts.

"Get me out of here for a while," she says.

"I know where there's water."

She remains quiet until they hit Sedalia and turn west onto Jarre Canyon Road, and when the road turns up into the Rockies her shoulders relax. Their dalliance last night was not their first, but their relationship, if it can be called that, is one of lazy convenience. She imagines that he thinks of her seldom but fondly. That's how she thinks of him.

Mia leaves out the parent-virginity surprise but rattles on about her sister and the army, how Camila betrayed her – she leaves it unspecified – and wonders out loud what she can do for revenge. Raul speaks with calm, and this fits Mia's picture of him: soft-spoken, a funky dresser, with a confidence and an intelligence that enable him to stay at the top of their class despite his frequent unexplained absences. As he drives his eyes dart to his rearview mirror, then to the side mirrors and back to the road, a routine he performs every thirty seconds or so.

"She should go into the navy. Boats are cool, and no one ever shoots at them," he says in a southern drawl that still surprises Mia. For all she knows, he was born and raised in Colorado. He glances at her and notes her disappointment.

"You could lock her out. Your parents are gone."

"Lock her out? She'd be upset for two seconds, then go back to the Burtons'."

"It's something."

"Yeah."

"You could run away."

"Not much of a revenge move. My folks might like it. They've said as much."

"No parents want that."

"You're wrong. Parents don't have to beat the shit out of you to show they don't love you."

"True."

"Sometimes they just do nothing."

"But yours get pissed at you. That's supposed to mean something. It might not be as bad –" He stops his sentence and, without transition, says, "House is on fire. You can grab two things. Go."

"Besides people?"

"So you still love them."

"Don't screw with me."

"Fine. What would you take? Everyone gets out okay."

The silence lingers so long that Raul asks, "Don't like fire? Okay. A flood."

Both quiet, they drive south along Highway 67, and the South Platte River joins them. Fly-fishermen in waders whip their lines out and back. Raul cracks his window and the rushing air smells fresh and warm. They pass through Deckers and keep south toward Pikes Peak, and a few miles farther Raul guides the truck over to a meager turnout and turns off the engine.

"Water," he says, and points at a humble stream down an embankment. The stream is maybe six feet across and shallow. "Let's go."

Raul grabs a backpack and a dusty wool blanket and

leads Mia down the gentle slope. They pause on the bank of the stream, and Raul excuses himself and comes back with a boulder that he throws in the middle of the water.

"Step."

They both cross, and Raul unfurls the blanket on a level patch of ground partially obscured from the road by a stand of flowering reeds. He reaches into the backpack and pulls out a flask and tosses it to her. She unscrews the top and tilts it back and shakes her head.

"Water?" she says, not all that disappointed.

"I have to drive back."

Raul pats the blanket beside him. A puff of dust rises.

"I don't feel like sitting," Mia says, and while she recognizes his intentions, she waits and basks in the high-altitude sun. She stands next to the creek and watches the clear water and smells the pine. She picks up a smooth rock and tosses it into the stream, and the tiny but explosive splash makes her laugh. Raul throws one. He sheds his hunting vest and his black shirt, then puts the vest back on.

"You look ridiculous," Mia says.

"I do it for attention. It works."

"Yeah."

"What do you do for attention?"

"I make out with guys in closets. Then I have my mom come in and beat the shit out of them. It's a fun routine we've perfected."

They gather large rocks and throw them in, and before long their efforts focus on building a dam across the stream. The lazy project takes fifteen minutes, and near completion, they decide to leave a space where the water runs unimpeded.

"You've never asked me about my name," he says as they sit on the blanket. Mia crosses her legs and touches his arm.

"What about it?"

"It means 'wolf counsel.'" He growls, claws his left hand, and laughs.

"Who told you that?"

"My parents."

Mia edges closer and places her hand on his.

"Are you trying to be funny?" she asks.

"Yes."

"You tell the truth too much."

Raul reaches for her, and she leans over and kisses him. She feels warm and electric and reaches down to the bottom of her shirt and teasingly lifts it up, then back down. She loves the look in his eyes, mistaking his desire – and her past boyfriends' – for something ineffable and singular in her. Their collective eyes and eager hands convince her that she will never be alone.

While she reaches for the back of Raul's neck, Mia picks up something in her peripheral vision, a misshapen brown blur through the trees. She stands and brings her index finger to her lips.

"Shhh," she says, and it comes into focus: a bear, far enough away to excite but close enough to unnerve. "Bear," and she points.

They gather their things as quietly as possible, tiptoe across their dam, and jump into the Ford. Their anxiety lessens the longer they watch the bear from the cab. They follow the brownish bear as it meanders downstream and disappears.

On the drive back to Castle Rock, dusk settles in and Raul puts on Barbra Streisand. He glances over at Mia, then back to the road. She thinks of saying something but stops herself, because she knows he wants her to comment on the music. Dusk is Mia's favorite time of day; there is some-

thing soothing about the diminishing visuals. She wonders
if she will sleep with Raul tonight, if he expects her to.

She watches the darkening road, the double yellow
lines curving in parallel, hears the hum of the mud tires,
and her mind drifts to her sister walking out of the house
that morning, wordless; to her parents – Estes Park, gulping
whiskey and wine; to Yellowstone; to the afternoon bear
meandering downstream, morphing into two bears. She's
fourteen on a chartered bus in Yellowstone, in a traffic jam
in northwestern Wyoming, and her science teacher points
at the top of a hill, where two bears feed on a felled bison,
and from her bus seat Mia sees the bears, then a flanneled,
bearded man with a camera who starts up the hill toward
the feeding, and already she senses something is wrong,
and her science teacher halts the lecture and yells out the
window to the advancing man "Stop!" but the man continues up the hill, so close to the wild that from her vantage
point it seems as if he could touch the bears with his hands,
and the man stands among the feeding animals and snaps
photos, then turns around, walks down the hill, and high-
fives his friends before giving the school bus two thumbs
up. This, Mia understands – even at fourteen – is exactly
the wrong lesson for a bus full of freshmen to learn. Later,
on the way back to Colorado, the bus stops unexpectedly
in Cheyenne during a manic snowstorm, and after a gripping internal debate she lets Marshall Knicks into her hotel room, and how thrilled and breathless and confused she
was when most everything hurt. Then, a week later, swinging back and forth in her snowy neighborhood park, with
Camila listening intently to her sex story and nodding along
because she understood – how Mia never thought she had
to say, "Don't tell anyone."

They drive into her dark neighborhood, then down her

street. Mia sizes up the Burton home, the house lit perfectly so night passersby can appreciate the trimmed hedges and clean brick. Mia's home is dark, and as they pull into the driveway she thinks she will invite him in, but she hears herself say, "Thanks, Wolfman. We'll catch up some other time."

She smiles.

"'Night," he says. "Just know you're breaking my heart."

"It's not your heart."

Alone, Mia turns on the kitchen light and sits on her worn barstool, second from the left. She checks her phone, but there are no messages. She's tired, and the house is a sauna. When she opens the fridge to cull some leftover mushroom pizza, she spots a sixer of Dogfish, her father's favorite, but she leaves the beer. She opens the living room windows, plops down, and catches the last half of *The Princess Bride*.

Surprised that she hasn't seen Camila, for a moment she doubts her judgment about the Burtons' being a sanctuary; maybe Camila is wandering the streets right now, lonely and scared, walking in the empty golf course down the road. Mia stares at the Burtons', at the light reflecting off the silver basement window wells. *She's there.* Mia closes her eyes and puts Camila in her parents' bedroom, betraying her, telling them about Yellowstone, the hotel in Cheyenne, and then she remembers Raul's suggestion. Not up for a big production, she simply walks to the front door and locks the deadbolt and handle, and does the same to the side and back doors. She closes the windows. A minor deterrence, perhaps, but Camila never has her keys on her.

Mia turns off her phone and turns off the lights. She guesses that Camila will wake her up with some knocking, then pounding, maybe some cursing, and then, sooner or later, she will leave, and they can go at it tomorrow. It may get ugly, and maybe it should.

Years later Mia will regret none of this. Not locking the doors and windows nor the vicious fistfight she'll win the following morning. She will not regret leaving home halfway through her senior year to live with soft-spoken Aunt Kathy in Aztec, New Mexico, or having a daughter at eighteen – she knew it would be a girl – or raising the child on her own, telling her daughter everything she promised herself she would. In fact, most days she will wish she had burned down the house that night, or at least threatened the fire. Her parents will continue to lose themselves in the bottles they move from the kitchen cabinets and scatter about the house – beneath their bed, in the bathroom vanity, the glove compartment, boxes of Christmas decorations, the outdoor grill. They will not call or write after Mia's daughter is born. After a year working checkout at the local CVS, Camila will skip the army and join the air force, hoping for desk job but receiving a wrench-turning gig on helicopters, and she will carry the cheek scar Mia gouges into her skin during the morning tussle after the lockout. Six months after the birth of her daughter, Mia will move, because her aunt's new boyfriend pushes Kathy around the house on paydays. When Mia sends an urgent letter, then dials a desperate midnight call from Shiprock asking for money for herself and her infant child, for rent, for clothes, for anything, Camila will say that she has none to give. Mia will plead, and Camila will ask if Mia is proud of her choices. Camila will ask if Mia has called their parents. Camila will ask if Mia has gone to a homeless shelter, and when Mia says no, Camila will say, "You're not desperate enough," and hang up.

• • •

Mia settles in Cortez, Colorado, working as a teller at First National Bank. The high-desert town plays host to a variety of tourists, mainly folks in the summer months who need a place to stay while exploring the ruins at Mesa Verde National Park or heading down for photos at Four Corners. In this rural and self-reliant community filled with ranchers and trucks and people planning on never moving again, Mia rents a narrow two-bedroom apartment, and after twelve years of upkeep, of weekly vacuuming and watching her daughter grow, the humble place now feels like her own. Most of her bank customers smile and gossip with her as she takes, and sometimes retrieves, their money. They call her "Me," and at thirty she still notices and appreciates the local men sizing her up as she counts out their cash one bill at a time on the blue counter. She has tried to date, though prospects are limited, but she has her eye on a stocky policeman named Kevin who skips the outside ATM and nervously lingers when making cash withdrawals from Mia's station.

Mia's daughter, Taylor, has the face of a young Camila and already has two inches on Mia. With her long, not-quite-under-control frame, Taylor navigates the seventh-grade hallways uneasily but challenges her teachers daily with a sunny curiosity that amazes Mia, who has not set or demanded superior performance. While Taylor brings home top grades, Mia rarely sees her study, but sometimes Mia returns home and discovers her at the tiny kitchen table, drawing, Journey softly playing from an old stereo. It is one of the few ancient CDs Mia owns, and surprisingly, Taylor has never asked her for music of her own, so Mia listens and notes how her favorites become Taylor's favorites. They share a favorite book (*Jacob Have I Loved*), the way they relax on the couch (lean back with one leg over the armrest), nervous tic (right earlobe pinch), how they want to be held (tightly, pinning their ears over the holder's heart). Theirs is an emotionally stout bond, and while their relationship is about caring and friendship and soccer games and piano lessons Mia barely affords, it's also about the occasional biting argument: the evening Mia learns that Taylor has cheated on multiple tests, the mustached ninth grader who leaves hickeys on her daughter's neck, and the incredible fragility of one-deep dependency.

Mia receives rare updates about her parents and sister from Aunt Kathy down in Aztec but makes no effort to contact them. Last she heard, her dad was trying a risky surgery on his back and Camila was stationed on an island off Japan, but that was some time ago, so it's with genuine astonishment that she returns home on a warm April afternoon and finds Taylor sitting in the apartment with Camila. For a full minute Mia has no words, just images: *Camila, alive, present, hair pulled back, odd, puffy cheeks, the scar, a blue T-shirt with* Independence *in white letters, jeans, on my couch, in my apartment, in Cortez, right now.* Mia looks over at Taylor, who touches her own cheek and gives a negative swivel of her head, which Mia doesn't know how to interpret.

"She looks like I did," Camila says with confident energy. She smiles, and her scar curls.

Mia debates saying "Get out," but she hears herself say, "Japan. How is Japan?" She wishes her voice were stronger.

"I don't live in Japan, Mia. In fact, I'm in the middle of a move."

"That's good."

Camila stands, and her comfort in the space already unnerves Mia.

"Should we hug?" Camila asks, but she keeps her arms at her sides. "Are you glad I'm here?"

"I don't know why you're here."

"Repentance, Mia. There's a lot to repent for."

Mia stands by the closed door. She tilts her head and folds her arms.

"I don't know what to say."

"How about introducing me to your daughter?"

"How long have you been here? How long have you been in my home?" To Taylor: "How long has she been here?"

"Aunt Camila's been here about twenty minutes."

"Aunt Camila?"

"That's my name, Mia."

"No. Your name is Camila."

"I'm here to ask for forgiveness."

"Give me a minute."

"Why don't you sit down?"

"You're telling me to sit in my own home?"

"I'm not telling, Mia."

"Stop saying my name."

Mia tries to compose herself. She sets her purse down on the wooden console and runs her right hand down her left arm. She asks Taylor to give them some time, and Taylor nods and heads for the door, but before she gets to the threshold Camila speaks.

"I want her to hear what I have to say."

Taylor pauses.

"Give us a minute," Mia says, and her daughter exits.

To Camila, shaking: "My God. I don't know why you're here. What do you need?" Pointing: "You don't come here and talk to me and my daughter like you control anything." Stepping forward: "You have something to say? Say it right now. You have ten minutes. I'm here. Go. And sit the hell down. Now. And when your time is up you will leave my home."

"That's fair."

"I make the rules."

Camila sits, and her confident aura dissolves into the sofa beneath her. She folds her hands in her lap and her chin quivers, and she cries. Mia commands herself to stay put, five feet from the sofa, standing, staring, in charge, but in her sister's contorted face Mia recognizes profound fear, and it's too much to take in so she moves to the kitchen for a paper towel. Mia inhales, tears off the towel, walks back, and hands Camila her makeshift Kleenex. While wiping clumsily at her face Camila pours out apologies in choppy fragments, first for telling their mom about Mia's Yellowstone encounter, then for the fistfight, then for the "You're not desperate enough" phone call, for not visiting, for not acting like an older sister, like an aunt, and she unloads her wreckage with startling acuity, recalls events years past, minor squabbles, meaningless slights, things Mia has forgotten or misremembered, and Camila sobs and trembles. Then: "I got a guy after me."

Mia dredges up her dire call to Camila from a dirty pay phone in Shiprock, how later that night she had to beg a female bartender with pink hair tending an empty room to let her and her daughter sleep on the sticky, carpeted stage. It disgusts her that Taylor and Camila were here alone. Mia looks around the room, at her modest, sane life, and finds the resolve to say, "Two minutes left."

A backfire or a firework or a gunshot sounds in the distance. Camila's eyes focus and her face changes in a way that alarms Mia. She thinks of the baseball bat she keeps by the refrigerator. A minute has passed, but Mia will not continue the countdown.

"I need help," Camila says. "Do you think I'd be here if I didn't need help?"

"I think it's time for you to go." Mia strides toward the kitchen. "Now."

"I need a thousand dollars or I'm dead."

"Why?" Mia takes another step toward the refrigerator. Her right foot touches linoleum.

"Does it matter?"

"Yes."

"Five hundred will do it. You gonna make me beg?"

A rustle on the porch, and the door opens. Taylor asks, "May I come in?"

"This is your home, honey. Camila was leaving."

Camila rises, shoulders down, but she lifts her chin.

"You like this, don't you? You like it that I finally need something. You're pathetic. And I know in your mind you think we're even. I didn't help you, you don't help me. Genius."

Mia crosses the room to Camila's side. She has yet to touch her, but she considers placing her hand on Camila's back, pushing her just enough so she takes her first step away, and then Mia notices a little stream of blood coming from Camila's right nostril. She clears it with a sniff. Taylor sneaks past them.

"She looks like I did," Camila says. "It's true."

"I'm going to give you forty dollars. It's for a bus ticket. Go anywhere. Don't come back."

Mia reaches into her purse, removes four crisp ten-dollar bills, hands them to Camila, and opens the door. There is enough light in the day to see the new growth on the ash trees across the street.

"I meant what I said," Camila says. "I've done wrong to you. You think I don't mean it, but I do. I'm not this person."

"That's not true. We're only what we've been. What you want to be means nothing."

After Mia closes the door Taylor rushes to the window

to watch her aunt walk away, and she sees Camila turn right, away from the bus station, and disappear into the dusk.

A week after Camila's intrusion, Mia drives to the western edge of town, to the community college, and signs up for classes. She hasn't thought the school thing all the way through, but she remembers her father telling her that one of the best things parents can do for their children is have homework of their own. His theory went that if your kids saw you studying, they would internalize the importance of the act, and Mia did observe her father and mother reading, almost every night, even if it was the comics, and yet it's only now that she appreciates their attempt to set a positive example. It certainly didn't stick in high school. Mia also remembers seeing her parents with alcohol every night, but somehow her father left that out of his do-as-I-do mantra.

Kevin the cop stops in the bank and Mia informs him about her college venture, and he grins and offers to take a class with her. Even though they've been on two dates that have gone well, she neither declines nor accepts his offer, which he interprets as an invitation. He has a degree in interdisciplinary studies from Adams State over in Alamosa, where he was raised, but Mia won't know this until later.

Mia starts with an English night class. As she walks into the aged classroom with poorly erased blackboards, she eyes the people scattered throughout the room. The scene isn't what she pictured when she thought of the word *college:* a couple of high schoolers in the front row in khakis (trying to get a jump on college credit), a rancher in a brown, wide-brimmed hat (he will not say four words all semester), three Hispanics spouting lightning-quick Spanish and laughing loudly (two will turn out to be brilliant), a few fiftyish women fidgeting with their already bought books, five white college-aged kids, Kevin (seated next to her, wearing too much cologne), and her.

Mrs. Kelley, the instructor, is about Mia's age, slightly hunched and heavy, with a cheerful face locked in a smile. Her accent is hard to place, but Mia is sure it is east of the Mississippi. Immediately Mia likes her, and that first night when they introduce themselves, Mrs. Kelley asks them to name their favorite book – "Even," she says, "if you haven't had time to finish it all the way." From the high schoolers: *Othello, Brave New World*. One of them reconsiders: "*1984*. Well, any dystopia."

"Thank you, sweetie," says Mrs. Kelley, with a raise of her eyebrows to acknowledge their zeal. The rest of the room names their favorite books, and besides the Bible – three times – Mia doesn't recognize the titles. Mrs. Kelley calls everyone "sweetie," and this will be the one thing that irks Mia. She's no one's sweetie, especially not of a woman of like age, regardless of education. When it's Kevin's turn he says, "*Slaughterhouse-Five*," and glances over at Mia for approval, but Mia is already saying her book title before Mrs. Kelley's "sweetie."

"*Jacob Have I Loved*," Mia says, and Mrs. Kelley smiles.

"Thank you, sweetie," Mrs. Kelley says, but before she can move on – before Mia can pinch her right ear to ease the nerves – from the front of the room, barely audible but there, loud enough for most to hear, a teenager's voice: "A kid's book? I read that in seventh grade." Sarcastic laughter arises among the small group of high schoolers. "Sixth grade," a girl says, looking back at Mia.

A void builds; the laughter grows, then stops abruptly. The teenagers – decent local kids, but immature – feel the initial pings of awkwardness, and everyone glances at Mia for her reaction, but all they see is her open mouth, her pink face, her confidence edging toward defeat. Kevin rises from his seat, but before he steps forward Mrs. Kelley points at the kids.

"Not again. You hear me?" She steps close. "You do anything like that again and you're gone."

"Not my worst first class," Mrs. Kelley says after class has ended and only Mia and Kevin remain. She forces a laugh. "No knives this time." She smiles. "If we were in Denver, those kids would come after me." Another smile. To Mia, "Sweetie, I love that book. I miss the open water and fish for breakfast."

Mia will never forget that night or the night after, when she lets Kevin kiss her in his patrol car outside her apartment. He's supposed to be making rounds, but it's a slow Tuesday night, so he escorts Mia to the Dairy Queen for ice cream and drives her back to her apartment, but instead of leaving he tells her about his four years in the Marines, pushing paper at Pendleton, his degree, and his ex-wife in Alamosa, and, surprising to Mia, admits fault with his ex. He describes his pastor father: honest, harsh, and proud. How he himself has never been east of Kansas City, how he has hidden an unpredictable but severe ringing in his right ear – caused by a kick to the head in basic training – from his boss. Mia tells him about her family, her rush to leave Castle Rock, about meeting her daughter's father while he worked on a paving project outside Aztec, about his disappearing a week after she told him she was pregnant. Kevin leans over and they both go silent, and Mia closes her eyes and plugs into the energy of anxious desire. His police radio interrupts them with numbers and codes that Kevin pauses to hear, then says can wait.

Later that night, still high from Kevin and his gentle hands, she hauls out the trash and dumps the plastic bag into the dumpster under their streetlight. The bag tears open, and while Mia glances at the exposed contents, something catches her eye. She looks closer and spies small clumps of bloodstained toilet paper among the dirty plastic and crushed cereal box. Soon it will all seem too obvious to Mia, but as she walks the forty steps back to her apartment she can't wrap her mind around the sight. She wonders if Taylor accidentally caught herself on something sharp – Mia imagines a broken glass and a slit index finger. She enters her place and Taylor leaves the bathroom, Band-Aid-less, in her bathrobe. The truth rushes to Mia. She'd always imagined a Safeway moment, with her daughter running to her, asking for advice and comfort and celebration. Taylor walks across the brown carpet towel drying her hair and Mia thinks, *This might not be her first period.* Mia strides to her daughter, intercepting her before she reaches her bedroom, and hugs her tight.

"I like him," Taylor says. "I'll say yes if you want to marry him."

Mia feels absorbed into Taylor's arms.

"You won't lose me," Taylor says. "Mom?"

Mia has her head glued to her taller daughter's chest. She notices a half-dollar-sized hickey above Taylor's collarbone.

"Mom? He's good for us."

Mia doesn't say, "Tell me everything"; she doesn't ask, "Is this your first period?" She will bring the topic up a month later, and they'll sit on Taylor's twin bed and Mia will remind her never to be ashamed of her body, to try to be patient with her boyfriend. Mia will learn that Taylor started her period five months earlier, and at that moment she will wonder what she has done wrong, what would cause her daughter not to tell her, but tonight, in her living room, she smells the strawberry-scented body lotion on her twelve-year-old and slides a step back and says, "Thanks, honey," and watches Taylor nod, then enter her bedroom and close the door.

During the day Mia works her teller slot and turns her head at the sound of "Me," and she pushes through the rough days and helps tourists with directions to Four Corners, reminding them that it costs ten dollars to spread-eagle into four states and the Navajos prefer cash. Most nights Mia and Taylor study at their kitchen table, Mia pushing through math, history, and science courses, Taylor drawing or daydreaming or waiting for her phone to ring. They put on their Journey and hit Repeat, and although they concentrate on their separate worlds, they always sit next to each other, each offering an occasional leg bump to keep the other awake. Some nights Kevin comes over, even though he's stopped taking classes, and he helps Mia with her math problems or tries to spark discussion with Taylor, who occasionally engages. While Kevin's flaws appear – he always answers his ex-wife's calls, he keeps a messy home and cusses too vehemently at the television when the Broncos or Avalanche lose – he hits the major checklist items: patient, knows how Mia likes to be held and touched, light drinker, good worker, educated, and takes to Taylor like a caring but not over-authoritative father. Still, even with Taylor's blessing, Mia is conflicted about marriage. She can't imagine – no matter how close she and Kevin get – a permanent addition to her and Taylor's life. She's content with companionship without the ring.

The night of community college graduation, Aunt Kathy drives up from Aztec. She brings Mia a massive white rose corsage and informs her that she's single now and happy.

When Mia's name is announced in the cramped auditorium, her legs go numb and she sees Mrs. Kelley tearing up and hears Kevin and Taylor scream out – it's been so long since someone has clapped for her that the noise overwhelms her – and as she leaves the stage with the paper diploma and hugs Taylor, Mia remembers her as a newborn with a misshapen head and purple eyelids, and herself at eighteen, ignorant and somehow perfectly content to go at motherhood alone, resigning herself to hard work and modest living, and now, she realizes, she's done something right. And not in a small way: she has raised a healthy, cheering daughter, and she has earned a diploma that says she finished something she never thought she would start.

Before she leaves the auditorium, her aunt hands her a letter.

"From your parents," she says. "Please don't be mad, but I've been keeping them up to date."

Later that night she opens the letter. It's her father's handwriting.

Mia,

Mom and I are so very proud of you. It's impossible for me to tell you how much. You are a great example for Taylor. Aunt Kathy tells us of your success, how Taylor is the smartest and most beautiful girl in the county. I should have written this letter years ago. You are always welcome here. You are wanted here. Things are different from what you remember. Better. Much better. There's not a right or appropriate way to say we're sorry. We regret a lot. We also remember our greatest joys are when we had you close. What I'm trying to say is that I can understand why you'd be angry. Rightfully so, Mia, but I hope the time will come when you will let us back into your life. You need to know your mother isn't well. I don't want to say too much, only that she may not have long to live and I wanted you to know.

Her health has me thinking a lot about my life, about our family. Things I'd change and things I wouldn't. Mia, I know it was tough for you that I was gone when you were young. I'd like to think that my time away was worth it somehow, but I'm not sure I'll ever get there. I used to think that my choices weren't about loyalties. That's what I'd tell myself, but I know that's not true. There are only choices, and I chose a job that took me away from you, your mother, and your sister, even after the accident. I don't know what that says about me, or the old me, but I want you to know there was an honest belief in what I was doing. It may not make sense to me now, but it did then. Mia, that may not make it any easier for you, but it is what keeps me from heading back to some dark places. I don't know if I ever was a soldier or a father. With every day that passes I feel I know myself less.

Mia, your mother and I are back at church and it's helping in the ways we've needed for a long time. I am more like my father than I care to admit, and I hope that in moments of happiness you find some connection to me or your mother.

Mia, this is the most important part – we love you. Please, when the time is right for you and Taylor, please come and visit.

Dad

One summer, a couple months after Mia hears that her mother has died, she decides to drive east across the state with sixteen-year-old Taylor to visit her father during Fourth of July weekend.

When Mia tells Kevin about the trip, he asks to come along – he expects to, as they've been together four years –

but Mia tells him no, and after a couple days of pouting he comes around to the idea and helps them pack their Honda.

Mia and Taylor leave on a Saturday, and an hour out of Cortez, Mia chooses to take a back way, and when they arrive in Woodland Park, she turns the car north on Highway 67 toward Deckers.

Taylor has been unusually silent, so Mia puts on some country music and daydreams about her father, but all that comes to her is his wheelchair, memories of a green army uniform with shiny pins, and disappointing departures.

Their route soon takes them along a small roadside stream. Mia remembers this place, and she tells Taylor about coming up here, describing the time she saw a bear, then the rock dam, and something moves in her, and she slows down at every turnoff, searching for her pile of rocks, her ninety-percent dam, but after a number of frustrating slowdowns and pull-offs, she keeps the car on the pavement, and she asks her quiet daughter what two things she would grab from a burning house, and Taylor takes a breath, then brings her hands to her face.

Before Taylor can answer, Mia considers her own response, imagines their Cortez apartment on fire, the two-room place alight, and she watches herself rush into the home to save Taylor, but when she enters, the place is empty, only fire and smoke.

Mia hears Taylor's voice, hears the words *I'm pregnant,* but nothing happens for a while, just the mountain road in front of them, leading them both to a place and a father Mia used to know.

15

Wyoming Is a Gun in His Waistband

W INTRIC HOPES IT'S the girl who arrives. Let it
be the girl. Let her walk the dirt road. Put her in
pink pants. Put her arms up in a *V*. Put her in skin. Give her
bones and blood. Give him her chest to target. Let him see
the line of the bullet all the way through her heart. Scope
that chest. Breathe that power. Squeeze that trigger.

The tomatoes are wrapped in a plastic bag on the seat
next to him. He feels the onset signs—the skull-pounding
pressure and muscle lock—here in the parking lot of the
Holiday market. The anxiety and warped recall are near.
He's long forgotten the moment, years ago, when the memories joined the physical pain. He reaches beneath his seat
and uncaps the plastic bottle. Although he has two pills in
his system, he slips four more into his mouth. They'll take a
while to work, so he waits.

He doesn't have a choice of scene, but the girl he'll be
able to process. He can tap into the decades-old mayhem
and the I-die-or-you-die judgment. He can access his flurry
of decisions—to squeeze the trigger, to raise his rifle, to don
his uniform, to sign up for the army, to leave his hometown.
Let it be the girl. Even though she'll puncture the peace of
a Wednesday afternoon, he can deal. With the drugs he can

deal with a silver vest and pink pants. He was a boy then. He's convinced himself of that. It should matter that he was there to deliver justice for attacks on American soil, but outside of a few crazies, all he saw were people searching for food. His mind grinds as it has for years: *What do you call someone who kills? Murderer. What do you call someone who kills a girl? Hero.* Let it be the girl. He attempts to guide his horror there, but he can't conjure the dirt road, Big Dax and Torres at his side.

No matter what comes it won't be easy, but the girl is easier than the darkness, the smell of burning trash, a push in the back, ripping flesh. Wintric won't close his eyes. Darkness takes him there. He attempts to focus, to stay here in the parking lot, in Chester. The tomatoes are next to him. He'll wash them when he gets home. The steering wheel is in front of him. He grabs it. A bread truck pulls to the back of the store for delivery. Kristen is in the store working. It's almost time for her to come home.

Wintric sits in the tenth and highest row of Chester High School's bleachers and wonders if Daniel will throw the next pitch at the batter's head. Since the time Daniel started Little League, Wintric has preached that he should throw a couple wild pitches each game to keep the batters nervous about where the next one might end up. This method worked well during Little League, but Daniel, now seventeen years old, with a fastball that reaches the low eighties, has the control to aim his "wild" pitches, and when appropriately pissed off, as he is today, down 4–0, the heaters come in high and tight. Just last week Daniel cracked a kid's helmet.

The batter digs his back foot in, and Wintric senses the energy in the afternoon, unsure what to do with it. Back from rehab and clean for a month, he rubs his hands together, still acclimating to the sharp sensation of unmedicated touch. The feeling keeps him busy, his hands moving from his pockets to his hips to the back of his neck, from sitting to standing to sitting to walking, nothing ever comfortable or calm enough. The acupuncture, meditation, and aspirin do nothing for his bad back and right hip, although they have helped decrease the frequency of his devastating memories. Most of his waking hours his bones feel misplaced and heavy. The counselors told him that this was what recovery felt like, that the promise of sobriety isn't about comfort, it's about being present, facing the moment aware, but Wintric is convinced that awareness isn't worth the price of pain, at least not yet. It's not like the drugs make him blind. He could be here, at this exact spot, present but pain-free, and still watch Daniel drill this kid with the next pitch.

Wintric stands and pockets his hands.

In front of him, the outfielders shade in a bit too much for the three-hole batter from Greenville. The infield grass is mostly yellow, and along the outfield fence thin pockets of April snow melt. Several of the town's homes still have their fireplaces going, and the smell of burning wood mixes with early pollen.

Daniel adjusts his cap low, then spits. A few inches short of six feet and thick across the shoulders, he readies himself on the mound and peers in at the catcher. His windup is slow and compact, his hands waist-high as he starts his move, rocking back, then upright, left leg rising, right arm reaching back low, then whipping forward, the baseball delivered hard and cutting inside, the batter turning just in time, turning his back toward the sting, the flat smack of a fastball to the kidneys and the collective groan of the thirty people in the stands. The batter feels the pain, arches his back, and his hands go there as he falls to his knees.

Wintric studies Daniel, who has taken two steps toward the plate. Straight-faced, he runs his pitching hand along the side of his thigh and studies the batter, who fights to hide his distress. Wintric searches for the slightest smile on his son, a glance his way in the bleachers, but Daniel stands still, now chatting with the catcher while the batter rises slowly and twists and trots down to first.

Wintric wasn't surprised when it was Daniel who picked him up from rehab down in Sacramento. Kristen's threat to leave had forced him to go in the first place, and the threat still retains its tangible power as he curses the aspirin bottle three times a day. She hasn't asked a single question about his time with the counselors or what he confessed or learned in the small group sessions. All she cares about is that he's clean, that he'll stay clean. On the way home from Sacramento, Daniel was exuberant, and he flung questions at Wintric one after another: How was the food? Not bad, actually. What was the worst you saw? Meth – never screw with meth, son. Did you catch any Giants games on TV? God, no power in the middle of the lineup. How do you feel? Hollowed-out but happy. We going deer hunting this fall? We'll put in for out-of-state, get us a big one.

Daniel drove and they rode 99 up through Yuba City, Gridley, and Chico, through the miles of almond orchards, before they turned northeast on 32 into the mountains. Wintric listened to his son go on and on, asking questions, then shooting off on tangents about his ex-girlfriend, about an English teacher who had it in for him, about maybe becoming a firefighter after finishing school. Wintric realized that he knew so little about his son and finally wanted to know everything. He understood then that his son had always worshipped him, and still did at seventeen, that there was no justice or redemption in that. His son didn't know him at all – he loved the idea of a dad and not the father that

Wintric had been. It was pathetic and beautiful and easy. Sitting next to Daniel, Wintric was suddenly grateful and scared that Daniel would forgive all of his future sins.

In the stands Wintric rubs his hands together and hears a logging truck downshift beyond the outfield fence. His fingertips and scalp ache, and he shakes his head at the thought of forty tiny needles pressed into the skin along his vertebrae. Will he always yearn for the drugs? Even now, watching his boy play ball? If he could only leave his body somewhere else for a couple hours and come back to this place. He fights the thought, but he knows he can get the pills a quarter mile from the bleachers where he stands. He remembers the address. He saw the guy at the gas station two days ago. He has enough money in his wallet.

From two rows down, someone from Greenville says, "The kid meant to do it. Look at him. Didn't even say sorry."

The mother of Chester High's third baseman says, "Come on. It slipped," and glances back at Wintric and grins.

One of the counselors had bright orange hair, which annoyed Wintric, but the guy, Jeff, had been to the far bottom of heroin and back up and he talked straight and cussed, so Wintric listened. Jeff took Wintric on walks down to the American River, where they'd watch the whitewater rafters and where Jeff repeated his sign-up message: "Pain isn't a fucking choice. Neither are the flashbacks. They're there. Comfort, happiness, all that weird shit we say when we mean 'not in pain,' that's a choice. A hard choice. If you ever stop choosing it, you're fucked. Optimists are deluded but sign up. You want in that club. Whatever it takes, sign up."

To Wintric, Jeff's speeches came off as too simplistic, even juvenile, but the guy was adamant and would occasionally sneak him a Lucky Strike. Wintric didn't notice anyone else getting the American River treatment, and Jeff kept reminding Wintric that he was one of the blessed ones: a family waiting for him, not suicidal, no heroin or meth.

On the mound, Daniel wears his baseball hat low on his forehead as Wintric used to do when he was a boy playing Little League centerfield. Daniel licks his fingers and twists the baseball in his hand. The crowd has settled down, but everyone is anxious for this first pitch after the wild pitch. Was it really an accident? Has the pitcher lost control?

When Wintric returned home, Kristen told him to come to her at the supermarket and interrupt her whenever he needed help, but he holds on to the beginning of newfound pride in not having gone to her once since his return to town. If Kristen ever does ask him, he'll tell her why he'll never relapse. He'll tell her about his small group sessions, how he saw the whole spectrum from lifelong fucked-up meth heads to three-drinks-a-night country-club house-wives. It didn't matter whose turn it was to speak; the stories all ended up at the same fear – being alone.

When he thought about what he would say to the group when it was his turn to speak, he expected to bring up the war, how much of the war he wasn't sure, but as he sat silently in the folding chair day after day, it dawned on him that his time in Afghanistan was nearly twenty years past. Something about the number twenty jarred him: twenty years of waking up, living, sleeping, repeat and repeat. Maybe it wasn't the war or the girl he shot or the rape or the foot, or maybe it was that, but twenty years of other shit as well. Maybe it wasn't cumulative, not twenty years, not even one year, perhaps just twenty-four-hour segments as they passed. Maybe an hour or a second or how he felt right then. How was he supposed to know? Where's the turn? The bottom? The point where things start getting better and always get better? Twenty years later and what's new? The hundreds of roofs he's nailed down, shingle by shingle. A son that's not like him in any meaningful way. A wife he loves threatening to leave him – he was at the sink washing tomatoes when she grabbed his arm, gently at first, then harder. Still in her Holiday market clothes; her mascara had run, and she wouldn't let him look away as she spoke.

The next batter, the cleanup hitter, a muscled boy who hit a double his first time up, walks to the plate and pauses outside the batter's box and studies the third-base coach. If Daniel hits this kid, there will probably be a fight.

When Wintric rose to speak to the small group in rehab, he didn't know what he'd say, but Jeff was there, and that helped somehow, and he heard himself confess: holding his son for the first time after his birth while high on Percocet. Loading up on Oxy before going to a party for Kristen when she was promoted to general manager at the Holiday market. Dropping pills before sex with her. These were moments when elation should have been enough, and may have been, if he'd just let them happen. As bad, he didn't know what hurting meant anymore. Sure, his back and hip had been giving him problems for years, even after the foot stopped, and sure, the flashes of war hit hard and unpredictably, but what was legitimate pain versus haunting versus routine? And he loves his wife more than anything, more than drugs or pain, and maybe it was only now that he understood that they were all linked, that he should have understood long ago. And he knew he was talking a good game in Sacramento, hours from home, coming clean, promising the world, but he feared what all of them feared. He now knew that the pain of the war, of the past two decades, of yesterday, would never recede all the way; the hurt simply finds new things to infect, things he has always loved – Christmas lights, interstate signs, hunting campfires, baseball games – but happiness and release also live somewhere among these things. He knew it was just a matter of finding them.

Wintric moves down the bleachers over near the Chester dugout and fingers, then squeezes, the chain-linked backstop. The outfielders have moved back, and the bruised boy at first takes two steps off the bag and waits.

Someone yells, "Throw strikes."

The cleanup hitter steps into the batter's box and toes his Nike cleats up close to the inner line, right next to the plate, but then, in short scoots, works his way back, further back from the plate than the first two times he was up.

Wintric sees it: this boy on his heels, the horrible recognition that he's not in control, the safe space on the outer edge of the plate. And Wintric looks out to his son and wonders what he knows.

Where's the next pitch going, Daniel?

The good nerves in Wintric's body spark, and he doesn't question whether he's choosing this or how long it will last. He squeezes the fence and brings his face close and looks through the holes. He is close enough now to see Daniel's eyes underneath his hat, close enough to see Daniel pause and look at him. There's no nod or wink, only three seconds when his son's eyes meet his.

Northbound on Highway 32, two miles past Potato Patch campground during the summer season, Wintric and Daniel stare at an injured, thrashing deer blocking the road. Its back haunches smashed, the panicked doe scratches at the double yellow lines with her front legs, but she can't stand.

The man who hit the deer sits in his car with the windows up. The front left bumper is dented, but it's drivable. He rests his forehead on the steering wheel, unable to look.

Of the five stopped cars, only Wintric, Daniel, and a woman in a Chico State T-shirt stand near the animal.

The deer swings her head into the air and back down, making frantic attempts to gain momentum, but it's hopeless, and the three of them hear the slap of her head against the pavement, the scraping front hooves.

"Crap," the woman says.

Wintric realizes what has to happen—knew soon after he got out of the truck and saw that the deer wasn't going anywhere. He'd hoped that the doe had been hit well enough to be on her last breath by the time he walked up, but the car had caught her back end, which meant working lungs and heart.

Wintric runs his hand over the pocketed knife that he's had for years. His cardiovascular system pounds inside him. He reaches out and touches Daniel's arm.

"Son," he says.

"I know," Daniel says. "Shit. I got nothing in my truck."

"Nothing," the woman says, and shakes her head.

"It's okay," Wintric says. "I got something. It's not great." He reaches into his pocket and pulls the knife out. He opens the three-inch blade and shows it to the woman, who purses her lips.

"It's okay," Wintric says.

Another car pulls to the back of the southbound lane lineup, and a man gets out, takes in the scene, then gets back in his car.

The deer exhales in short, violent bursts, her black eyes huge in her head.

"Poor damn thing," the woman says, still shaking her head.

"Dad," Daniel says.

"What do you want me to do?" the woman says.

"One second," Wintric says.

"What can I do?" says the woman.

"Dad," Daniel says. "I can do it."

Wintric looks at the deer, at the deer's neck, the fur there, and he can't remember the last time he sharpened his knife.

He had felt good today, not perfect, but good. As long as he keeps the car rides under two hours, he can manage. He could stop everything now and wait for someone with a gun, but who knows how long that will take, and already there are enough people stopped to make a scene. They may be in their cars, but they'll watch.

"She'll kick like hell," Wintric says. "You two hold her."

"Step on her?" Daniel says.

"We'll have to lean," the woman says. "She's strong."

"That's right," Wintric says. "Lean on her. Get ready."

He kneels down a few feet away from the doe, the knife light in his hands. Underneath him he sees the tons of tiny rocks that make the road. They dig into his knees. Black flies dart past his ears. While Daniel and the woman get into position he presses the knife against his left thumb, but it just dents the skin.

"Stay on the body," Wintric says. "I'll go fast." He clenches his teeth. "I'll go fast. Okay. Now."

Daniel and the woman kneel on the deer's flailing body and Wintric presses his knee down on the deer's head and he feels the muscled power underneath him, the neck strong, trying to twist up, to breathe, lifting his knee, and him pressing back down with all his weight and his hand under the deer's jaw grabbing at the folds there, feeling the deer throb, and his knife already at the throat, sawing, sawing into the neck fur, the knife edge disappearing into the fold and the shit smell and he saws the blade deep, but there's no blood, and he presses harder into the animal, sawing the blade, and the deer heaves, and he searches for an opening where he saws, but there's nothing, and he yells "Shit" and with his right arm already tiring and his back flaring he drives the blade hard into the neck and the fur now opens, but only a little, and he yanks at the sliced fold but he can't grab enough to pull it back, and the sweat in his eyes and the black flies, and he saws hard and fast at the space there, and his arm is giving out and the deer yanks and bounces his knee into the air, and he yells "Shit" and slams his knee back down on the deer's head, and he holds the knife up into the afternoon and shakes his arm out, and "Fuck," and he stabs at the deer's neck twice, and the first spots of blood appear on the road, and he saws, his arm and lungs and back giving out, and the shit smell every-where, and his vision turns and he saws and feels the blade through the skin now and blood, warm blood on his hands, but not enough, not spurting, and the shit smell on him, and the blade against cartilage, and his arm numb and weak, and the sparks in his vision, and the breath he can't draw, and he looks over at Daniel, who slides to him fast and takes the knife from Wintric's hand, and Wintric lunges over the deer's body, straddling the thrash, pressing the front legs down, breathing in the shit, shoulder to shoulder with the woman, flies at his face, hearing Daniel's loud grunts, eyes focused on the road, the millions of rocks, the thrashing and wheezing underneath him, and Daniel grunting and a thin crack and Daniel yanking the deer's head back, and Dan-iel's voice, "Through," and the rocks of the road, a stream of bright blood, a desperate whistle-wheezing and thrash, the woman's voice, "Can we get up? Can we get up?" and Daniel, "Yes," and Wintric rises, and the deer's front legs scratch at the road and Wintric's hands are wet and dirty, he's wiping them on his jeans, and the deer's legs scratch at the road, then slow and stop, and Wintric looks at Daniel, at Daniel's blood-soaked hands, Wintric's knife in his hand.

Lately Torres has talked about his international speaking gigs, memories of Big Dax, the Denver Broncos, the weather, the Rockies, and his wife, but Wintric hasn't heard him talk about his daughter, Mia, in over a year. Wintric closes his bedroom door and lies on his bed, phone on speaker. Torres seems sober.

"I don't know about regrets," Torres says. "It's the great thing about life. You don't know the alternative. Make your decisions and press on. Mia made her choices. She wants to raise that poor child on her own, let her. She wants to live in Cortez and do it alone, let her. When you walk away from family, you walk away. Life is hard, but some people like it that way."

"Yeah," Wintric says. "Doesn't make it easy."

"Nothing's easy, I guess."

"I don't know," Wintric says.

"I thought she'd come back. It's been four years. I haven't seen my granddaughter. Most days I don't care, but sometimes I do."

"That makes sense."

"Does it?"

"It's family," Wintric says. "Everything and nothing makes sense. It's your kid, doesn't matter if they're six or twenty-six."

"They're not always your kid."

"No?"

"Mia doesn't get that you have to choose to be in a family. After a while it's not guaranteed. If she were to show up right now, I don't know if I'd let her in. I'd like to think that I wouldn't. There have to be consequences. Listen, I don't pretend there's justice in the world. Only fools think that. She'll probably win the damn lottery or something."

"I don't know," Wintric says.

"There's no justice, but there are rules. You don't have to like them, but they're there. You want to get pregnant, move out, turn your back on your family, fine, but you're not going to be sailing the Mediterranean on your yacht. And I get it. It's not all about money. But she chooses the hardest way possible."

"I get it."

"All of that, and if she showed up, I'd probably let her in. Why wouldn't I?"

"I guess you would," Wintric says.

"It wouldn't be about forgiveness, just about the kid. It's my only grandkid."

"Old man."

"Old enough."

"Drop her a note and see what happens."

"A note?"

"Write it out, old school," Wintric says. "You might be surprised."

"You'd forgive everyone. That's your rehab talking."

"You never know. Things grow out of control, but sometimes there's a good reason. I mean that things may be okay after a while. Maybe she comes back different and things are good."

"Do you feel different?"

"I feel how I feel. I try to remember how I used to feel, but I never know if it's better or worse. I don't believe people when they say, 'This is the worst I've ever felt.' I don't think anyone remembers how good or bad things were."

"Maybe."

"I think about being on the drugs," Wintric says. "I remember being calm. I remember feeling good, but I don't know. I don't trust myself." He pauses. "What if it felt good but it could've been better? The only way to know would be to try it again."

"Dangerous."

"That's the problem with drugs," Wintric says. "They work."

"I was on good stuff after the accident. You're damn right they work. I'd be lying there in the hospital thinking that I'd walk again, I felt that good. I remember weeks after, still thinking I'd walk. Get me drunk enough and I'd probably tell you I still imagine it. It's not good to think that way."

"You never know."

"Stop. It's been long enough to know. But put it this way – if a miracle happens and I stand again, I'll throw a party. I'll fly out all the friends I can find. We'll all hold hands and go on a walk together."

"Am I on the list?"

"Hell, you are the list."

"I don't believe you," Wintric says.

"I'm not drunk."

"How's your liver?"

"How's yours?"

"That fair, I guess," Wintric says.

"It's not about fairness."

"Okay."

"I don't know what it's about."

"We're older now. It can be about anything."

"I remember being a kid on the playground at school and watching the cars driving by and wondering where all of them were going. It fascinated me that all these people could just go wherever the hell they wanted. And come to find out it's true. You grow up and you can go wherever the hell you want. Just hop in the car and go. You get older and all of a sudden you have all these choices."

"Independence," Wintric says.

"In a way."

"Yeah."

"But you still have places to be."

"Hopefully, places you want to be," Wintric says.

"Your choice, my friend. Grab the family, hop in the car, and go. That easy. One-way trip. But I've been preaching at you for years. You know this. You aren't going anywhere, because you like it there."

"You're guessing."

"What's the name of the lake?"

"Almanor."

"You love it."

"You're guessing."

"I've known you a long time."

"That's true," Wintric says.

"You like getting up in the morning?"

"What?"

"Do you like waking up and thinking you have a day in front of you?"

"Sure."

"My father used to rant all the time about random crap and most of it was worthless, but as I got older one thing he used to ask me was, 'Why are you waking up today?' I guess what he meant was that I'd better have something worth waking up for, and if I ever got to a place where I didn't, I'd better make a change quick. But you ask that question too often and it gets tough. Doesn't matter what you've been through. Don't ask me to answer my own question."

"You don't have to think like that when you're a kid."

"You don't ever have to think about it, but it helps sometimes."

"We all got reasons to get up," Wintric says.

"Do you know yours?"

"Maybe he didn't mean the big stuff. Maybe it's a small thing."

"Could be."

"Something simple," Wintric says.

"It has to be simple or no one would understand. Has to be enough to get you out of bed."

"Yeah," Wintric says. "Something simple."

The game is on ESPN2. An afternoon bowl game five days before Christmas. Channel flipping, home alone and bored, Wintric sees the game appear, and an unrecognized moment of peace passes before he focuses on the screen. Wyoming versus Oregon State. Flung into paralysis, he stares at Wyoming's brown-and-yellow uniforms, the helmets: the saddled cowboy and bronco. Wyoming. Jettisoned to Nelson's white door, Nelson's dog, now huge and savage, the white door in the heat, the *AFG* sticker on Nelson's Jeep, the dog pressing him, the McDonald's parking lot, a white door, a garbage truck, desert and gunpowder, a postcard in his hand. He won't write his name on it. He won't send it. Wyoming is a white door. Trapped, Wintric holds the remote in his living room. He can't move his fingers. He holds the remote. Wyoming is an exit off I-80. He stares at the television through credit card and beer commercials, through a missed field goal and an ACL tear. Wyoming is a gun in his waistband. He won't use it. Wyoming is a white door. No one is there.

Wintric stands. He's off the couch. His coat is on. He's on a nearby street, squinting. The sun reflects off the ice-packed road.

The dealer's house is in a row of shotgun homes. Someone has left a square of red Christmas lights on around the front window. The fence has been fixed and the home has been painted yellow since Wintric was last here, ten months ago. There used to be kids' toys everywhere, but now there's only this sturdy fence and two feet of snow.

Wintric doesn't go inside. He waits on the steps. When he gets the pills, he selects four from the bottle, then tosses them into his mouth. He tries to swallow them dry, but the pills stick in his throat. He gulps twice, but they're still stuck, so he rushes down the three stairs and cups snow from the yard into his mouth and waits for it to melt enough to swallow.

"What the hell?" says the dealer. "Get the fuck on."

Wintric walks away, but not home. He turns down Second Avenue, past an empty lot where as a kid he used to break empty Budweiser bottles. Every step he takes seems to propel him a block. Rushing and ready for the Oxy to be absorbed, he walks past the old homes and families he's always known: the McIntires, the Garretts, the Roulands, the Killingsworths. His breath plumes out wide into the cold. He doesn't know where he's walking, but he wants to be outside. Already he believes he could walk forever, go anywhere.

Down First Avenue now; a minivan and a blue Chevy truck pass him and he walks the road past the Salversons' and the Hardigs'. The cold and anticipation push Wyoming away and he searches for the self-pity that will make all this worth it, and he thinks about his life, how he's lost it, how the days don't get better fast enough, how he's seen the world but none of the parts he wanted.

Wintric steps and slips, but he steadies himself. He stops in front of the Waldrons' place, a house he roofed in the fall. An inflatable Santa sits on the porch by the front door. Family friends for years; he'd only cleared three hundred on the five-day job. The snowpack lays thick on the roof, and Wintric finds himself here, in Chester, before the drugs have hit.

He'll always be here. He won't get younger. He's walked this street forever. The drugs haven't hit, but he can wait. It's him, alone on First Avenue. The Waldrons' place right here. He's alone but alive, and the drugs haven't hit yet. He's here, alone, and suddenly there's enough time to fear.

When he enters the Holiday market, he pauses inside the automatic doors. The store is busier than normal in the winter months, and he frantically searches the check-out stations for Kristen, but she's not there. He digs his nails into his palms and keeps his head down and paces fast down the cereal aisle to the back of the market. Wintric turns the corner near the frozen apple juice and sees her and stops. Her back is toward him, hands at her hips. Her hair is longer than he remembers.

Kristen is talking to Mrs. McIntire. She shifts her weight and brushes Mrs. McIntire's arm.

Wintric steps forward, then pulls back near the freezers and grabs the back of his neck. He presses his forehead on the cold glass. Kristen loves him and he doesn't know why. He's starting to feel light and he's scared to go home and scared to step out into the aisle, but he knows what alone means. He's heard their stories.

He pulls his head off the freezer door. He steps out into the aisle.

It's Mrs. McIntire who waves to him first, and Wintric waves back, but he can't force a smile. His heart pumps the poison and Kristen turns toward him. She raises her hand to wave, and when she sees him her hand stops its move upward. Her mouth opens. Her hands fall to her sides.

Out back by the delivery dock, in an employee bathroom, Wintric jams two fingers down his throat for the second time. He cut the roof of his mouth with his fingernails on the first attempt and he tastes his own blood and gags, then throws up into the toilet. His head floats over the putrid water and he cries and waits for what's next. His stomach clenches and he dry-heaves. He stands and washes his hands and face with hand soap. He exhales, then sprays a lavender-scented air freshener.

On the back of the bathroom door hangs a green-and-white Chester Volcanoes basketball calendar. Kristen must have put it here. He stares at it for a while as he gets his legs under him.

Wintric listens for his wife on the other side of the door, but he doesn't hear her. A weak exhaust fan works above him and he searches for the switch to turn it off, but he finds only one switch, so he flips it off and it kills the light and the fan. It's quiet now and he listens. What's he opening this door to?

Wintric listens inside the dark bathroom. He feels the drugs. He smells the pungent lavender. He places his hands on the door. In the darkness he could be anywhere.

He waits for Kristen's voice asking if he's okay.

He waits and he cries and his chest is soft and the drugs warm the space behind his temples and all along his back.

He can wait. If he wants, he can wait right here. He can choose to stay in this place.

He thinks about flipping on the light switch, about saying his wife's name. He thinks about turning the doorknob.

"Kristen?" he says.

He listens. He hears his own staggered breathing and squeezes his mouth. He waits. He feels for the doorknob. It's small in his hand.

"Kristen?" he says, and opens the door.

Out on the delivery dock, a man Wintric recognizes unloads crates of milk. An announcement garbles over the store's loudspeaker.

In the far corner, behind stacks of paper towels, Kristen sits on a stool with her face in her hands. She's pulled her hair back into a ponytail. Wintric walks to her and stands close. He can smell her vanilla perfume. It's cold and he doesn't know if he should touch her or speak, so he wipes at his wet face and stands there and watches her. Her wedding ring covers her left eye. A bracelet he's never seen is on her left wrist.

Behind him, the sound of milk crates being stacked. An announcement from the speaker somewhere above them. The voice calls his wife's name.

Wintric reaches out and touches Kristen's shoulder. His numb fingertips press against her cotton shirt.

He knows what's happening. He'll leave his hand here. He's aware. He's facing the moment. He'll stay right here.

"Please," she says. She stands up, shaking his hand off her.

She exhales hard and runs her hands down her chest and belly, over to the outside of both hips. She pulls at the bottom of her shirt. She stands close, her shoulder inches from Wintric's chest.

"Kristen," he says. He stands, motionless, her smell in his nose. The shape of her neck. The curves of her ear. She could turn to him. So close, she could turn his way. He watches her face. He waits for the turn.

Over the store's loudspeaker, someone's calling her name.

She keeps her eyes forward as she walks away and rounds the corner back into the store.

Wintric grabs the back of his neck, then folds his arms.

Someone is calling her name.

He listens to the sound.

Acknowledgments

My deepest appreciation for

  –my incredible agent and friend Chelsea Lindman.

  –my brilliant editor and friend Ben Hyman.

  –the wonderful Houghton Mifflin Harcourt team, especially Leila Meglio, Hannah Harlow, Brian Moore, Laura Brady, and Liz Duvall.

  –my parents

  –the Goolsby, Archibald, Hunt, Rouland, Moss, and Walton families.

  –my dear friend, colleague, and sounding board Brandon Lingle.

  –the many people who opened the doors to my professional dreams, especially Donald Anderson, Kathleen Harrington, Thomas McGuire, Blaine Holt, Erin Conaton, Peter Bloom, Lance Bunch, Jessica Wright, Karen Pound, Troy Perry, and Debra Shattuck.

  –my great friends and brilliant readers of this book: J. A. Moad II, Brian Turner, Siobhan Fallon, Kristen Loyd, Kerry Linfoot, Gretchen Koenig, Kyle Torke, Charlie Beckerman, CJ Hauser, and Mike Warren.

  –my Florida State University family, especially Robert Olen Butler, Bob Shacochis, Mark Winegardner, Diane Roberts, Elizabeth Stuckey-French, Michael Garriga, Brandi George, and Jennine Capó Crucet.

  –my University of Tennessee family, especially Allen Wier, Marilyn Kallet, and Michael Knight.

–my Air Force Academy family, especially Jim Meredith, George Luker, Richard Lemp, Ann Reagan, Thomas Bowie, Gary Mills, Wilson Brissett, Bill Newmiller, Max Despain, James Bishop, Kathy Binns, and Jeanette Millar.

–my Wolfpack family.

–Tom and Jackie Quinn.

–Ben Oneto, Tim Campbell, Matt Bateman, Nicholle Tognotti, Glenda Grant, Dave Willhardt, and Kurt Martinson.

–Greg Killingsworth, Paul Hardig, Phil Bryant, and Dave Taylor.

–the Hambidge Center for the Creative Arts and Sciences.

–the community of writers, artists, journals, and magazines that has supported my work.

Most importantly, with all my heart,

–my wife, Sarah, and children, Ella, Owen, and Abby.